HIT ME

ALSO BY LAWRENCE BLOCK

The Matthew Scudder Novels

The Sins of the Fathers • Time to Murder and Create • In the Midst of Death A Stab in the Dark • Eight Million Ways to Die • When the Sacred Ginmill Closes • Out on the Cutting Edge • A Ticket to the Boneyard • A Dance at the Slaughterhouse • A Walk Among the Tombstones • The Devil Knows You're Dead • A Long Line of Dead Men • Even the Wicked • Everybody Dies • Hope to Die • All the Flowers Are Dying • A Drop of the Hard Stuff

Keller's Greatest Hits

Hit Man • Hit List • Hit Parade • Hit and Run

The Bernie Rhodenbarr Mysteries

Burglars Can't Be Choosers • The Burglar in the Closet • The Burglar Who Liked to Quote Kipling • The Burglar Who Studied Spinoza • The Burglar Who Painted Like Mondrian • The Burglar Who Traded Ted Williams The Burglar Who Thought He Was Bogart • The Burglar in the Library The Burglar in the Rye • The Burglar on the Prowl

The Adventures of Evan Tanner

The Thief Who Couldn't Sleep • The Canceled Czech • Tanner's Twelve Swingers • Two for Tanner • Tanner's Tiger • Here Comes a Hero Me Tanner, You Jane • Tanner on Ice

The Affairs of Chip Harrison

No Score • Chip Harrison Scores Again • Make Out with Murder The Topless Tulip Caper

Other Novels

A Diet of Treacle • *After the First Death* • *Ariel* • *Campus Tramp* *Cinderella Sims* • *Coward's Kiss* • *Deadly Honeymoon* • *Getting Off* *The Girl with the Long Green Heart* • *Grifter's Game* • *Killing Castro* *Lucky at Cards* • *Not Comin' Home to You* • *Random Walk* • *Ronald Rabbit Is a Dirty Old Man* • *Small Town* • *The Specialists* • *Such Men Are Dangerous* • *The Triumph of Evil* • *You Could Call It Murder*

Collected Short Stories

Sometimes They Bite • *Like a Lamb to Slaughter* • *Some Days You Get the Bear* • *Ehrengraf for the Defense* • *One Night Stands and Lost Weekends* *The Lost Cases of Ed London* • *Enough Rope* • *The Night and the Music*

Books for Writers

Writing the Novel: From Plot to Print • *Telling Lies for Fun and Profit* *Spider, Spin Me a Web* • *Write for Your Life*

Written for Performance

Tilt (episodic television) • *How Far?* (one-act play)
My Blueberry Nights (film)

Memoir

Step by Step

Anthologies Edited

Death Cruise • *Master's Choice* • *Opening Shots* • *Master's Choice 2* *Speaking of Lust* • *Opening Shots 2* • *Speaking of Greed* • *Blood on Their Hands* • *Gangsters, Swindlers, Killers, and Thieves* • *Manhattan Noir* *Manhattan Noir 2*

First published in Great Britain in 2013 by Orion Books,
an imprint of The Orion Publishing Group Ltd
Orion House, 5 Upper Saint Martin's Lane
London WC2H 9EA

An Hachette UK Company

1 3 5 7 9 10 8 6 4 2

A CIP catalogue record for this book is available from the British Library.

ISBN (Hardback) 978 1 4091 2484 9
ISBN (Export Trade Paperback) 978 1 4091 2485 6
ISBN (Ebook) 978 1 4091 2486 3

Printed in Great Britain by
CPI Group (UK) Ltd, Croydon, CR0 4YY

The Orion Publishing Group's policy is to use papers that are natural, renewable and recyclable products and made from wood grown in sustainable forests. The logging and manufacturing processes are expected to conform to the environmental regulations of the country of origin.

www.orionbooks.co.uk

HIT ME

LAWRENCE BLOCK

This one's for
all my
Tweasured Tweeps
&
FeeBee Jeebees
all you
Wild.Web.Workers
&
Cyberzerkers
and especially for
JAYE
&
JULIA

KELLER IN DALLAS

ONE

The young man, who would have looked owlish even without the round eyeglasses, unfolded a piece of paper and laid it on the counter in front of Keller. "The certificate of expertization for Obock J1," he said. "Signed by Bloch and Mueller."

He might have been a Red Sox fan invoking Ted Williams, and Keller could understand why. Herbert Bloch and Edwin Mueller were legendary philatelists, and their assertion that this particular stamp was indeed a genuine example of Obock's first postage due stamp, designated J1 in the Scott catalog, was enough to allay all doubt.

Keller examined the stamp, first with his unaided eye, then through the magnifier he took from his breast pocket. There was a photograph of the stamp on the certificate, and he studied that as well, with and without magnification. Bloch and

Mueller had sworn to its legitimacy in 1960, so the certificate was old enough to be collectible in and of itself.

Still, even experts were sometimes careless, and occasionally mistaken. And now and then someone switched in a ringer for an expertized stamp. So Keller reached for another tool, this one in the inside pocket of his jacket. It was a flat metal oblong, designed to enable the user to compute the number of perforations per inch on the top or side of a stamp. Obock J1 was imperforate, which rendered the question moot, but the perforation gauge doubled as a mini ruler, marked out in inches along one edge and millimeters along the other, and Keller used it to check the size of the stamp's overprint.

That overprint, hand stamped on a postage due stamp initially issued for the French Colonies as a whole, had the name of the place—Obock—in black capitals. On the original stamp, the overprint measured 12 1/2 millimeters by 3 3/4 millimeters. On the reprint, a copy of which reposed in Keller's own collection, each dimension of the overprint was half a millimeter smaller.

And so Keller measured the overprint on this stamp, and found himself in agreement with Mr. Bloch and Mr. Mueller. This was the straight goods, the genuine article. All he had to do to go home with it was outbid any other interested collectors. And he could do that, too, and without straining his budget or dipping into his capital.

But first he'd have to kill somebody.

The Dallas-based firm of Whistler & Welles conducted auctions of collectibles throughout the year. At various times they sold coins, books, autographs, and sports memorabilia, but the partners had started out as stamp dealers, and philatelic holdings remained the largest component of their business. Their annual Spring Equinox Sale, held each year in the Hotel Lombardy on the third weekend in March, was one Keller had wanted to attend for years. Something had always prevented him from attending. He'd marked up copies of their catalogs over the years, sent in unsuccessful mail bids on a few occasions, and one year had a hotel room reserved and a flight booked before something or other came up and forced him to cancel.

He'd lived in New York when Whistler & Welles put him on their mailing list. Nowadays he lived in New Orleans, and the name on their mailing list was one he'd borrowed from a local tombstone. He was Nicholas Edwards now, and that was the name on his passport, and on all the cards in his wallet. He lived in a big old house in the Lower Garden District, and he had a wife and a baby daughter, and he was a partner in a construction firm specializing in purchasing and rehabilitating distressed properties.

A year earlier, he'd looked with longing at the Whistler & Welles catalog. Dallas was a lot closer to New Orleans than to New York, but he and Donny Wallings were putting in twelve-hour days and seven-day weeks, just trying to keep up with everything they had going on.

But that was a year ago, before the collapse of the subprime mortgage market and everything that followed on its heels. Credit dried up, houses stopped selling, and they'd gone from more business than they could handle to no business to speak of.

So he could afford the time. A couple of days in Dallas? Sure, why not? He could even take his time and drive to Dallas and back.

And there were plenty of stamps on offer that he'd be eager to add to his collection, with Obock J1 at the very top of his wish list.

Now, though, he couldn't afford it.

* * *

The Lombardy, an independent, locally owned older hotel trying to survive in a world of modern chains, was starting to show its age. The carpet in Keller's room, while not yet threadbare, was due for replacement. A sofa in the lobby was worn on the arms, and the wood paneling in one of the elevators needed touching up. None of this bothered Keller, who found the hotel's faded glory somehow reassuring. What better venue for men of a certain age to compete for little pieces of paper that had done their duty carrying the mail long before any of them were born?

Whistler & Welles had booked a large conference room on the mezzanine for their three-day sale, which would begin promptly at nine Friday morning. New Orleans and Dallas were a little over five hundred miles apart, and Keller drove most of the way Wednesday, stopping for the night at a Red Roof Inn off a handy exit from the interstate. He checked into his room at the Lombardy a little after noon, and by one o'clock he was signing *Nicholas Edwards* on the bidder register and walking over to the long table where they were showing the auction lots.

By two thirty he'd had a look at all the lots that interested him, and had made cryptic notes in his auction catalog. Every sales lot was illustrated with a color photograph, so he didn't absolutely have to see them up close and personal, but sometimes you got something that way that you couldn't get from a photo in a catalog. Some stamps reached out to you while others put you off, and it probably didn't make any real sense, but the whole hobby was wacky enough to begin with. I mean, spending a fortune on little pieces of colored paper? Picking them up with tongs, putting them in plastic mounts, and securing them in albums? Why, for heaven's sake?

Keller had long since come to terms with the essential absurdity of the pastime, and didn't let it bother him. He was a stamp collector, he derived enormous satisfaction from the pursuit, and that was all he needed to know. If you thought about it, just about everything human beings did was pointless and ridiculous. Golf? Skiing? Sex?

Upstairs in his room, Keller reviewed the notes he'd made. There were stamps he'd initially considered and now decided to pass on, others he might buy if the price was right, and a few for which he'd be bidding competitively. And there was Obock J1. It was rare, it didn't come up that often, and this particular specimen was a nice one, with four full margins. Imperforate stamps had to be cut apart, and sometimes a careless clerk snipped off a bit of the stamp in the process. That didn't keep a letter from reaching its designated recipient, but it made the stamp considerably less desirable to a collector.

According to the Scott catalog, Obock J1 was worth $7500. In their catalog, Whistler & Welles had estimated the lot conservatively at $6500. The actual price, Keller knew, would depend on the bidders, those in the room and those participating by mail or phone, or via the Internet, and the hammer price wouldn't tell the whole story; to that you'd have to add a 15 percent bidder's premium and whatever sales tax the state of Texas saw fit to pile on. Keller, who wanted the stamp more than ever now that he'd had a look at it, figured he might have to bid $12,000 to get it, and the check he'd write out would be uncomfortably close to $15,000.

Would he go that high?

Well, that's why they had auctions, and why bidders showed up in person. You sat in your chair, and you'd decided in advance just how high you'd go and when you'd drop out, and then they got to the lot you were waiting for and you discovered how you really felt. Maybe you did exactly what you planned on doing, but maybe not. Maybe you found out your enthusiasm wasn't as great as you'd thought, and wound up dropping out of the bidding early on. Or maybe you found yourself hanging in far beyond your predetermined limit, spending considerably more than your maximum.

No way to guess how it would be this time. It was Thursday, and tomorrow's morning and afternoon sessions would both be devoted to U.S. issues, and thus of no interest to Keller. He wouldn't need to be in the auction room until Saturday morning, and the French Colonial issues, including Obock J1, wouldn't come up until early Saturday afternoon.

He went downstairs, walked outside. It was cool, but not unpleasantly so. Football weather, you'd call it, if the calendar didn't insist that it was March. Cool, crisp—a perfect October day.

He walked a couple of blocks to another hotel, where there was a queue of waiting cabs. He went to the first one in line, settled into the backseat, and told the driver to take him to the airport.

TWO

He'd been working on his stamps when the phone rang. He was alone in the house, Julia had left to pick up Jenny at day care, and he very nearly let the machine answer it because calls were almost invariably for Julia. But there was always a chance it was Donny, so he went and picked it up half a ring ahead of the machine, and it turned out to be Dot.

Not that she bothered to identify herself. Without preamble she said, "Remember that cell phone you had?" And she broke the connection before he could respond.

He remembered the phone, an untraceable prepaid one, and even remembered where he'd left it, in his sock drawer. The battery had long since run down, and while it was charging Julia and Jenny came home, so it was a good half hour before he was back in his den with the phone.

For years he'd lived in New York, a few blocks from the United Nations, and Dot had lived north of the city in White

Plains, in a big old house with a wraparound porch. That house was gone now, burned to the ground, and the same wind that had blown him to New Orleans had picked up Dot and deposited her in Sedona, Arizona. Her name was Wilma Corder now, even as his was Nicholas Edwards, and she had a new life of her own. Back in the day she had arranged the contract killings he had performed, but that was then and this was now.

Even so, he closed the door before he made the call.

"I'll just plunge right in," she said. "I'm back in business."

"And the business is—"

"Holding its own. Not booming, but a long way from flatlining, which seems to be what everybody else's business is doing."

"What I meant—"

"I know what you meant. You want to know what business I'm in, but do you have to ask? Same old."

"Oh."

"You're surprised? You're not the only one. See, there's this thing I joined, Athena International."

"It sounds like an insurance company."

"It does? It's what they call a service club, like Rotary or Kiwanis. Except it's exclusively for women."

"Can't women join Rotary?"

"Of course, because it would be sexist to keep them out. But men can't join Athena."

"That doesn't seem fair."

"Keller, if it bothers you, you can put on a dress and a wig and I'll drag you along to a meeting. If you're still awake at the end of it I'll buy you a pair of high heels."

"But you enjoy it."

"The hell I do. I must have been brain-dead when I joined.

We do things like pick up trash once a month around Bell Rock, and I approve of that, since I've got a view of the damned thing from my bedroom window, and it looks better without the beer bottles and gum wrappers. I'm not crazy about walking around in the hot sun hunting for other people's garbage, but I go once in a while. And we raise money to give some deserving girl a scholarship to college, and if I'm not out there running a table at the bake sale, or God forbid baking something, at least I'll write out a check. But I mostly pass on the monthly meetings. I've never been a meeting person. Endless talking, and then the damn song."

"What song?"

"The Athenian song, and no, I'm not about to sing it for you. But that's how we close the meeting. We all stand in a circle and cross our arms over our chests and clasp hands and sing this Mickey Mouse song."

"Minnie Mouse," he suggested.

"I stand corrected. The thing is, most of the members have careers of one sort or another, and we don't just pick up garbage. We network, which means we take in each other's laundry."

"Huh?"

"Beth's a travel agent, Alison's a real-estate agent, Lindsay does Tupperware parties."

"So you've been buying Tupperware," he suggested. "And houses."

"No houses. But when I went to Hawaii for a week I let Beth make the booking," she said, "and one of our members is a lawyer, and when I need a lawyer she's the one I go to. And of course I bought the Tupperware. You go to the party, you buy the Tupperware."

"And drink the Kool-Aid. I'm sorry, go on."

"Anyway," she said, "there they all were with their careers, and there I was, with all the money I needed, and it couldn't keep me from feeling time was passing me by."

"That's what time does."

"I know. But I couldn't shake the feeling that I ought to be doing something. But what? Volunteer at a hospital? Help out at a soup kitchen?"

"Doesn't sound like you."

"So I picked up the phone," she said, "and made a few calls."

"How'd that go? I mean, officially, aren't you dead?"

"As a doornail," she agreed. "Shot in the head and burned up in a fire. You Google Dorothea Harbison and that's what you'll find out. But the people who would call me to arrange a booking, they never heard of Dorothea Harbison. A few of them knew me as Dot, but most of them didn't even have that much. I was a phone number, and a voice on the phone, and a mail drop where they sent payments. And that was as much as anybody needed to know."

"And how much did you know about them?"

"My customers? Next to nothing. But I did have a couple of phone numbers."

And one day she drove to Flagstaff and rented a private mailbox at a franchise operation on South Milton Road, a block from the Embassy Suites hotel. On her way home she picked up a prepaid and presumably untraceable phone, and over the next few days she made a couple of calls. "I wondered what happened to you," the first man said. "I tried your number, but it was disconnected."

"I got married," she told him, "and don't bother congratulating me, because it didn't work out."

"That was quick."

"For you, maybe. You weren't there. Long and short, I'm here for you when you need me. Let me give you the number."

She had other numbers, too, of men who'd done what Keller used to do. Not all of those numbers worked anymore, but she was able to reestablish a contact or two, and one fellow said he could really use the work. Then she sat back and waited for something to happen, not entirely sure she wanted her new phone to ring, but it did, and within the week.

"And here's something interesting, Keller. The call was from someone I hadn't called myself, someone I hadn't even worked with before. One of my old clients passed the word, and here was this guy calling me out of the blue, with a piece of work to be done in the great state of Georgia. So I called the guy who'd told me how he needed work, and he couldn't believe I was getting back to him so quick. And I sat back and got paid."

Like old times, Keller suggested, and she agreed. "I'm still me," she said. "I'm a rich lady, and I look better than I used to. I moved to Sedona and the pounds started to drop off right away. The place is crawling with energy vortexes, except I think the plural is vortices."

"What are they?"

"Beats me, Keller. I think it's something like an intersection, except the streets are imaginary. Anyway, some of the women I know are fat as pigs, and they've got the same vortices I do. I belong to a gym, can you believe it?"

"You told me."

"And I've got a personal trainer. Did I tell you that, too? His name is Scott, and I sometimes get the feeling he'd like to get a little more personal, but I'm probably wrong about that. It's not as though I turned into whistle bait, and what would he want with a woman old enough to use a term like that? Whistle bait, for God's sake."

"I guess people don't say that anymore."

"They don't whistle much, either. Look, this is a mistake, isn't it? I shouldn't have called."

"Well."

"For God's sake, you've got your life to live. You've got a beautiful wife and an amazing daughter and you're the rehab king of New Orleans real estate. So why don't you just wish me luck in my new venture and hang up, and I'll leave you alone."

THREE

Keller limited himself to monosyllables en route to the airport, and gave the driver a tip neither large nor small enough to be memorable. He walked through the door for departing flights, took an escalator one flight down, and a bubbly girl at the Hertz counter found his reservation right away. He showed her a driver's license and a credit card, both in the same name—one that was neither J. P. Keller nor Nicholas Edwards. They were good enough to get him the keys to a green Subaru hatchback, and in due course he was behind the wheel and on his way.

The house he was looking for was on Caruth Boulevard, in the University Park section. He'd located it online and printed out a map, and he found it now with no trouble, one of a whole block of upscale Spanish-style homes on substantial landscaped lots not far from the Southern Methodist campus. Sculpted stucco walls, a red tile roof, an attached three-car garage. You'd think a family could be very happy in a house like that, Keller thought, but in the present instance you'd be wrong, because the place was home to Charles and Portia Walmsley, and neither of them could be happy until the other was dead.

Keller slowed down as he passed the house, then circled the block for another look at it. Was anyone at home? As far as he could see, there was no way to tell. Charles Walmsley had moved out a few weeks earlier, and Portia shared the house with the Salvadoran housekeeper. Keller hadn't learned the housekeeper's name, or that of the man who was a frequent overnight guest of Mrs. Walmsley, but he'd been told that the man drove a Lexus SUV. Keller didn't see it in the driveway, but he couldn't be sure it wasn't in the garage.

"The man drives an SUV," Dot had said, "and he once played football for TCU. I know what an SUV is, but—"

"Texas Christian University," Keller supplied. "In Fort Worth."

"I thought that might be it. Do they have something to do with horny frogs?"

"Horned Frogs. That's their football team, the Horned Frogs. They're archrivals of SMU."

"That would be Southern Methodist."

"Right. They're the Mustangs."

"Frogs and Mustangs. How do you know all this crap, Keller? Don't tell me it's on a stamp. Never mind, it's not important. What's important is that something permanent happens to Mrs. Walmsley. And it would be good if something happened to the boyfriend, too."

"It would?"

"He'll pay a bonus."

"A bonus? What kind of a bonus?"

"Unspecified, which makes it tricky to know what to expect, let alone collect it. And he'll double the bonus if they nail the boyfriend for the wife's murder, but when you double an unspecified number, what have you got? Two times what?"

Keller drove past the Walmsley house a second time, and didn't learn anything new in the process. He consulted his map, figured out his route, and left the Subaru in a parking garage three blocks from the Lombardy.

In his room, he picked up the phone to call Julia, then remembered what hotels charge you for phone calls. Charles Walmsley was paying top dollar, bonus or no, but making a call from a hotel room was like burning the money in the street. He used his cell phone instead, first making sure that it was the iPhone Julia had given him for his birthday and not the prepaid one he used only for calls to Dot.

The hotel room was okay, he told her. And he'd had a good look at the stamps he was interested in, and that was always helpful. And she put Jenny on, and he cooed to his daughter and she babbled at him. He told her he loved her, and when Julia came back on the phone he told her the same.

Portia Walmsley didn't have any children. Her husband did, from a previous marriage, but they lived with their mother across the Red River in Oklahoma. So there wouldn't be any kids to worry about in the house on Caruth Boulevard.

As far as the Salvadoran maid was concerned, Dot had told him the client didn't care one way or the other. He wasn't paying a bonus for her, that was for sure. He'd pointed out that she was an illegal immigrant, and Keller wondered what that had to do with anything.

* * *

That first night, he hadn't called Dot back right away. First he and Julia had tucked Jenny in for the night—or for as much of it as the child would sleep through. Then the two of them sat over coffee in the kitchen, and he mentioned that Donny had called earlier, not because some work had come in but on the chance that he might want to go fishing.

"But you didn't want to go?"

He shook his head. "Neither did Donny, not really. He just wanted to pick up the phone."

"It's hard for him, isn't it?"

"He's not used to sitting around."

"Neither are you, these days. But I guess it must be like old times for you. You know, with lots of time off between jobs."

"Stamp collecting helped take up the slack."

"And I guess it still does," she said. "And that way there's no fish to clean."

He went upstairs and sat down with his stamps for a few minutes, then made the call. "So you're back in business," he said. "And you didn't call me, and then you did."

"And I guess it was a mistake," she said, "and I apologize. But how could I be in the business and not let you know about it? That didn't seem right."

"No."

"And it's not like you're a recovering alcoholic and I'm opening wine bottles in front of you. You're a grown-up. If you're not interested you'll tell me so and that's the end of it. Keller? You still there?"

"I'm here."

"So you are," she said. "And yet you haven't told me you're not interested."

One of his stamp albums was open on the table in front of him, and he looked at a page of Italian stamps overprinted for use in the Aegean Islands. There were a few stamps missing, and while they weren't at all expensive they'd proved difficult to find.

"Keller?"

"Business dried up," he said. "There's no financing. We can't buy houses and we can't sell them, and nobody's hiring us to repair them, either, because there's no money around."

"Well, I'm not surprised. It's the same everywhere. Still, you've got enough money to see you through, haven't you?"

"We're all right," he said. "But I've gotten used to living on what I earn, and now I'm dipping into capital. I'm not about to run through it, there's no danger of that, but still..."

"I know what you mean. Keller, I've got something if you want it. I had a guy lined up for it and I just learned he's in the hospital, he flipped his car and they had to yank him out of there with the Jaws of Death."

"Isn't it the Jaws of Life?"

"Whatever. His own jaw is about the only part of him that didn't get broken. I guess he'll live, and he may even walk again, but there's no way he can get it all together by the end of the month and spare my client the agony of divorce."

"And the heartbreak of community property."

"Something like that. It has to happen before the first of April, and either I find somebody who can take care of it or I have to send back the money. You probably remember how much I like doing that."

"Vividly."

"Once I have it in hand," she said, "I think of it as my money, and I hate like the devil to part with it. So what do you think? Can you get away for a few days in the next couple of weeks?"

"My calendar's wide open," he said. "All I've got is a stamp auction I was thinking about going to. That's the weekend after next, if I go at all."

"Where is it?"

"Dallas."

There was a thoughtful silence. "Keller," she said at length, "call me crazy, but I see the hand of Providence at work here."

FOUR

The Lombardy had a buffet breakfast they were proud of, and in the morning Keller went down to give it a try. The problem with buffets, he'd found, was that you wanted to get your money's worth and wound up eating too much. He resolved not to do that, and helped himself to a moderate amount of bacon and eggs and a toasted bran muffin. When he was through he sipped his coffee and thought about the other items he'd noticed, and how good they'd looked. He sighed and went back for more.

And took another plate, as the sign advised him to. "I don't get it," he said to a fellow diner, a heavyset man with an oversize mustache. "Why does the state of Texas forbid me to pile new food onto an old plate?"

"Health regulation, isn't it?"

"I guess, but why? I mean, what am I going to do, pass germs to myself?"

"Good point."

"And this way they've got an extra plate to wash."

"Even more," the man said, "if you make enough return trips, and that smoked salmon is worth a try, believe me. They feed you a hell of a breakfast here at the Venetia. But maybe there's another reason for fresh plates. Maybe it's like putting new wine in old bottles."

"Well, that's something else I've wondered about," Keller said. "I know it's a metaphor, but what are you supposed to do with old bottles? Just throw them in a landfill?"

He went back to his table and ate everything on his plate, but didn't even consider going back for thirds. Instead he let the waitress pour him more coffee, signed his check, and carried the coffee over to the table where the mustachioed gentleman was working on his smoked salmon.

Keller put a hand on an unoccupied chair, and the man nodded, and Keller sat down. "You're here for the auction," he said.

"I have that look, do I?"

He shook his head. "The hotel," he said. "You called it the Venetia."

"I did? Well, that's a giveaway, isn't it? A very philatelic slip of the tongue. Or should that be slip of the tongs?"

Because he collected stamps, Keller knew that in the mid-nineteenth century Lombardy-Venetia had been a kingdom in the north of Italy forming part of the Austrian Empire. Starting in 1850, Austria produced stamps for Lombardy-Venetia, essentially identical to regular Austrian issues but denominated in centesimi and lire and, after 1858, in soldi and florins. Then in 1859 Lombardy was annexed to Sardinia, and seven years later Venetia became a part of the kingdom of Italy.

"But for philately," the fellow said, "I might never have heard of Lombardy or Venetia, let alone know to link the two of them with a hyphen."

"I haven't done much with Lombardy-Venetia," Keller admitted. "All those reprints, and so much counterfeiting. It's confusing, so I always find it easier to buy something else."

"Your Lombardy-Venetia's probably well ahead of mine, considering that I don't own a single stamp from the benighted place. Nothing but U.S. for me, I'm afraid."

"And that's the one thing I don't collect," Keller said. "I'm worldwide, to 1940."

"That way there's always something for you to buy. Which is a blessing or a curse, depending how you look at it. I don't even collect all of my own country. I did, but then I sold everything after 1900, and then I narrowed that down to the 1869 issue. I don't know if you know the stamps..."

Keller knew them well enough to hold up his end of the conversation. By the time they left the table they were Nicholas and Michael, sharing the comfortable camaraderie of fellow hobbyists who wouldn't be competing with one another in the auction room. In fact they wouldn't even be occupying the room at the same time, with U.S. on the block today and the rest of the world waiting its turn.

"Stamps in the morning, covers in the afternoon," Michael said. "There's a block of Scott 119, the fifteen-cent type two, that I wouldn't mind having. And this afternoon, well, this wouldn't mean much to a nonspecialist, but..."

Keller heard him out, wished him luck.

"Ah, but what's luck, Nick? I'm too old to chase 'em nowadays, but when I used to go out looking to pick up a woman, I'd tell myself maybe I'd get lucky. But you reach a point where getting lucky means going home alone. You know, you ought to drop by when the 1869 lots come up. Share in the drama without having a stake in the outcome. All the excitement and none of the risk—like watching a murder mystery on television."

Keller slipped into the auction room a half hour after the start of the morning session. The first several dozen lots were nothing too exciting, job lots and accumulations, and then the first of the Postmasters' Provisionals came up and the proceedings got more interesting. Sort of like watching a mystery on television, come to think of it.

He stayed longer than he'd planned, waiting for the large block of number 119 to be offered, and watched as his new friend hung in gamely while bidding climbed to four times the estimated value. Then Keller's friend dropped out, and the block was knocked down to a telephone bidder.

Not quite like a murder mystery on television, because it didn't end the way you wanted it to.

Keller slipped out of the auction room, left the hotel, and picked up his rental car. He'd brought his map along, but never took it out of his breast pocket. He had no trouble remembering the route to the house on Caruth Boulevard.

He drove past the house, taking a quick look at it, and all he really managed to establish was that it was still there. He couldn't stake the place out and watch the comings and goings, not in this neighborhood, where a man lurking in a parked car would be reported to the police in no time at all. Nor could he park a few blocks away and approach on foot, because if there was a single pedestrian over the age of six anywhere in the area, he'd managed to keep out of Keller's field of vision.

The right way, he thought, was to take a week or two, but the hell with that. This wasn't some well-guarded mafioso in a walled castle, with a moat full of bent-nosed alligators. This was a woman who had no idea just how much her husband wanted to be rid of her, and no reason to fear a stranger at her door.

Keller went back to a strip mall he'd passed earlier, with a Walgreens at one end and an Office Depot at the other. Park near one and walk to the other? No, he told himself. Why bother? Nobody was going to look at his license plate, and what difference did it make if they did?

He parked in front of the Office Depot and was in and out of it in ten minutes, paying cash for the clipboard and the pad of yellow paper. Duct tape? No, not necessary. He was going to buy a pen, then remembered that he already had one of his own.

What else? A box cutter, a letter opener, something sharp and pointed? No. He had his hands, and there would be knives in the kitchen if he felt the need.

He drove back to the Walmsley house and parked in the driveway, where anyone walking by could see his car and take note of the license plate. Fat chance, he thought, and walked up to the door and rang the bell.

Nothing.

Maid's day off, he thought. Getting lucky, he told himself, was when you rang a doorbell and nobody answered. That was even better than going home alone, and—

Footsteps, approaching the door. He waited for it to open, and when it didn't he poked the bell again, and this time the door opened immediately, and he found himself looking at his own reflection in the mirror that faced the door. Just for an instant, albeit a disconcerting one; then he lowered his eyes and looked down at the Salvadoran maid.

"Ah, good morning," he said. "Mrs. Walmsley?"

"No," the maid said, in Spanish or English, it was impossible to tell. "Her no *aquí,*" she said, in a combination of the two.

"And Mr. Walmsley?"

"Him not *vive aquí.*"

A shake of the head, good enough in either language.

"Is anyone else at home?"

Another head shake. The simple thing to do, Keller realized, was kill the woman, stuff her in a closet—or a laundry hamper, or a big hatbox. She was innocent, but then so was Portia Walmsley, for all he knew.

But Jesus, she was so tiny.

The client, he recalled, didn't care one way or the other about the woman. He wasn't paying a bonus for some illegal immigrant, and—

Bingo.

He brandished the clipboard, gave her a look at it. He hadn't thought to write anything on the top sheet of paper, but it didn't matter.

"INS," he said.

Her face remained expressionless, but eloquently so.

"Green card," he said.

"No hablo inglés."

"Carta verde," Keller said, straining his command of the language to the limit. *"¿Tienes un carta verde?"*

Una, he thought. Not *un,* for God's sake. *Una*. An INS man would know that, right? Jesus, you couldn't live in New York without knowing that much, let alone Texas, and—

Un, una, what difference could it possibly make? Her shoulders slumped, and she managed somehow to become even smaller. Keller felt horrible.

"I will be back," he said. "I'll go away now to have my lunch, and when I come back you can show me your green card. Your *carta verde, comprenez-vous?*"

Comprenez-vous? That was French, for God's sake, yet another language he was unable to speak. But it was clear that she *comprenezed* just fine.

"You come back?"

"In an hour," he said, and turned away, unable to bear the sight of her expressionless face.

He drove to the strip mall, parking this time near the Walgreens, and tossed the clipboard into a trash bin alongside the entrance. He wasn't hungry and he couldn't think of anything to buy, so he returned to his car and sat behind the wheel. Nothing to read, nothing to do, really, but let time pass. He fiddled with the radio, but couldn't figure out how to get it to play without running the engine. There'd be a way to do it, there always was, but every car maker felt compelled to work out its own way of doing things, and when you rented cars you could never figure out how to adjust the seats or play the radio or work the air-conditioning or dim the lights, and when you went to signal a left turn you generally wound up switching on the windshield wipers. The steering was always more or less the same, and so were the brakes, and it was a good thing or everybody would crash into everybody else.

They'd have newspapers in the drugstore. Magazines, maybe even paperback books.

No, the hell with it.

He gave her an hour and a half, then returned to the Walmsley house and parked once again in the driveway. He walked up to the door and rang the bell, and wondered if he might have been a shade precipitous in ditching the clipboard, because what if she opened the door with Portia Walmsley on her left and some slick immigration lawyer on her right? *Hang on,* he'd say. *Be right back, soon as I get my clipboard—*

No one came to the door. He rang the bell again, and listened carefully, and heard no footsteps. The car, the rented Subaru, had now become a problem, and he wished he'd left it at the strip mall and approached on foot. But that was a long way to walk in a neighborhood where everybody drove.

He couldn't leave the thing in the driveway. There was probably room for it in the three-car garage, since the estranged husband wouldn't have left on foot, but Portia Walmsley would almost certainly notice his car when she parked her own beside it, and—

He backed out of the driveway, drove fifty yards down the street, parked, and walked back. Rang the bell, listened for footsteps, knocked, listened again. He tried the doorknob, because you never know, but it was locked.

No problem.

FIVE

Keller had never been a thief, let alone a burglar. In his youth he'd been one of several young men who'd hung around the Old Man's place in Yonkers. The Old Man was Giuseppe Ragone, dear to the hearts of tabloid journalists, who wrote about him as Joey Rags. Keller had never called him that, or anything like it. In direct conversation, if he called the man anything it was Sir. To others, he'd refer to him as Mr. R. In his own mind, though, his boss was the Old Man.

And Keller liked hanging around. The Old Man would give him errands to run, packages to pick up and deliver, messages to pass along. Eventually he sent Keller along when disciplinary actions were called for, and something he saw led him to devise assignments that, in retrospect, Keller was able to recognize as little tests. Keller, unaware he was being tested, passed with flying colors. What the Old Man managed to establish was that Keller didn't flinch when called upon to pull the trigger. The Old Man had suspected as much, that was why he'd devised the tests, but it was all news to Keller.

So Keller went from being an errand boy to taking people out, and at first the people he took out were men who had somehow managed to get on the Old Man's hit list, and then the Old Man realized what a fine, dependable asset he had, and began renting Keller out to interested parties. Not many people knew Keller's name, the Old Man saw to that, but an increasing number of people knew he was out there somewhere, at the beck and call of Joey Rags, and that he did good work. So from that point on that was the only kind of work he was called upon to perform. There were no more packages or messages to deliver, no more errands to run.

A more conventional apprenticeship would have seen Keller grow into a jack-of-all-criminal-trades, with a working knowledge of various felonious enterprises. But Keller, forced to improvise, had picked up what he needed to know. Without ever becoming a disciplined student of the martial arts, he'd read books and rented videos, taken the odd class here and there, and was as proficient as he had to be with the usual run of weapons, and with his bare hands. Similarly, he'd become reasonably good at breaking and entering, and it didn't take him long to get into the Walmsley house.

It was the sort of house that would have a burglar alarm installed, and there was a decal to that effect, along with metallic tape on the ground-floor windows. But the alarm had not been engaged when the maid opened the door to him, and he didn't believe for a moment she'd have taken the time to set it before fleeing a house she'd never be likely to see again. If the Walmsleys had ever taken the trouble to teach her how to set it in the first place.

No alarm, then. The front door was locked, probably because it locked of its own accord when you pulled it shut. Keller could have forced it but didn't, nor did he force the door leading to the garage. He went around to the rear of the house, took one of the windows off its track, and let himself in.

The maid wouldn't be coming back. The house was a large one, and Keller went through it room by room, and it was easy to tell the maid's room, because it was the smallest room in the house, tucked in under the back stairs and alongside the kitchen. There was a wooden crucifix hanging from a nail on one wall, and there was a week-old copy of *El Diario,* and that was pretty much all there was aside from the bed and dresser. She'd thrown everything else in a suitcase and now she was gone, and she wouldn't be coming back.

The crucifix, he decided, had been a parting gift from her mother in El Salvador. That was the name of the country, while the capital city was San Salvador, but she probably came from somewhere else. Cutuco, he decided. Puerto Cutuco was the only other city he knew in El Salvador, and he knew it because one of the stamps of the 1935 series pictured the wharf at Cutuco. Another stamp in the same series showed a volcano, and he knew its name, but couldn't remember it.

As if it mattered. Her mother in Cutuco had given her the crucifix, he continued thinking, telling her to keep it with her forever and it would always protect her, and she'd dutifully mounted it on the wall, and in her haste she'd forgotten it. Terrified of the faceless Immigration and Naturalization Service (except it wasn't so faceless now, it had Keller's face on it), she'd abandoned the one thing she owned that tied her to her home and family. She wouldn't come back for it, she didn't dare, but its loss would always bother her, and—

Jesus, get over it, he told himself. She could let go of the crucifix a lot easier than he could relinquish the fantasy he was spinning, complete with a hometown from a stamp in his collection.

It bothered him, though. That he'd scared her the way he did. Still, what else was he supposed to do? He couldn't snap her neck just because she was in the way. She was tiny, she'd have to stand on a box to be five feet tall. It would be like killing a little kid, and that was something Keller had never done. Once or twice someone had offered a contract on a child, and he and Dot had been entirely in accord on the subject. You had to draw a line, and that was where you had to draw it.

But that was a matter of age, not size. The woman—and he found himself wishing he knew her name, now that he'd played such a role in her life—was certainly over twenty-one. Old enough to vote, old enough to drink...and old enough to be killed? Was he being politically incorrect by giving her a pass on the basis of her height? Was he being...well, he wasn't sure the word existed, but was he being a sizeist? A heightist? Was he altitudinally prejudiced?

What he was being, he told himself, was severely neurotic, and that was the occasional consequence of breaking into an empty house with nothing to do but wait for someone to appear. He'd done this sort of thing before, but that was in an earlier life. Now he had a wife and a daughter, now he lived in a big old house in New Orleans and had a business repairing and renovating other people's houses, and the new life suited him, and what was he doing here, anyway?

He looked at his watch, and every ten minutes or so he looked at it again.

Keller had read somewhere that all of man's difficulties stemmed from his inability to sit alone in a room. The line stayed with him, and a while ago he'd Googled his way to its source. Someone named Pascal had made the observation, Blaise Pascal, and it turned out he'd said a lot of other interesting things as well, but all but the first one had slipped Keller's mind. He thought of it now as he forced himself to sit alone in the maid's room, waiting for Portia Walmsley to come home.

And pictured the woman. When he was living in New York, he'd have taken the train to White Plains, where Dot would have given him the woman's photograph, which someone would have sent to her by FedEx, in the same package with the first installment of his fee. Instead, he'd booted up his computer, clicked on Google Images, typed in "Portia Walmsley," and clicked again, whereupon Google served up a banquet of pictures of the oh-so-social Mrs. Walmsley, sometimes alone, sometimes with others, but all of them showing a big-haired full-figured blonde with what Keller had once heard called a Pepsodent smile. Or was it an Ipana smile? Keller couldn't remember, and decided he didn't care.

Sitting alone in a room, with only one's own mind and an abandoned crucifix for company, wasn't the most fun Keller had ever had in his life. There was nothing in the room he could read, and nothing to look at but suffering Jesus, and that was the last place Keller wanted to aim his eyes.

Which, no matter where he pointed them, he was finding it increasingly difficult to keep open. They kept closing of their own accord. He kicked off his shoes and stretched out on the bed, just for comfort, not because he intended to sleep, and—

And the next thing he knew he was in an auction room, with one lot after another hammered down before he could get his hand in the air to bid. And a man and a woman were sitting on either side of him, talking furiously in a language he couldn't understand, and making it impossible for him to focus on the auction. And—

"Where is that damn girl? For what I pay her you'd think she could do what she's supposed to. *Margarita!*"

"Maybe she's in her room."

"At this hour?"

His eyes snapped open. A man and a woman, but now they were speaking English, and he could hear them on the stairs. He sprang from the bed, crossed to the door, worked the bolt. No sooner had it slid home than they had reached the door, and the woman was calling the maid's name—Margarita, evidently—at the top of her brassy voice.

"Give it up," the man said. "Ain't nobody home."

A hand took hold of the doorknob, turned, pushed. The bolt held.

"She's in there. The lazy bitch is sleeping."

"Oh, come on, Portsie." Portsie? "Couldn't nobody sleep through the racket you're making."

"Then why's the door locked?"

"Maybe she don't want you rummaging through her underwear."

"As if," Portia said, and rattled the doorknob. "This is something new, locking the door. I don't think you *can* lock it, except from inside. You slide a bolt and it goes through a little loop, but how can you do that from outside?"

"Maybe she's in there with a boyfriend."

"My God, maybe she is. Margarita! God damn you, open the fucking door or I'll call the fucking INS on you." There was a pause, and then Keller heard them moving around, and some heavy breathing.

"Hey," the woman said. "And what do you think you're doing, sport?"

"Rummaging through your underwear, Portsie."

"It's distracting me."

"That's the general idea."

"If she's in there fucking some pint-sized *cholo*—"

"She's not. She was in there, all by herself, and she locked the door."

"So where is she now?"

"Out."

"Out? How'd she get out?"

"Through the keyhole."

"You're terrible, baby."

"C'mon," he said. "I need a drink, and so do you. And that's not all we need."

And Keller stood there while their footsteps receded.

Once he'd had time to think about it, Keller realized he'd missed an opportunity. There they were, the target and the bonus, all ready to walk right into the room where he was waiting for them. And what had he done? He'd locked the door, as if he were not a hired assassin but the timid little chambermaid who'd been the room's rightful if unlawful occupant.

He was half asleep, and unprepared, and that's why he'd been so quick to lock the door. Alert and prepared, he'd have flung it open and yanked them inside, and in no time at all he'd have been around the block and out of the neighborhood, and they'd be working their way toward room temperature.

Now, because he hadn't been clever enough to let them burst in on him, he'd have to do the bursting.

SIX

It wasn't hard to find them. From the hallway outside Margarita's room, he could hear them—laughing, grunting, sounding for all the world like a pair of drunken lovers. He made his way to the door of the master bedroom, which they had not troubled to close, and there they were, doing the dirty deed. One glance established as much for Keller, and he quickly averted his eyes.

The woman was Portia Walmsley; Keller had glimpsed more than enough of her to match her with her pictures. Not that he'd been in much doubt, with her companion calling her Portsie. And the man looked vaguely familiar as well, though Keller couldn't think why. Had he seen him in the auction room? Jesus, was the sonofabitch a stamp collector?

He could take another look, but he didn't really want to. Keller had never regarded lovemaking as a spectator sport. When he was in high school a classmate had brought some dirty pictures to class, and Keller had looked at them, and found them erotic enough. But he wasn't in high school anymore.

Even without watching them he could tell they were pretty well wrapped up in each other, and unlikely to offer much resistance if he went in there and did what he was supposed to do. He rehearsed it in his mind, visualized himself moving purposefully into the room, taking the lover out of the play with a judo chop to the side of the neck, grabbing the woman and breaking her neck, then doing the same for the immobilized man. It would all be over before they knew it, almost before *he* knew it.

Go on, he thought. *Don't just stand there. You know what you're supposed to do. So why aren't you doing it?*

Maybe there was a better way.

If he just went in there and got the job done, he'd have earned his fee—plus a bonus for the boyfriend. But he'd also be leaving the kind of mess that would make headlines, and the cops would be all over their client. It was Walmsley's responsibility to provide himself with an alibi, and he'd probably come up with a good one, but would he have the sense to lawyer up right away and keep his mouth shut? Or would he fall apart when it became clear that he was the sole suspect?

Not Keller's worry. Walmsley could hang himself by talking, but he didn't know enough to hang anybody else.

Still, what if Keller left the Dallas cops a case they could close as soon as they opened it? He could see a way to do it, and earn a double bonus in the process.

It would take time, though. So he went back to Margarita's room to wait.

Was it the same crucifix? He could swear it was larger than he remembered.

He left the door open. He didn't really want to hear the two of them—though that wasn't nearly as bad as seeing them. But he wanted to know when they fell silent.

And, while he waited, he ran an amended scenario through his mind. He liked it, he thought it would work, but there was still one question he couldn't answer.

Could he do it?

For a couple of years now he'd been leading a very different life, and it struck him as possible that he'd become a different person in the process. He had a wife, he had a daughter, he had a house, he had a business. He might cross the street against the light, and he and Donny managed to keep their cash receipts a secret from the tax man, but all in all he was a law-abiding individual, a reasonably solid citizen. He'd always had a penchant for civic responsibility; he'd served on a jury when called, and volunteered at Ground Zero in the aftermath of 9/11. But all along he'd had this dark side, this other life, and he'd left that part of himself behind when he settled in New Orleans.

So maybe that was what had led him to throw the bolt and lock himself in the maid's room. And maybe he wasn't waiting now for a better opportunity. Maybe he was stalling, and waiting for a chance to pull the plug on the whole operation.

He mulled it over, running various possibilities through his mind. And then it struck him that he couldn't hear them anymore, and in fact hadn't heard them for a while now.

How long? Could they have put their clothes on and gone out? If so, he decided, then he was going to say the hell with it. He'd climb out the window and drive away, and leave Portia Walmsley to work out for herself what had happened to her maid and her window, one having jumped the track and the other having disappeared altogether. But she'd get to stay alive, at least until her husband hired somebody else, and she'd never know what a close call she'd had.

Scratch that, he told himself. Because there she was in the bedroom, lying on her back with her mouth open, snoring away in a very unappealing fashion. And, lying beside her and snoring twice as loud, was the oaf she'd picked to be her boyfriend. He still looked familiar, and Keller figured out why. It was the mustache, identical in shape to that of Michael, his companion at breakfast.

Keller found his way to the kitchen, and came back with a knife.

SEVEN

"Oh, it was a lazy day," he said. "I got to talking with a U.S. collector over breakfast, and wound up hanging out in the auction room to see how he did when his lots came up. I meant to call earlier so I could talk to Jenny before her bedtime, but I guess it's too late now."

His first call, when he got back to his hotel room, was on his other cell phone, the one he used only for calls to Dot. When there was no answer he put that phone away, got out the other one, and called Julia, and when he heard her voice he felt a great sense of relief.

After the phone call, after she'd told him about her day and he'd made up a day for himself, he tried to figure out what that sense of relief was all about. He hadn't been aware of any anxiety until the sound of her voice dispelled it.

It took him a few minutes to sort it out, but what he decided was that he'd been afraid his whole new life was gone, that he'd somehow thrown it away in the Spanish-style house on Caruth Boulevard. Then he'd heard her voice and been reassured.

Now, though, he wasn't sure how he felt.

He tried Dot again, watched a half hour of television, tried Dot one more time, and tried to decide if he felt like getting something to eat. He hadn't eaten since breakfast, so he ought to be hungry, but he didn't have much of an appetite. He checked the room-service menu and decided he could eat a sandwich, but when the waiter brought it he knew it was a mistake. There was coffee, and he drank that, but he left the sandwich untouched.

Years ago he'd learned how to clear his mind after a job. Very deliberately he let himself picture the master bedroom on Caruth Boulevard as he had last seen it. Portia Walmsley lay on her back, stabbed through the heart. Beside her was her unnamed lover, comatose with drink, his fingers clenched around the hilt of the murder weapon. It was the sort of image you'd want to blink away, especially if you'd had something to do with it, but Keller fixed it in his mind and brought it into focus, saw it in full color and sharp relief.

And then, as he'd learned to do, he willed the image to grow smaller and less distinct. He shrank it, as if viewing it through the wrong end of a telescope, and he washed out the bright colors, dimming the image to black and white, then fading it to gray. The details blurred, the faces became unrecognizable, and as the image disappeared, the incident itself lost its emotional charge. It had happened, there was no getting around it, but it was as if it had happened years and years ago, and to somebody else.

* * *

Keller, in line for the breakfast buffet, knew he was going to get his money's worth. He'd put the room-service tray outside his door without taking the first bite of the sandwich, and went to bed uncertain if he'd be able to sleep on an empty stomach. The next thing he knew it was morning, and one of the first things that came to mind was an expression his mother had used now and then: *My stomach thinks my throat's been cut.* Keller was shaving when the line came to him, which might have given him a turn, but he used a twin-blade safety razor, hardly something you'd use to cut a throat, your own or anybody else's.

He piled his plate high and looked around for an empty table, and there was his friend of yesterday morning, mustachioed Michael, wielding a fork with one hand and beckoning to Keller with the other. Keller, glad for the company, went over and joined him.

"Saw you yesterday morning," Michael said. "If I remember correctly, you were in the room when that big block got away from me."

"Quite a price it brought."

"Way more than my maximum, so I wisely sat back and let it go. And guess what?"

"You've been kicking yourself ever since."

"Around the block and back again. Oh, I know I was right to let it go, but when am I gonna get a shot at a piece like that again? Not until they auction off the collection of the sonofabitch who bought it, and by then it'll probably go for three times what it brought yesterday. Nick, I've bought some things I shouldn't have over the years, and I've paid too much for some of them, but that sort of thing never bothers me for more than a minute or two. It's the ones that get away that drive you crazy."

Obock J1, Keller thought.

He worked on his breakfast while Michael told him about the afternoon session, where he'd made up for the loss of the block by picking up all the covers he'd had his eye on, most of them at good prices. "But I wanted that block," he told Keller, "and I still want it. How about yourself? What are you looking to buy today?"

Keller had a seat in the auction room and was studying his catalog when he realized he'd forgotten to call Dot. He hadn't called Julia, either, to wish her a good morning. Should he duck out and make the calls? He thought about it, and then they started the sale and called the first lot, and he decided to stay where he was.

By the time they got to France and French Colonies, Keller had bid on ten lots and acquired six of them, letting the others go when the bidding climbed out of his range. As Michael had observed, a general collector always has plenty of things to buy, and Keller spent a few dollars and added a few stamps to his collection, issues from Albania and the Dominican Republic and Eastern Rumelia and Ecuador, none of them bringing more than a few hundred dollars. Then they got to the French section, where Keller's collection was strongest and where the lots he needed were higher in price, and harder to find. He sat calmly in his chair, but he felt anticipation and excitement coursing through him like an electric current.

The Obock stamp was valued at $7500 in Keller's Scott catalog, while his Yvert et Tellier specialized catalog of France and its colonies listed the stamp at €12,000, or almost double the price in Scott.

Both Scott and Y&T mentioned the reprint, Scott pegging it at $200, Y&T at €350. Keller couldn't remember what he'd paid, but thought it was around $150. Now he'd have the chance to bid on the original, and had a feeling it was going to bring a high price.

Back in New Orleans, before Dot's phone call, Keller had already had his eye on the stamp. At the time he'd decided the stamp was worth $10,000 to him, but wasn't sure he could rationalize spending that much money. Now, with his business on Caruth Boulevard successfully concluded, the money was there to be spent. He picked up a couple of lots—an early stamp from Diego-Suárez, an inverted overprint from Martinique—and when Obock J1 came up, he was ready.

Moments later, the stamp was his.

There were other lots that he'd marked in his catalog, but he was no longer interested in bidding on them. He felt as though he'd just fought a prizefight, or run a marathon, and all he'd done was raise a forefinger and keep it raised until he was the only bidder left.

The hammer price was $16,500, and he'd have to pay a 15 percent bidder's premium on top of that, plus whatever sales tax the state of Texas felt it deserved. Close to $20,000 for a homely little square of paper, but it was his to have and to hold, his to protect in a black-backed plastic mount, his to place in his album alongside the $200 reprint to which it looked essentially identical.

In the elevator he felt a twinge of buyer's remorse, but by the time he was in his room it had dissipated, leaving him with a warm glow of accomplishment. He'd had to hang in there, had to keep his finger in the air while other bidders in the room gave up and dropped out, then had to hold on until the phone bidder finally gave up and let go. It was a rare stamp, and other people wanted it, but the whole point of an auction was to see who wanted something the most, and this time around it was Keller.

He called Julia from his room. "I got the stamp I wanted, and it's a beauty. But I had to spend more than I expected, so I'm going to skip the afternoon session and hit the road early. I'll break the trip somewhere, and I should be home some time tomorrow afternoon."

She told him the latest cute thing Jenny had said, and a little gossip about the young couple who'd moved into the old Beaulieu house, and when the conversation ended he switched phones and called Dot, and this time she answered.

"I tried you yesterday," he said, "and then I was going to call first thing this morning but it slipped my mind, and I was all caught up in the drama of a stamp auction."

"With all the pulse-pounding excitement thereof."

"What I wanted to tell you," he said, "is it's all taken care of, and it couldn't have gone better."

"Is that so."

"Double bonus," he said.

"Oh?"

They were using a pair of untraceable phones, but even so he felt it best to be cryptic. "The primary is down," he said, "and the secondary objective is fully implicated."

"Do tell."

He frowned. "Is something wrong?"

"From a dollars-and-cents standpoint," she said, "I'd have to say there is. There's not going to be a bonus, let alone a double bonus."

"But—"

"As a matter of fact, we can forget about the second half of the basic fee. You know, the portion due upon completion of the assignment?"

"But the assignment was completed."

"I'll say."

"Dot, what's the matter?"

"You got up this morning, had a cup of coffee—right so far?"

"I had breakfast," he said, mystified. "And then I went to the auction room."

"Read the paper while you ate your breakfast?"

"No. I joined this fellow and we got to talking."

"About stamps, I'll bet. Good breakfast?"

"Yes, as a matter of fact, but—"

"And then you went to the auction room."

"Right."

"And bought some stamps, I suppose."

"Well, yes. But—"

"The Dallas morning newspaper," she said, "is called the *Dallas Morning News,* and don't ask me how they came up with a name like that. You can't beat Texans for imagination. Go buy the paper, Keller. You'll find what you're looking for right there on the front page."

EIGHT

He picked up the lots he'd won, paid for them, and packed them along with his other belongings in his small suitcase. He checked out of the Lombardy and drove off with his suitcase next to him on the front seat. Traffic was light, and he didn't have any trouble finding his way to the interstate. He headed for New Orleans, and found a country music station, but turned it off after half an hour.

He broke the trip at the same Red Roof Inn, used the same credit card. In his room he wondered if that was a good idea. But the trip was a matter of record, and one he had never attempted to conceal. Portions of it, of course, were off the record—the car rental, the visit to Caruth Boulevard—but he had no reason to hide the fact that he'd been to Dallas, and had the stamps to prove it.

He ate next door at a Bob's Big Boy, and it seemed to him that half the men in the room had mustaches. Like his philatelic friend Michael, and like the man whose fingers he'd curled around the hilt of Portia Walmsley's kitchen knife.

They'd found him like that, Keller had learned on page one of the *Dallas Morning News*. Still in a drunken stupor, still holding the knife, and still sprawled out next to the dead body of a woman.

Reading the paper, Keller had learned why the sonofabitch looked familiar. Keller had seen him before, and not in the auction room, or around the Lombardy. He hadn't seen the man himself, not really. He'd seen the guy's picture—online, in some of the photos that popped up when he asked Google Images for a peek at Portia. And it was entirely natural that he be photographed at her side. After all, he was her husband.

Charles Walmsley. The client.

A reconciliation, Dot had explained. Charles Walmsley had gone over to his wife's house, perhaps in the hope of getting one last look at her before he got to see her in her coffin. And evidently the old magic was still there, and, well, one thing led to another. And somewhere along the way he remembered that he'd better call off the hit.

So he made a phone call and figured that was that. A single phone call had put the operation in motion, so wouldn't a second phone call nip it in the bud?

Absolutely. But the person Walmsley called had to make a call of his own, and the person *he* called had to call Dot, and the new directive took its time working its way through the system. By the time Dot got the word, it was already too late.

Back home, Keller held his daughter high in the air. "Tummy!" she demanded, and he put his lips to her stomach and blew, making an indelicate sound. Jenny laughed with delight and insisted he do it again.

It was good to be home.

Later that evening, Keller went upstairs and settled in with his stamps. After he'd mounted Obock J1, he called Julia in and showed it to her, and she admired it extravagantly.

"It's like when somebody shows you their new baby," Keller said. "You have to say it's beautiful, because what else are you going to say?"

"All babies are beautiful."

"And all stamps, I suppose. That's the original on the right and the reprint next to it. They look the same, don't they?"

"I bet their mother could tell the difference," she said.

Two days later, Keller bought a new phone and called Dot. "Take down this number," he said, and read it off to her. She read it back and asked what was wrong with the old number.

"It's no good anymore," he said, "because I smashed the phone and threw the pieces down a storm drain."

"I smashed a pay phone once," she said, "when it flat-out refused to give me my dime back. What did this phone do to piss you off?"

"I figured it would be safer to get a new phone."

"And I figure you're probably right. You okay, Keller? Last time we talked you were a little shaky."

"I'm all right."

"Because you didn't do anything wrong."

"Our client fell in love with his wife all over again," he said, "and I killed her and framed him for it. If I'd known what was going on, you can bet I'd have handled it differently."

"Keller, if you'd known, you wouldn't have handled it at all. You'd have bought some stamps and come home."

"Well, that's true," he allowed. "Obviously. But I still wish I hadn't made the phone call."

"To me?"

"To the cops, after I got out of there. I wanted to make sure they showed up before he could come to his senses and head for the hills."

"Hills would be hard to find," she said, "in that part of the country. Look, don't worry about it. You had no way of knowing he was the client, or that he'd canceled the contract. One way to look at it, he's a lucky man."

"Lucky?"

"You wanted the double bonus, right? That's why you left him with the knife in his hand."

"So?"

"So otherwise you'd have killed them both. This way at least he's alive."

"What a lucky guy."

"Well, yes and no. See, he's consumed with guilt."

"Because he didn't call it off soon enough?"

"Because he got drunk and killed his wife. He doesn't actually remember doing it, but then he can't remember much of anything after the third drink, and what's a man supposed to think when he comes out of a blackout with a knife in his hand and a dead woman next to him? He figures he must have done it, and he'll plead guilty, and that's the end of it."

"And now he's got to live with the guilt."

"Keller," she said, "everybody's got to live with something."

KELLER'S HOMECOMING

NINE

Keller, his suitcase unpacked, found himself curiously reluctant to leave his hotel room. He turned on the TV, channel surfed without finding anything that held his attention, threw himself down on the bed, picked himself up, test-drove every chair in the room, and finally told himself to get over it. He wasn't sure what it was that he had to get over, but he wasn't going to find it sitting in his room. Or lying down, or pacing the floor.

One explanation occurred to him in the elevator. Keller, who'd lived all his life in and around New York, had never had occasion to stay at a New York hotel before. Why would he? For years he'd had a wonderfully comfortable apartment on First Avenue in the 40s, and unless he was out of town, or had been invited to spend the night in the bed of some congenial female companion, that was where he slept.

Nowadays the only female companion in his life, congenial

or otherwise, was his wife, Julia, and he lived in her house in New Orleans's Garden District. His name in New Orleans—and, for that matter, everywhere he went—was Edwards, Nicholas Edwards. He was a partner in a construction business, doing post-Katrina residential rehabilitation, and his partner called him Nick, as did the men they worked with. Julia called him Nicholas, except in intimate moments, when she sometimes called him Keller.

But she didn't do that so often anymore. Oh, the intimate moments were no less frequent, but she was apt to call him Nicholas then. And, he thought, why not? That was his name. Nicholas Edwards. That's what it said on his driver's license, issued to him by the state of Louisiana, and on his passport, issued to him by the United States of America. And that was the name on every credit card and piece of ID in his wallet, so how could you say that wasn't who he was? And why shouldn't his wife call him by his rightful name?

His daughter, Jenny, called him Daddy.

He realized that he missed them both, Jenny and Julia, and it struck him that this was ridiculous. They'd driven him to the airport that morning, so it had been only a matter of hours since he'd seen them, and he went longer than that without seeing them on any busy workday. Of course there'd been fewer busy workdays lately, the economy being what it was, and that in fact had a little to do with this visit to New York, but even so...

How you do go on, he told himself. And, shaking his head, walked through the lobby and out onto the street.

His hotel, the Savoyard, stood at the corner of Sixth Avenue and West 53rd Street. He took a moment to get his bearings, then headed uptown. There was a Starbucks two blocks from his hotel, and he waited at the counter while a young woman with a snake coiled around her upper arm—well, the inked representation of a snake, not an actual living reptile—made sure the barista understood exactly what she did and didn't want in her latte. Keller couldn't imagine caring quite that much about the composition of a cup of coffee, but neither could he imagine getting tattooed, so he let it go. When it was finally his turn, he asked for a small black coffee.

"That would be a 'Tall,'" said the barista, herself sporting a tattoo and a few piercings. She drew the coffee without waiting for his reply, which was just as well, because Keller didn't have one. The tables were all taken, but there was a high counter where you could stand while your coffee cooled. He did, and when it was cool enough to drink he drank it, and when he was done he left.

By then he'd come up with another explanation for his disinclination to leave his hotel room. He wasn't used to being in a hotel in New York, and consequently he wasn't quite prepared for what they cost. This one, decent enough but hardly palatial, was charging him close to $500 for no more space than they gave you in a Days Inn.

Spend that much on a room, you wanted to get your money's worth. If you never left the room, it would only be costing you $40 an hour. If, on the other hand, you used it solely to sleep and shower...

At 56th Street he crossed to the west side of the avenue, and at 57th Street he turned to his left and walked about a third of a block, stopping to look into the window of a shop that sold watches and earrings. Once Keller had heard one woman tell another on QVC that you couldn't have too many earrings, a statement that he had found every bit as baffling as the snake tattoo.

Keller wasn't really interested in looking at earrings, and it wasn't long before he'd turned to gaze instead across 57th Street. Number 119 West 57th Street was directly across the street, and Keller stayed where he was and tried to pay attention to the people entering and leaving the office building. People came and went, and Keller didn't see anyone who looked familiar to him, but 57th was one of the wide crosstown streets, so he wasn't getting a really good look at the faces of those who were coming and going.

It wasn't the hotel room, he realized. The price of it, the novelty of being in a New York hotel. He hadn't wanted to leave the room because he was afraid to be out in public in New York.

Where there were people who used to know him as Keller, and who knew, too, that one fine day in Des Moines, that very Keller had assassinated a popular, charismatic midwestern governor with presidential aspirations.

TEN

Except he didn't. It was a frame, he was the fall guy, and it cost him his comfortable New York life and the name under which he'd lived it. When all was said and done he didn't have any regrets, because the life he now led in New Orleans was worlds better than what he'd left behind. But that hadn't been the plan of the man who set him up.

That plan had called for Keller to be arrested, or, better yet, killed outright, and it had taken all Keller's resourcefulness to keep it from turning out that way. The man who'd done the planning was dead now, thanks to Keller, and so was the man who'd helped him, and that was as far as Keller saw any need to carry it. Someone somewhere had pulled the trigger and gunned down the governor, but Keller figured that faceless fellow was probably dead himself, murdered by the man who'd hired him, a loose end carefully tied off. And if not, well, the best of luck to him. He'd just been a man doing a job, and that was something Keller could relate to.

And Keller? He had a new name and a new life. So what was he doing back in New York?

He walked back to the corner of Sixth and 57th, waited for the light to change, then crossed the street and walked to the entrance of 119 West 57th. This was a building he'd entered a dozen or more times over the years, and always for the same purpose. There had been a firm called Stampazine on the second floor, and every couple of months they held a Saturday auction, and there was always some interesting and affordable material up for grabs. Keller would sit in a wooden chair with a catalog in one hand and a pen in the other, and every now and then he would raise a forefinger, and sometimes he'd wind up the high bidder. At six or six thirty he'd pick up his lots, pay cash for them, and go home happy.

Stampazine was gone now. Had they closed before or after he'd left New York? He couldn't remember.

He recognized the uniformed lobby attendant. "Peachpit," he said, and the man nodded in recognition—not of Keller but of Keller's purpose. "Seven," he said, and Keller went over and waited for the elevator.

Peachpit Auction Galleries was a cut or two above Stampazine. Keller had never visited them during his New York years, but after he was settled in New Orleans an ad in *Linn's Stamp News* sent him to the Peachpit website. He bid on a couple of lots—unsuccessfully; someone else outbid him—but, having registered, he began to receive their catalogs several times a year. They were magnificently printed, with a color photograph of every lot, and he always found an abundance of choice material.

There was a way to bid online in real time, during the actual floor auction, and he'd planned on doing so but always seemed to be at work during their midweek auctions. Then a few months ago he'd had the day off—he and Donny had the whole week off, actually, although they'd have preferred it otherwise. And he remembered the Peachpit sale, and logged on and went through what you had to go through to bid, and he found the whole process impossibly nerve-racking. An auction was anxiety-ridden anyway, but when you showed up in person you could at least see what was going on, and know that the guy with the gavel could see you in return. Online, well, he supposed a person could get the hang of it, but he hadn't, and wasn't inclined to try again.

Then, a couple of weeks ago, Julia and Jenny walked into his upstairs office—Daddy's Stamp Room—to find him shaking his head over the new Peachpit catalog. Julia asked what was the matter.

"Oh, this," he said, tapping the catalog. "There are some lots I'd like to buy."

"So?

"Well, the sale's in New York."

"Oh," she said.

"Daddy 'tamps," said Jenny.

"Yes, Daddy's stamps," Keller said, and picked up his daughter and set her on his lap. "See?" he said, pointing at a picture in the catalog, a German Colonial issue from Kiauchau showing the kaiser's yacht, *Hohenzollern*. "Kiauchau," he told Jenny, "was an area of two hundred square miles in southeast China. The Germans grabbed it in 1897, and then made arrangements to lease it from China. I don't imagine the Chinese had a lot of choice in the matter. Isn't that a pretty stamp?"

"Pity 'tamp," Jenny said, and there the matter lay.

Until the phone rang two days later. It was Dot, calling from Sedona, and the first thing she did was apologize for calling at all.

"I told myself I'd just call to see how you're doing," she said, "and to find out the latest cute thing Jenny said, but you know something, Keller? I'm too damn old to start fooling myself."

Dot still called him Keller. And that figured, because that's who she was calling to talk to. Not Nick Edwards, who fixed houses, but Keller. Who, in a manner of speaking, fixed people.

"The last thing I should be doing," she went on, "is calling you. There's two reasons why this is a mistake. First of all, you're not in the business anymore. I dragged you back in once, that business in Dallas, and it wasn't your fault that it didn't go off perfectly. But it wasn't what you really wanted, and we both agreed it was what the British call a one-off."

"What does that mean?"

"One time only, I think. What's the difference what it means? You went to Dallas, you came back from Dallas, end of story."

But if it was the end of the story, what was this? A sequel?

"That's one reason," she said. "There's another."

"Oh?"

"Three words," she said. "New. York. City."

"Oh."

"What am I even thinking, Keller, calling you when I've got a job in your old hometown? I didn't throw New York jobs your way when you lived there, *because* you lived there."

"I worked a couple of New York assignments."

"Just a couple, and they weren't exactly what you'd call problem-free. But at least you could walk around the city without wearing a mask. Now it's the one place in the world where it's not safe for you to be you, where even a waitress in a coffee shop can take a second look at you and reach for a telephone, and here I am calling you with a New York assignment, and that's as far as this is going, because I'm hanging up."

"Wait a minute," Keller said.

The receptionist at Peachpit told him to have a seat, and he leafed through an old auction catalog while he waited. Then a stoop-shouldered man with his sleeves rolled up and his tie loosened came to show him inside and seat him in a stackable white plastic chair at a long table. He had already prepared a slip of paper with the numbers of the lots he wanted to inspect, and he looked them over carefully when they were brought to him.

The stamps were tucked into individual two-inch-square pockets of a chemically inert plastic, each plastic pocket stapled to its own sheet of paper bearing the lot number, estimated value, and opening bid. Keller had brought a pair of tongs, and could have taken out a stamp for closer inspection, but there was no need, and the tongs remained in his breast pocket. Given that the catalog had already shown him clear color photos of all of these stamps, it probably wasn't necessary that he look at them in the first place. But he'd learned that actually looking at a stamp, up close and personal, helped him decide just how much he really wanted to own it.

He'd requested a dozen lots, all of them stamps he needed, all of them stamps he genuinely wanted—and he didn't want them any less now that he was getting a look at them. But he wasn't going to buy them all, and this would help him decide which ones to buy if they went cheap, and which ones deserved a firmer commitment. And, finally, which ones he'd go all out to get, hanging on like grim death, and—

"Hello, there! Haven't seen you in a while, have I?"

Keller froze in his white plastic chair.

"She loves watching you work with your stamps," Julia said. "'Daddy 'tamps,' she says. She has a little trouble with the *s-t* combination."

"I suppose philately is out of the question."

"For now. But before you know it she'll be the only kid in her class who knows where Obock is."

"Just now I was telling her about Kiauchau."

"I know. But see, I know how to pronounce Obock."

He was silent for a moment. Then he said, "There's something we have to talk about."

ELEVEN

They sat at the kitchen table with cups of coffee and he said, "I've been keeping something from you, and I can't do that. Ever since we found each other I've been able to say whatever's been on my mind, and now I can't, and I don't like the way it feels."

"You met someone in Dallas."

He looked at her.

"A woman," she said.

"Oh, God," he said. "It's not what you think."

"It's not?"

If he had to kill this man, how would he do it? He was close to sixty, and he looked soft and pudgy, so you couldn't call him a hard target. The closest thing Keller had to a weapon was the pair of stamp tongs in his breast pocket, but he'd made do often enough with nothing but his bare hands, and—

"I guess you don't recognize me," the fellow was saying. "Been a few years, and it's safe to say I put on a few pounds. It's a rare year when I don't. And the last time we saw each other the two of us were on a lower floor."

Keller looked at him.

"Or am I wrong? Stampazine? I never missed their auctions, and I'd swear I saw you there a few times. I don't know if we ever talked, and if I ever heard your name I've long since forgotten it, but I'm pretty good with faces. Faces and watermarks, they both tend to stick in my mind." He stuck out a hand. "Irv," he said. "Irv Feldspar."

"Nicholas Edwards."

"A damn shame Stampazine's gone," Feldspar said. "Bert Taub's health was bad for years, and finally he closed up shop, and then the word got around that he missed the business and wanted to get back into it, and the next thing we knew he was dead."

"A hell of a thing," Keller said, figuring something along those lines was expected of him.

"Plenty of other auctions in this city," Feldspar said, "but you could just show up at Stampazine and there'd be plenty of low-priced material to bid on. No fancy catalogs, no Internet or phone bidders. I don't think you and I ever bumped heads, did we? I'm strictly U.S. myself."

"Everything but U.S.," Keller said. "Worldwide to 1940."

"So I was never bidding against you, so why would you remember me?"

"I didn't come all that often," Keller said. "I live out of town, so—"

"What, Jersey? Connecticut?"

"New Orleans, so—"

"You didn't come in special for Bert's auctions."

"Hardly. I just showed up when I happened to be in town."

"On business? What kind of business are you in, if I may ask?"

Keller, letting a trace of the South find its way into his speech, explained that he was retired, and then answered the inevitable Katrina questions, until he cleared his throat and said he really wanted to focus on the lots he was examining. And Irv Feldspar apologized, said his wife told him he never knew when he was boring people, and that she was convinced he was suffering from Ass-Backward syndrome.

Keller nodded, concentrated on the stamps.

Julia said, "I knew there was something. Something's been different ever since you got back from Dallas, and I couldn't say what it was, so I had to think it was another woman. And you're a man, for heaven's sake, and you were on the other side of the state line, and things happen. I know that. And I could stand that, if that's what it was, and if what happened in Dallas stayed in Dallas. If it was going to be an ongoing thing, if she was important to you, well, maybe I could stand that and maybe I couldn't."

"That wasn't it."

"No, it wasn't, was it?" She reached to lay her hand on top of his. "What a relief. My husband wasn't fooling around with another woman. He was killing her."

"I don't know what to say."

"Do you remember the night we met?"

"Of course."

"You saved my life. I was taking a shortcut through the park, and I was about to be raped and killed, and you saved me."

"I don't know what got into me."

"You saved me," she said, "and you killed that man right in front of me. With your bare hands. You grabbed him and broke his neck."

"Well."

"That was how we met. When Jenny's old enough to want to know how Mommy and Daddy met and fell in love, we may have to give her an edited version. But that's not for a while yet. How was it? In Dallas? I know it went smoothly enough, and I think it's pure poetry that the man you framed wound up confessing."

"Well, he thinks he did it."

"And in a sense he did, because if he hadn't made that first phone call you would never have left the hotel."

"I probably wouldn't even have gone. I'd have sent in a few mail bids and let it go at that."

"So he got what was coming to him, and it doesn't sound as though either of them was a terribly nice person."

"You wouldn't want to have them to the house for dinner."

"I didn't think so. But what I wanted to know was how was it for you? How did it feel? You hadn't done anything like this in a long time."

"A couple of years."

"And your life is different from what it was, so maybe you're different, too."

"I thought of that."

"And?"

He thought it over for a moment. "It felt the same as always," he said. "I had a job to do and I had to figure out how."

"And then you had to do it."

"That's right."

"And you felt the satisfaction of having solved a problem."

"Uh-huh."

"At which point you could buy that stamp without dipping into capital."

"We only collected the first payment," he said, "but even so it more than covered the cost of the stamps I bought."

"Well, that's a plus, isn't it? And you didn't have any trouble living with what you'd done?"

"I had trouble living with the secret."

"Not being able to mention it to me, you mean."

"That's right."

She nodded. "Having to keep a secret. That must have been difficult. There are things I don't bother to tell you, but nothing I *couldn't* tell you, if I wanted to. How do you feel now?"

"Better."

"I can tell that. Your whole energy is different. Do you want to know how I feel?"

"Yes."

"Relieved, obviously. But also a little troubled, because now I seem to be the one with a secret."

"Oh?"

"Shall I tell you my secret? See, the danger is that you might think less of me if you knew." Before he could respond, she heaved a theatrical sigh. "Oh, I can't keep secrets. When you told me what happened in Dallas? What you did?"

"Yes?"

"It got me hot."

"Oh?"

"Is that weird? Of course it is, it's deeply weird. Here's something I'm positive I never told you. It got me hot when you killed the rapist in the park. What it mostly did was it made me feel all safe and secure and protected, but it also got me hot. I'm hot right now and I don't know what to do about it."

"If we put our heads together," he said, "maybe we can come up with something."

Back in his room at the Savoyard, Keller figured it out. Asperger's syndrome—that's what Feldspar had, or what his wife said he had.

Though Ass-Backward syndrome wasn't a bad fit.

"If I'd known what it would lead to," he said, "I'd have told you right away."

"But you didn't."

"No. I was afraid, I guess. That it would ruin things between us."

"So you didn't say anything."

"No."

"And then you did."

"Right."

She didn't say anything, but he felt besieged by her thoughts, bombarded with them. He said, "I figured I was done with it, I'd never do it again, so why bother mentioning it? I could just keep my mouth shut and seal off the episode and let it fade out into the past."

"Like the faces you picture in your mind."

"Something like that, yes."

"I guess you got another phone call."

"This afternoon."

"I noticed something was different," she said, "when Jenny and I got home from Advanced Sandbox. How's Dot these days?"

"She's good." He cleared his throat. "I reminded her what I'd told her right after Dallas. That I didn't want to do this sort of thing anymore."

"But she called you anyway."

"Well," he said, "it's complicated."

TWELVE

Keller, who'd found it hard to leave his hotel room earlier, now found it impossible to spend any time in it. He showered, got dressed, turned the TV on and then off again, and went out.

In New Orleans, Keller drove his pickup truck for business and Julia's car on other occasions. If he walked north for a couple of blocks, he could hop on the St. Charles Avenue streetcar. And there was a fair network of buses, and it was never hard to get a cab.

For all the choices available to him, Keller did a lot of walking. New Orleans was one of a relatively small number of pedestrian-friendly American cities. Not only could you get around on foot and find interesting things to look at while you did so, but New Orleanians—total strangers—would actually greet you in passing with a smile and a kind word. The ones who didn't might well draw a gun and hold you up, post-

Katrina street crime being a definite problem, but among the law-abiding citizenry you were apt to encounter a high level of politeness and genuine warmth. "Lovely morning, innit?" "Just grand! And how are y'all keeping this fine day?"

New York was at least as much of a city for walkers, to the point where Keller couldn't understand why some people lived in the city and still felt compelled to own cars. The sidewalks might not be as quaintly friendly as those of New Orleans—there was, after all, good reason for the popularity of the line "Can you tell me how to get to the Empire State Building or should I just go fuck myself?"—but nevertheless it was a walker's city, and Keller didn't have to think about it. He left his hotel and started walking.

After his shower, he'd checked in the mirror to see if he needed a shave. He'd decided he could wait until morning, and looked a moment longer at the face Irv Feldspar had been able to recognize. It had changed some since Feldspar (or anyone else in New York) had last had a look at it. Back then his hair had been dark brown, almost black, and it had grown further down on his forehead. When he surfaced in New Orleans, with his face in newspapers and on TV, not to mention on post office walls, he wore a cap all the time, and tried to figure out how to dye his hair gray.

Julia had dyed his hair for him, not gray but a sort of tan shade she called mouse brown. And she had cut his hair short, and had given him a receding hairline. He'd had to shave the stubble where the hairline grew back, but he didn't have to do that anymore, as Time had worked its own barbering tricks on him. Julia still touched up the dye job periodically, but the dark roots she'd had to lighten were now evolving into gray roots she needed to color.

And yet for all that transformation, worked by Julia and by

the years, a guy Keller didn't recall at all had placed him immediately. Of course he'd seen him in context, he knew him from one stamp auction and recognized him at another, so if they'd run into each other on a subway platform, say, Feldspar might not have given him a second glance.

If he had, Keller could have thrown him in front of a train.

"You may have read about the case," Dot said. "Or caught it on the evening news. Political corruption in northern New Jersey."

"I'm shocked," Keller said.

"I know. It's almost impossible to believe. Elected public officials taking bribes, laundering money, selling kidneys—"

"Selling kidneys?"

"So I understand, though who'd want to buy a politician's kidney is a question I'd be hard put to answer. You must have seen something in the paper or on TV."

"In New Orleans," he told her, "we don't pay much mind to political corruption in faraway places."

"Y'all like to eat your own cooking?"

"There you go," he said.

"A lot of people got arrested, Keller, and a couple of them went so far as to resign, but most of them are out on bail and still collecting their municipal paychecks. But it looks as though they'll all have to step down sooner or later, and the abbot will probably have to give up his position, and—"

"The abbot?"

"Well, I don't see how he can go on heading the monastery."

"There's an abbot heading a monastery?"

"Keller, that's what they do. Not all of them can be partners with Lou Costello." She paused, and he realized too late that she'd been waiting for him to laugh. When he didn't, she said, "I don't know how any of this works. I guess he can go on being a monk, unless he gets defrocked. And as for the other monks, well, I guess they'll go on doing what they do. What do they do, anyway?"

"Pray," Keller guessed. "Bake bread. Make cordials."

"Cordials?"

"Bénédictine? Chartreuse?"

"Monks make those? I thought that was Seagram's."

"Monks started it. Maybe they sold the business. I think basically they pray, and maybe work in the garden."

"The garden-variety monks work in the garden," she suggested. "The laundry-variety monks keep themselves occupied with money and kidneys. See, the abbot was in cahoots with all the politicians."

"Felonious monks," Keller said. "Dot? You don't think that was funny?"

"I chuckled a little," she said, "the first time I heard it."

"I just made it up."

"You and every newscaster in the country."

"Oh."

"Long story short," she said, "here's the long and the short of it. The abbot's the guy who knows where all the kidneys are buried. If he talks, nobody walks. Keller? You beginning to get a sense of what your role's going to be?"

To Keller, the word *monastery* called up an image of a walled medieval building, set off somewhere in a secluded rural location, its design combining elements of a Romanesque cathedral and a fortified castle. There'd be those narrow windows, to shoot arrows out of, and there'd be places to sit on the battlements, whatever exactly battlements were, while you poured boiling oil on people. And there'd be a dungeon, and there'd be little individual cells where the little individual monks slept. And there'd be grains of rice, to kneel on during prayer.

And singing, there'd be lots of singing. Gregorian chants, mostly, but maybe some sea chanteys, too, because Keller tended to mix up chants and chanteys in his mind. He knew the difference, but he mixed them up anyhow.

You wouldn't look for a monastery on a quiet residential block in the East 30s. You wouldn't expect to find a monastic order housed in a five-story limestone-front row house in Murray Hill.

Yet there it was.

It stood on the downtown side of East 36th Street between Park and Madison, flanked on either side by similar structures. A small brass plaque identified one of them as the Embassy of the Republic of Chad, while the other looked to be what all of these houses had once been—an elegant private residence. Between them, the building whose plaque read simply THESSALONIAN HOUSE looked no more monastic than either of its neighbors.

Dot had referred to Paul Vincent O'Herlihy, abbot of the Thessalonians, as a fine figure of a man, giving the words a touch of stage-Irish lilt. Keller knew why when he checked him out via Google Images. The abbot was tall and broad-shouldered, heavily built but not fat, with a leonine head and a full mane of white hair. He had one of those open faces that tend to inspire trust, often unwarranted, and Keller could see right away how, if this man were to become a monk, he might very well wind up as the man in charge. With the same looks and bearing, he could as readily have become some city's commissioner of police, or chairman of the board of a Wall Street firm, or an insurance company CEO. Or, back when Tammany Hall ran New York, he might have been mayor.

Likes his food, Keller had thought, noting O'Herlihy's bulk, the fit of his jacket, and in his head he heard the voice of a middle-aged Irishwoman: *"Ah, but doesn't he carry it well?"* Likes a drink, Keller added, taking note of the florid complexion, the network of broken blood vessels in the cheeks and nose. *"Ah, shure, and don't they call that a strong man's weakness?"*

He was in there now, this fine figure of a man. He'd been there when a crew of federal agents came to the door and rang the bell. (If there was one; Keller noted a great brass door knocker mounted in the middle of the door, and perhaps that had been what the Feds used to make their presence known.)

Keller liked the idea of them using the knocker. When they rounded up drug dealers, they generally used a battering ram and knocked the door down. That was how they did it on TV, anyway, and it was impressively dramatic. But when they had to pay a call on a man of God, they didn't even need to disturb the tranquillity with a doorbell's chime. A discreet knock would serve.

So they'd knocked, Keller decided. And he knew that the visit had been no surprise to Father O'Herlihy, that he'd been forewarned by a phone call and was accordingly forearmed, with his attorney at his side when the door opened.

Had they cuffed him for the ride downtown? It was usually mandatory, but maybe they'd spared him that indignity. Keller couldn't remember seeing news photos of a priest in handcuffs, and it was the kind of image that tended to stay with you.

Keller walked to the end of the block, crossed the street, and looked back at where he'd been. Having posted bond,

Father O'Herlihy was now free to go where he pleased, but Keller was willing to bet he was under self-imposed house arrest, living the cloistered life in Thessalonian House. He'd be comfortable there, and those walls would keep him safe from reporters and photographers and other intrusive types.

And, of course, from Keller.

Suppose he just walked up and thumped away with the brass door knocker? Somebody would open the door. And who was to say it wouldn't be the man himself?

Keller, who was ordinarily inclined to take his time, had been in a hurry once in Albuquerque. And so he'd gone straight to the home of the designated victim, walked from his rented car to the front door, and rang the bell. The door was opened by the man in the photo they'd sent Keller, who'd promptly killed him and left. The girl at the Hertz counter said, "So soon? Is there something wrong with it?" He said something about a change in plans, and flew back to New York.

Keller couldn't believe the duty of opening the front door would fall to the abbot, not even in more ordinary circumstances. So Keller would have to deal with whoever came to the door, and then there'd probably be other people to deal with before he got to O'Herlihy.

He turned his back on the monastery and started walking.

Keller had lived for years in an Art Deco apartment building on First Avenue in the 40s. He had rented the apartment, then bought it when the building went co-op. Since then it had appreciated enormously in value, although he supposed it must have dropped some in the current recession.

Not that it mattered, because he was pretty sure he didn't

own it anymore. How could he? He hadn't paid the maintenance since his world turned upside down and left him running for his life. It had probably taken the co-op board a while to figure out how to proceed, but they'd have long since worked it out, and someone else would be living there now.

It was, he thought, stupid to walk over there, stupid to show his face in his old neighborhood. But he couldn't seem to help himself, and while his mind wandered here and there—thinking about O'Herlihy, thinking about stamps, thinking about Julia and Jenny—his feet insisted on carrying him to the block he used to live on, and planted him in a doorway directly across the street.

There was a light on in his window.

He felt very strange. Years and years ago, he'd had occasion to walk down the suburban street where he'd lived as a boy. By then it had been ages since he and his mother lived there, and he'd never had an urge to go back, and that unplanned visit hadn't had much impact. Someone had painted it another color, he'd noted, but the old basketball backboard was still mounted on the garage. It seemed to him that the shrubbery looked different, though he couldn't have said just how.

And he'd turned away and never given the place another thought.

Now, though, it was somehow different. He hadn't moved out of this apartment. He was just there, and then one day he wasn't. He'd sneaked back in the dead of night, slipped the doorman a few bucks to look the other way, and went upstairs to retrieve his stamp collection. Only he was too late for that…

And so he'd gone off, never to return. Until now, when he was suddenly back in New York. He wasn't Keller anymore, and he didn't live here anymore, and just what did he think he was doing here, anyway?

He walked halfway across the street until he could get a look at the doorman. The fellow was wearing the uniform they all wore, maroon with gold piping, but as far as Keller could make out there was nothing else familiar about him. It had been a couple of years, and a certain amount of staff turnover was to be expected. And if Keller didn't recognize the guy, why should the guy recognize Keller?

He probably wouldn't. That didn't necessarily mean Keller could get past him, but it seemed likely Keller could at the very least get close to him, close enough to get his hands on him. And there was the package room, right off the lobby. He could put the guy in the package room and they wouldn't find him until morning.

And then all he'd have to do was go upstairs, and give the doorbell a poke—no knocker on his door, not unless the new tenant had added one. *"Hi, I'm your neighbor from downstairs, I don't mean to disturb you but I've got water coming through my bathroom ceiling—"*

Then the door would open, and there'd be a man or a woman standing there—or a man *and* a woman, or two men, or two women, it hardly mattered. And he didn't have a weapon, but he had his hands, and that was all he'd need.

He drew back into the shadows, flattened himself against the brick wall of the building behind him. Across the street, the doorman stepped out onto the street for a quick cigarette break. He still didn't look familiar to Keller, who found himself wondering why he'd been contemplating snapping the guy's neck and sticking him in the package room.

Just so he could go upstairs and kill some stranger for no good reason at all.

The impulse—or fantasy, or whatever you might want to call it—was gone now. Go home, he told himself sternly.

He stepped over to the curb, held up a hand for a cab. One came along, its dome light lit, and headed his way, whereupon Keller shook his head and waved him off. Keller wasn't able to see the expression on the driver's face, but he could imagine it.

He started walking.

He walked all the way back to his hotel, and he took his time getting there. On the way, he stopped for a slice of pizza and ate it standing at the counter, drank a cup of coffee at the diner that had been his regular breakfast place. He bought a newspaper at a deli, dropped it unread into the next trash can he came to.

And wondered throughout just what he was doing.

He wasn't entirely certain whether or not he recognized anybody. There were faces that looked familiar, but the waitress at the diner wasn't the one who'd served him all those breakfasts. She'd have finished her shift hours ago.

There'd been changes in the neighborhood. He saw a bank that hadn't been there before, and a chain drugstore. What was missing? It seemed to him that a Chinese restaurant was gone, and a dry cleaner, and what happened to the shoe-repair guy? Or was he over on the next block?

He was exhausted by the time he got back to his hotel. He took a shower, drank a bottle of water from the minibar. And went to bed.

THIRTEEN

Keller's first thought was to have breakfast in the hotel. They had a huge buffet, but they charged $35 for it, and he couldn't see starting the day with $35 worth of food in his stomach. He went across the street to an imitation French bistro, where an Asian girl with her hair in pigtails brought him a croque madame, which was essentially a grilled ham-and-cheese sandwich with a fried egg on top. He had orange juice, and a side of home fries, and finished up with a two-cup pot of filtered coffee, and the check came to $31.25, plus tip.

But it was money well spent, he decided, because his attitude was better after breakfast. A good night's sleep had rid him of most of last night's mood, and the meal had finished the job.

And, speaking of jobs, it was time he got to work on his.

Abbot O'Herlihy, Paul Vincent O'Herlihy, was tucked away in the Thessalonian residence in Murray Hill. There were, as far as Keller could make out, only two ways to carry out his assignment. He could get the man to leave the building, or he could contrive to get himself inside it.

The first way was better, he decided, if he could find a way to manage it. The second way had two parts to it, getting in and getting out, and both of them could present problems. Not that getting O'Herlihy out of his refuge was a piece of cake, but there ought to be a way to manage it.

It was Tuesday morning, and, according to his watch, not quite a quarter to ten. The Peachpit auction would take the form of morning and afternoon sessions Wednesday and Thursday. All of Wednesday was given over to general foreign, with British Commonwealth in the morning and the rest of the world in the afternoon. Thursday morning was a specialized offering of U.S. issues, and the final session on Thursday afternoon was devoted to a remarkable collection of German offices and colonies, including that stamp from Kiauchau he'd pointed out to his daughter.

So he had all of Tuesday, and Wednesday night and Thursday morning. And he could miss one or both of the Wednesday sessions if he had to, but he really wanted to be in the room Thursday afternoon when they sold the German collection.

And Thursday night he wanted to be on his way to New Orleans. The last flight out was JetBlue's, at 8:59, and with luck he'd be on it.

He walked all the way to Thessalonian House, and it looked no different than it had the previous afternoon. The brass knocker was just as inviting, the heavy door just as forbidding. He looked over at it from the uptown side of the street, and barely slowed as he passed on by.

He didn't see a pay phone at the corner of 36th and Park,

and walked another block to Lexington. No pay phones there, either, and he walked a block uptown before he found one, and it didn't work. He had a prepaid cell phone in his pocket, which he'd bought at the New Orleans airport, and he'd hoped he could use it to call Julia, but it looked as though he was only going to be able to get one call out of it.

Well, too bad.

He punched in 911, spoke briefly, and disconnected. Then he walked over to the curb and slipped the inoffensive phone down a storm drain.

He retraced his steps slowly, south to 36th Street, west toward Thessalonian House. He was halfway to Park Avenue when he heard the first siren, but maintained his measured pace. By the time he reached the scene, three city vehicles had already arrived, two NYPD squad cars and an FDNY hook and ladder.

Not surprisingly, a crowd was gathering, with a couple of uniformed cops moving spectators to the uptown side of the street, and firefighters setting up barricades to block the sidewalk on either side of the monastery.

Keller picked out one of the cops and asked him what was going on. The man didn't answer, but a fellow spectator chimed in. "Guy broke in, shot two nuns, and he's holding the rest of 'em hostage."

The doors opened, and the monastery began to empty out, the sidewalk filling up with men, some of them in robes, some in business suits. The man who'd just spoken said he might have been wrong about the nuns, and a woman said you didn't have nuns in a monastery, and another man said, "What meat can a priest eat on Friday? None. Get it?"

Keller was the first to spot the bomb squad truck, but he let somebody else point it out. It looked like one of the Brink's armored cars used to transport large amounts of cash, but it said BOMB SQUAD on the side, in letters large enough to command attention. "Oh, it must be a bomb," someone said, and everyone immediately moved one step in from the street.

So did Keller, even though he couldn't imagine what protection an additional foot of distance from a blast could possibly afford. And in any event he knew there was no bomb, having called in the threat himself.

Another cop, younger and larger than the first, was standing off to the side. He was smoking a cigarette, and Keller got the impression that doing so was against department regulations, and that the man didn't give a damn.

Keller moved closer to him, but not too close, and asked if the building across the street was the Thessalonian monastery.

The cop bristled. "And if it is?"

"I just wondered," Keller said. "A fellow I went to school with, a good friend, actually, he was going to join the Thessalonians."

"Oh, yeah?"

"He thought very highly of them," Keller said. "But you know, you lose track of people. I don't know whether he joined up or not. Say, isn't that—"

"Father O'Herlihy," the cop said. "He hasn't got enough on his plate, he needs a bomb threat on top of everything else."

The man in question looked to Keller as though very little stayed for very long on any plate of his. He had a full face and an extra chin, and looked massive even though his robe hid his figure. His was a plain brown robe, but somehow it seemed less plain and even less brown than those worn by the other monks. He was quite clearly in command, and while Keller couldn't make out what he was saying he could see how the rest rearranged themselves according to his orders.

"And here comes *Eyewitness News,*" the cop said sourly. "Fuckin' media won't leave the man alone. Jersey's got a certain level of corruption, and it don't matter whether you're the Church or some local businessman, you gotta go along to get along. But maybe you see it different."

"No, I'm with you," Keller said.

"But as soon as a man of God's involved, and especially if he just happens to be a *Catholic* man of God, then it's all over the goddamn papers. These days, beating up on the Church is everybody's favorite sport. Not too many years ago this woulda got swept back under the rug, where it belongs."

"Absolutely," Keller said.

"What did the man do, for Christ's sake? I didn't hear no scandals about altar boys. All right, somebody goes and sells a kidney, that's gonna draw attention. I'll grant you that. But is it any reason to sling mud at a man who does as much good in the world as Father O'Herlihy?"

Keller was ready to express agreement, when someone off to the side said, "Hey, look, a dog!" And indeed a uniformed bomb squad officer was fastening a leash to the collar of a sprightly beagle.

"Jesus," somebody said. "Don't tell me the monks are selling drugs on top of everything else."

"It's a bomb-sniffing dog, you moron," someone else said.

"It's cute, whatever it is," a woman said.

"We had one just like that when I was a kid," a man said. "Dumber than dirt. Couldn't find food in his dish."

The dog disappeared into the building, and the conversation looked for other topics. The abbot continued to move among his corps of monks, patting this one on the back, touching this one on the shoulder, looking like an officer rallying the troops.

"Hey, O'Herlihy," someone called out. "I hear you're running a special on kidneys this week!"

The crowd had been buzzing with casual conversation, and it stopped dead, as if someone had unplugged it. Keller sensed his fellow spectators gathering themselves, brought up short by the combination of shock and a sense of opportunity. The speaker had clearly crossed the line, and they were deciding whether to disapprove or join in. It would depend, he figured, on whether they came up with things too clever to suppress.

But the abbot made the decision for them. He broke off his conversation, spun around to his left, and stalked up to the curb. He drew himself up to his full height and silenced the crowd with a stare.

Then he spoke. "Disperse," he said. "All of ye. Have ye nothing better to do? Go about your proper business, or return to your homes. There's no need for ye here."

And damned if they didn't do exactly that, and Keller with them.

FOURTEEN

"It was pretty impressive," he told Dot. "He just assumed command."

"I guess he must be used to it. Comes with the job, wouldn't you say?"

"I suppose so, but I got the feeling he's been like that all his life. I can picture him as a ten-year-old in the schoolyard, settling disputes in kickball games."

"I always wanted to play kickball," Dot said, "but at my school it was boys only. I'll bet it's different now."

He'd bought another prepaid phone, with a chip good for one hundred minutes or one call to 911, whichever came first. His first call was to Julia; he told her how it felt to be in New York, and how the auction was shaping up, and she filled him in on Jenny's day, and passed on some gossip about a couple two doors down the street. He hadn't told her anything specific about his assignment, and didn't talk about it now.

To Dot he said, "I'm not sure I accomplished anything with that call I made."

"Oh, I don't know, Keller. You got a look at him, didn't you?"

"It's not as though I hadn't seen enough pictures of him."

"But seeing him in person's a little different. You got a sense of the person."

"I guess."

"And you established for certain that he's in residence there. You'd assumed as much, but now you know it for a fact."

"I suppose you're right."

"You don't sound convinced, Keller. What's the matter?"

"The phone."

"Why'd you toss it? I know they log 911 calls, but I thought your phone's untraceable."

"They can't tie it to me," he said, "but they can tell what numbers I call with that phone. Then all they have to do is walk back the cat."

"To Sedona," she said, "and to New Orleans. No, you wouldn't want them to do that. So what's the problem? You bought a disposable phone and then you disposed of it."

"I paid seventy bucks for that phone," he said, "and I made one useless call with it, and now it's floating in the New York sewer system."

"I doubt it's floating, Keller. It probably sank like a stone."

"Well."

"And landed on the bottom," she said, "unless an alligator ate it. Remember Tick-Tock the alligator? In *Peter Pan*?"

"Wasn't that a crocodile?"

"Keller, I know there's a difference between alligators and crocodiles, but is it one we have to care about? Tick-Tock swallowed a clock once, and that's why you could always hear him coming."

"Probably how he got his name, too."

"Odds are. You know, I always wondered how come it didn't run down. You figure it was like a self-winding watch? Just swimming around was enough to keep it going?"

"Dot—"

"So here's your phone," she said, "and this alligator swallows it, and now what happens if somebody calls you?"

How did he get into conversations like this? "Nobody has the number," he said.

"Is that a fact?"

"Besides, I turned the phone off after I made the call. So it wouldn't ring."

"That was wise of you, Keller. Because all you need is an alligator in the sewer with a phone ringing inside his belly."

"And anyway it's a myth. There aren't really any alligators in the New York sewers."

She sighed heavily. "Keller," she said, "you know what you are? A genuine killjoy. You got any inside information about Santa Claus, kindly keep it to yourself. And I wouldn't worry too much about the seventy dollars. It's not gonna keep you from buying any stamps, is it?"

"No."

"Well, there you go. How's New York?"

"It's okay."

"You comfortable there?"

"Pretty much. At first I was worried someone would recognize me, but nobody did, so I stopped worrying."

"I guess so, if you actually started a conversation with a cop."

"Until this moment," he said, "it never occurred to me that I was doing anything risky."

"Maybe you weren't, Keller. The world has a short memory, and I have to say that's just as well. Look, you'll figure out a way to get the job done. You always do."

Keller had Thai food for lunch. You could get perfectly decent Thai food, and almost everything else, in New Orleans, but there was a Thai restaurant two blocks from his old apartment that he remembered fondly. He walked over there, and the hostess put him at a table for two on the left wall, about halfway between the front door and the kitchen.

He was studying the menu when the waitress brought him a glass of Thai iced tea before he could ask for it. How did she know that was what he wanted? He reached for it, and she said, "Papaya salad? Shrimp pad thai, very spicy?"

Was the young woman psychic? No, of course not. She remembered him.

And so had the hostess. Because, he realized, this was the table where he'd always sat years ago, and the meal was the one he'd almost invariably ordered.

Now what? He'd always paid cash, so they wouldn't know his name. Still, they would certainly have seen his photograph, in the papers or on the TV news. But would it have registered out of context?

More to the point, what should he do now? Get up and make a run for it? Or, more discreetly, invent a pretext: "Uh-oh, forgot my wallet, I'll be back in a minute." And they'd never see him again.

But wouldn't that create suspicion where it might well not already exist? And once he'd done that, they'd have reason to wonder what was the matter, and at that point one of them might link this old customer of theirs to a photo dimly recalled, and they could call 911 and it wouldn't even cost them a $70 phone.

On the other hand, he'd be gone by then.

But the authorities, who'd had years to get used to the idea that Keller the Assassin had been liquidated by his employers, would have reason to believe he wasn't dead after all. And there'd be a manhunt, and attention from the media, and what would happen to his life in New Orleans?

The papaya salad came. If he wanted to allay suspicion, he thought, then he ought to act like a man with nothing to hide. So he picked up his fork and dug in.

It was just as he remembered it.

So was the pad thai—the rice noodles nicely slippery on the tongue, the shrimp tender and flavorful, the whole thing fiercely hot. He'd lost his appetite when he realized he'd been recognized, but it returned in full measure once he started eating, and he cleaned both his plates. He might have ordered dessert, there was a baked coconut rice pudding he used to like, but he decided not to push it.

He scribbled in the air, and the hostess brought the check, took his money, and brought his change. He left a tip designed to be generous without being memorable, and on the way out the hostess said, "Long time we don't see you."

"I moved away."

"Ah, that's what I say! Somebody say maybe you don't like us no more, but I say he move. Where you now, Upper West Side?"

"Montana."

"Oh, so far! What city?"

The first thought that came to him was Cheyenne, but that was in Wyoming. "Billings," he said, pretty sure it was in Montana.

"My brother's in Helena," she told him. "Big problem getting people there to try Thai food. So he put sushi on the menu. Sushi very big in Helena."

"In Billings, too."

"They come for sushi," she said, "and then maybe they try something else. Smart guy, my brother. Almost went broke, thought of sushi, and now he's making lots of money."

"That's great."

"You get to Helena, you try Thai Pagoda. Nice place." She frowned. "Cheap rent, too. Not like here. You come back when you in New York, okay?"

"I will."

"You looking good," she said. "Lost some weight!"

"A couple of pounds."

"Almost didn't recognize. Then it comes to me. Table seven! Thai iced tea! Papaya salad! Shrimp pad thai!"

"That's me, all right."

"Very spicy! Make sure very spicy!"

Keller, back in his hotel room, sat in front of the television set watching NY1, the twenty-four-hour local news channel. It was pointless, he knew; if somebody at Thai Garden did make the connection and felt compelled to rat him out to the law, the media wouldn't be reporting it for at least a couple of hours. But he sat there for a half hour anyway, and learned more than he needed to know about the sports and weather, along with ongoing coverage of the bomb scare at Thessalonian House. Once again he got to hear the abbot thunder at the crowd, bidding them to disperse, and even spotted himself in the act of dispersal.

That gave him a turn, but he realized that no one could have identified him on the basis of what he'd just seen. He was part of a crowd shot, seen from a distance, and he had his back to the camera. If he hadn't known he was there, he doubted he'd have recognized himself.

There was, of course, no bomb to be found. The beagle's name turned out to be Ajax, which struck Keller as a pretty decent name for a dog, bomb-sniffing or otherwise. There was a brief interview with Ajax's handler, a light-side-of-the-news piece that Keller found reasonably interesting, and then the announcer's voice turned serious as she talked about the criminal nature of bomb threats, and the need to respond to each of them, and the high cost involved.

"Every call reporting a bomb is logged, and every caller identified," she said. "If you make a false report, it's just a question of time before the long arm of the law reaches out and takes hold of you."

Well, maybe not, Keller thought. Not unless the long arm of the law could reach all the way down into the sewers, and yank his phone out of the alligator's belly.

In the hotel's business center, Keller logged on to the Peachpit site and checked the current status of the lots he was interested in. With one or two exceptions, the opening bids were unchanged. He noted the changes in his catalog and was ready to return to his room when he thought of something.

Google. Who could imagine life without Google?

He was on the computer for fifteen minutes more, and made a few more notes. Then he pulled down the History menu and deleted that day's searches, his and everybody else's.

Then back to his room.

FIFTEEN

"I'd like to talk to Abbot O'Herlihy," Keller said. His voice, he noticed, was pitched higher than usual. He hadn't planned on it. It just came out that way.

"That would be Abbot Paul," said the monk who'd answered the phone. "And I'm afraid he's not taking any calls."

"I think it would be a good idea for him to take this one," Keller said, and he could only hope he'd said it ominously.

There was a thoughtful silence. Then, "Perhaps you could tell me the nature of your business with the abbot."

"It was almost thirty years ago," Keller said, "and he wasn't Abbot Paul then. He was Father O'Herlihy, with a parish in Cold Spring Harbor. And I was little Timmy Hannan, just ten years old, and, and—"

"I'm putting you on hold," the monk said, and Keller heard a click, and then spent a full five minutes listening to recorded Gregorian chants.

Keller was just beginning to get into the music when it cut out in the middle of a phrase, and the voice that took over was very different from that of the mild-mannered chap who'd answered the phone. He placed it at once, the timbre, the authority, the slight but unmistakable touch of brogue.

"Who is this?"

"Someone you knew in Cold Spring Harbor."

"Tell me your name." Not *What's your name?* but *Tell me your name.* This man, when he prayed, probably gave orders to God.

"Timothy Michael Hannan, Father, but you called me Timmy."

"Did I? And when was this, by God?"

"Almost thirty years ago. You did... bad things."

"Bad things."

"And I forgot! I blocked it all out, and last week I saw you on television, and I heard your voice, and—"

"And it all came back to ye, did it?"

Remarkable how the son of a bitch managed to put you on the defensive. Keller, in his high-voiced role as little Timmy Hannan, damn near cowered.

He drew a quick breath and said, "Father, they want me to go to the media, to the district attorney, to the diocesan office, but first I wanted—"

"Wanted what?"

"To meet with you. If I could just have a few private minutes with you this afternoon, or perhaps this evening—"

"Private minutes."

"Because, I don't know, maybe it's a false memory. God knows I want it to be. If we could just meet in person, in private—"

"Tomorrow."

"Uh, I was hoping we could find some time today."

"Tomorrow morning," the abbot said, "a car will call for me at nine forty-five to take me to the New York Athletic Club. Do ye know where that is?"

"I can find it."

"No doubt ye can. I am a member, and I will arrange for ye to be admitted as my guest. Spell your name for me."

"T-I-M—"

"Your last name, ye idiot."

Keller wasn't sure how to spell it, Hannan or Hannon, but he figured he was all right either way. He spelled it with two *a*'s.

"You'll arrive at ten fifteen, no sooner and no later. They'll give ye a pass and a locker key, and tell ye how to find the steam room. Strip to the skin, put your clothes in a locker, fasten the key around your wrist, and help yourself to a towel. I'll be taking the steam before my massage. You'll come join me, and we'll have our 'private time.'"

Keller wasn't sure how to reply to that. While he was working it out, the phone clicked in his ear.

Hell.

Wednesday morning's session at Peachpit would feature Great Britain and the British Commonwealth, and there were several lots that Keller was hoping to bid on. The starting time was ten o'clock, and he'd just agreed to show up at the New York Athletic Club at ten fifteen.

Or had he? It seemed to him that he, in the persona of little Timmy Hannan, hadn't been provided with much opportunity to agree or disagree. He'd been issued his instructions, and it seemed to be a given that he would follow them to the letter. And to the number, which was precisely fifteen minutes after the Peachpit crew began selling British stamps.

It was impossible to predict the pace of an auction; the more competitive the bidding, the longer it took to get through the lots. But no matter how you figured it, Keller couldn't keep his date with the abbot without missing the first half of the session, and the tyranny of alphabetical order placed British East Africa very much in that time span.

British East Africa was what philatelists designated a dead country. The first time Keller heard that term he visualized an arid wasteland, with the skulls of cattle scattered here and there, and noxious vapors rising from the occasional water source. In due course he learned that the term merely indicated that a particular stamp-issuing entity was no longer operating under that name.

Keller's collection had a cutoff date of 1940. He'd stretched that out to include British Commonwealth issues through 1952, the end of George VI's reign constituting a natural stopping point. And lately he seemed to be stretching his limits for other countries as well, to accommodate World War II issues. All in all, though, his collection held no end of dead countries, and the list kept growing. Even Czechoslovakia had become a dead country, once it divvied itself up into the separate Czech and Slovak Republics.

British East Africa had its philatelic birth in 1890, when the British East Africa Company overprinted three Indian stamps for use in the territory under its administration. The next eight years saw the appearance of just over a hundred British East Africa stamps, some of them created specifically for the colony, others overprinted on stamps of India or Zanzibar. Then British East Africa was incorporated as the East Africa and Uganda Protectorate, which was subsequently folded into the Kenya Colony, which gave way to what collectors knew as K.U.T., for Kenya Uganda and Tanganyika, which Keller always thought of as an African version of the Atchison, Topeka, and Santa Fe.

Dead countries, all of them.

Commencing in 1890, British East Africa issued seventeen stamps with the design of a crowned sun, ostensibly symbolizing light and liberty. The following year, a shortage of certain denominations led the postal authorities to surcharge others, changing their denominations either by hand stamp or by pen and ink and creating eight collectible stamps in the process. One of these, listed in the Scott catalog as number 33, consisted of a two-anna vermilion stamp surcharged half an anna in manuscript, and marked as well with the initials A.B., for Archibald Brown.

Keller had no idea who Archibald Brown might be, and didn't much care, but he wanted the stamp. It was unused, with only a trace of original gum, and the centering was not absolutely perfect, but the color was bright and unfaded, and an accompanying Sergio Sismondo certificate proclaimed it genuine and free of flaws.

Scott valued the stamp at $6000, and Peachpit's presale estimate was $3500. A mail or Internet bidder had submitted an opening bid of $2750, and no one had topped it when Keller had last checked. But there was no telling what would happen when it went under the hammer.

How much did he want it? How high would he go for it? Well, that was one of the things you found out when you sat in an auction room. You might have a top figure in mind, but when the time came you might find out you didn't really want it all that much. Or you might go much higher than you'd planned.

Could he get there in time? No, not a chance. British East Africa 33 was lot number 77, and would surely be sold in the first hour of the auction. At ten fifteen he'd show up at the NYAC, and by the time he was actually inside the steam room it would be ten thirty, and he couldn't envision a scenario that left Paul Vincent O'Herlihy dead and Keller dressed and in Peachpit's auction room by eleven o'clock.

Get real, he told himself. It's only a hobby.

It was only a hobby, and the stamp was only a stamp, but that didn't mean he could get it out of his head. He had dinner at a deli that was famous for giving you more food than you could eat, and it lived up to its reputation. The waiter was surprised, and seemed slightly offended, when Keller didn't want to take home the leftover half of his enormous sandwich. "That's a whole meal you're throwing away," the man told him. "Didn't your mother ever tell you they're starving in Africa?"

And there he was, back in the blighted landscape of British East Africa, with its long-horned cattle skulls and poisoned water holes. And now, thanks to this helpful son of a bitch, the picture included little black children, their stomachs bloated with kwashiorkor, flies buzzing around their mournful eyes. It was a hard image to get rid of, and the only solution was to resume thinking about the stamp.

And he went on thinking about the stamp for the rest of the evening, except when he forced himself to think about what he would do in the steam room. He could guess why O'Herlihy had chosen it as the venue for their meeting, as it combined convenience with security. He was going there anyway for his massage appointment, so there'd be no unexplained absence from the monastery. And how could Timmy Hannan, with only a towel to cover himself, wear a wire into a steam room?

Keller hadn't planned on wearing a wire, as a recording of the proceedings was the last thing he wanted. But it would be nice to have a weapon.

A gun, say. Keller wasn't that crazy about guns. They were noisy, unless you used a suppressor. They left nitrate particles on your hand, unless you wore gloves. Sometimes they jammed, and sometimes they misfired. And, unless you got fairly close to your target, there was always the chance that you would miss. If you were close enough to rule out a miss, well, you were probably close enough to get the job done without a gun.

Still, O'Herlihy was an awfully large man. Sheer bulk was part of what made him so imposing. It might be mostly fat, but simply carrying all that weight around could make a man strong, couldn't it? So there was a certain appeal in being a couple of steps away from him, maybe even three or four steps, and pointing a gun at him, and finding out if he could stop the bullets by sheer force of will.

Well, forget that. They wouldn't make you go through a metal detector to get into the New York Athletic Club, but there'd be other people in the locker room, and possibly in the steam room as well, and even if he took a second towel and wrapped the gun in it—no, never mind, he couldn't go in there with a gun.

Not that he had a gun, or knew offhand where to get hold of one.

Then what? A knife? Anything large enough to do the job would be a problem to conceal.

He walked around, letting his mind play with the problem. He remembered a television program he'd seen ages ago, in which the murder weapon was an icicle. A nice touch, he'd thought at the time. It was a locked-room murder, if he remembered correctly; the murderer and the victim were found in the room, the victim stabbed to death, and no murder weapon to be found. Because it melted.

Did they solve it? Find water droplets in the wound and put two and two together? Or did the killer get away with it? He couldn't remember, and didn't see that it mattered. Nor did he see where he was going to find an icicle at this time of year, let alone carry it into a steam room.

Maybe the best he could hope for from tomorrow's meeting was to lay the groundwork for another meeting at a more promising venue. And then what? Set up something for Thursday afternoon and miss his shot at the German Colonials?

He spent twenty minutes in a chain drugstore. Then he headed back to his room at the Savoyard and went to bed.

SIXTEEN

It was a quarter after seven when Keller opened his eyes, and he was grateful for the opportunity to get up and start the day. He'd set the bedside alarm clock for eight and backed it up with an eight fifteen wake-up call, and he shut off the first and canceled the second and got under the shower, hoping the spray would sluice away the residue of the dream.

He'd dreamed about the stamp, of course, and managed to incorporate the old naked-in-public-places dream that he'd had in one form or another for most of his life. It had pretty much stopped since he wound up in New Orleans, but here it was again, with him sitting in Peachpit's auction room and suddenly realizing that he was wearing a T-shirt and nothing else.

And all night long he kept realizing it was a dream, and turning over and going back to sleep, and slipping right back into the dream all over again, trying to find a way to make it come out right. He missed out on the lot he wanted to buy, and he made mistakes and bought other things that he didn't want or need, and throughout it all he was hoping nobody would notice that he didn't have any pants on.

Only a dream, he thought. Only a dream, only a hobby, only a stamp.

Hell.

Downstairs, he visited the business center and checked the stamp's current price. It was unchanged, still $2750. Keller had decided the most he was willing to pay was $4500, and he registered on the site and entered the bid. He waited a minute or two and refreshed the page, and saw that the opening bid had now increased to $3000. That meant he was the high bidder, and someone else would have to raise it another $1750 to top his maximum.

Was it time to meet O'Herlihy? No, not even close. He had plenty of time for breakfast, but he'd just committed himself to pay $4500 for a stamp, and it would cost him more than that by the time he was done. The auction gallery tacked on a buyer's premium of 20 percent, and there was New York sales tax on top of that, so a lot he bought for $4500 would cost him something over $5800, which wasn't that much less than its $6000 Scott valuation.

Shelling out $35 for breakfast never seemed like a great idea to Keller, but it was even less attractive after the bid he'd just made. So he passed on both the hotel's buffet and the ersatz bistro and found a vendor's cart on one of the side streets. He got a croissant and a cup of coffee, which was as much as he wanted, and the bright-eyed immigrant, no doubt from a dead country, gave him change back from his $5 bill.

The croissant was fine, and so was the coffee, and they had

pedestrianized Times Square since he moved away, so he was able to pull a little chair up to a little table and have his breakfast in—well, not peace and quiet, not exactly, but it was pleasant all the same.

When he was done he glanced at his watch. There was time, he saw, but he'd have to hurry.

He walked quickly back to his hotel. The business center had four people in it, but it had five computers, and Keller was grateful for that.

The New York Athletic Club was on the corner of Seventh Avenue and Central Park South, not far from the Savoyard and even closer to the Peachpit offices on 57th Street. Parked out in front, next to a convenient fire hydrant, stood a black limousine, its chauffeur chatting away on a no-hands cell phone. And waiting, Keller suspected, to drive the abbot back to the monastery.

Keller had put on a suit and tie, thinking the place might have a dress code, and realized the absurdity of it when a couple of overage preppies passed him wearing workout clothes. Still, the suit might make a decent impression on the desk attendant, who looked up at his approach. "Hannan," Keller told him. "I'm Father Paul O'Herlihy's guest."

"You have some ID?"

To sit in a steam bath? Keller had a full set of ID, but nothing that proclaimed him to be Timothy Hannan.

He patted his pockets. "No idea I'd need it," he said. "I don't like to leave my wallet in a locker."

The clerk, whose totem animal was clearly the weasel, explained that all guests had to show identification. "I'm afraid I can't make an exception," he said.

Oh, I'll bet you can, Keller thought. "Fine," he said, and

turned toward the door. "I'll just tell the abbot that the fellow behind the desk took his job a little too seriously."

He took three steps, but before he could take a fourth the weasel must have imagined the conversation he'd wind up having with Father O'Herlihy. In view of the abbot's prominence, he suggested, and because Mr. Hannan hadn't been informed of standard procedures, well, perhaps these were special circumstances. And here's a locker key, and to get to the locker room, all you do is...

Well, Keller thought, now for the hard part.

In the locker room, one flight below ground level, two men in their fifties were discussing a proposed corporate merger while they got back into their business attire. "These things always take too long," one of them said. "But then everything's like that these days. I'm with my girlfriend the other day and I realize I can't wait for it to be over. I didn't want the pleasure, I wanted the memory of the pleasure."

The other nodded. "Some days," he said, "all I want is to move everything in my life from the in-box to the out-box."

Keller picked up a towel and found the right locker. He stripped and loaded his clothes into it. There was a wooden hanger for his jacket, another for his shirt. Before he took off his pants, he drew his homemade weapon from his pocket. He'd bought a few yards of picture-hanging wire at the drugstore the night before, and in his room he'd bent it back and forth until he'd equipped himself with a piece two feet long. He'd fashioned a loop at either end and wound up with what ought to be a perfectly serviceable garrote, which he now wound around his left wrist.

It looked like a bracelet, an arts and crafts project from some facility for the developmentally challenged, but when

Keller slipped his hand through the locker key's elastic band, it pretty much blended in. And he could have it off his wrist and his hands in its loops in a matter of seconds. He'd spent half an hour last night trying, and if practice hadn't made him perfect, it had at least made his movements swift and sure.

He secured the towel around his middle and headed for the steam room.

And walked into a fog bank. One thing he somehow hadn't taken into account was the presence of steam, though it now seemed to him an obvious component of a steam room, like water in a swimming pool. The steam was hot, and right there in his face, and he couldn't really see anything, just colorless shapes looming in the colorless mist.

While he couldn't see much, that didn't mean he was himself invisible. He learned as much when a voice he recognized said, "Hannan? Over here."

He blinked, moved toward the voice. Either the steam was clearing or his eyes were getting used to it, because he could see a little better now. There were seven men—well, he could only assume they were men—seated on ledges on three of the room's sides. The abbot of the Thessalonians was all by himself at the extreme right of the far wall.

"Sit beside me, Hannan. No, get closer, but not so close that your leg is touching mine. Ye might fancy that but I would not."

Keller so arranged himself that there was a good six-inch gap between his leg and O'Herlihy's. He'd have preferred to be on the man's other side, so that his wire-wrapped wrist would be shielded from view, but there was a wall on that side.

"Now remove the towel."

Oh, Jesus, Keller thought.

"So that I may assure myself you're not wearing a wire, lad. I've no interest in any part of your wretched self that's beneath the towel."

But he was in fact wearing a wire, Keller thought, and then realized the man was talking about a recording device, not something Keller hoped to loop around his thick neck. Keller lifted the towel, and the man looked at him and looked away so quickly that Keller found himself feeling somehow inadequate.

"Now we can talk, Hannan. If we keep our voices at this level these other men won't hear us. The steam's an insulator. And it will probably keep ye from recording this, should ye be equipped with some new device I'm unable to detect."

"I'm not."

"Ah, well, I'm sure I can take ye at your word."

The sarcasm was razor-sharp, and came wrapped in the rank odor of yesterday's alcohol draining from the man's pores. That, Keller guessed, was the point of the steam bath; it drew out yesterday's poison and made room for today's.

And room would be needed, because O'Herlihy's breath carried a slightly different scent, one of alcohol not yet processed by that bulky body. So he'd had a drink to start the day. Some sort of whiskey, by the smell of it.

Ah, well. A strong man's weakness.

"Now I'll talk," O'Herlihy said, in a cloud of whiskey breath. "And ye'll listen. If ye'd called six months ago with the same sorry tale I'd have told ye to feck off. And hung up on ye, and taken no calls from ye afterward. Do ye know why?"

Keller shook his head.

"Because I'm not queer," he said, "and there's women who'd swear to it. There's a woman who was a housekeeper of mine, in Cold Spring Harbor and other parishes, and I'd still see her after I went with the Thessalonians. Not as often, as I was older and felt the heat less, and she's along in years herself, but still has her charms. But they'd be wasted on ye, wouldn't they? You're a gay boy yourself, are ye not?"

"No, I—"

"Of course ye are, and fixing to blame myself for your sorry state. Six months ago the press'd pay no mind to ye. They'd have heard rumors of this woman of mine, and one or two others who needn't concern you, and they'd dismiss your dirty talk out of hand. But now I'm in the public eye, and if nothing else they'd have to refute your bloody words, and she'd get dragged into it, and I won't have that. Do ye follow me, lad?"

"Father, I must have made a mistake."

"Indeed ye did, thinking to squeeze money out of myself."

"No," Keller said. "No, I honestly thought—Father, I have these memories, but they can't be true, can they?"

There was a pause. The door to the steam room opened. A man left, and two others entered.

"There might be something in those memories," O'Herlihy said grudgingly. "There was another priest in the same parish, as thin as I was stout, and as dark as I was fair. Father Peter Mullane was his name, and he had a weakness for boys, and—"

"Father Peter," Keller said, glad for a straw to grasp at.

"You recall him, lad?"

"I'd forgotten him completely, but as soon as you said his name I could picture him. Very slender, and dark-haired, and—God, I can see his face now!"

"Well, ye needn't start searching for him. The poor man's twenty years dead. And didn't he take his own life? Whatever grief he caused ye, he's paying for it many times over. Burning in hell for all of eternity, if ye believe the shite we taught ye."

Scotch, Keller thought, getting the strongest whiff yet of the man's breath. He said, "Father, I don't know what to say. I made a terrible mistake."

"Ye did, but at least spare me the burden of hearing your confession." A sigh. "Well, they'll get my testimony, the bastards, and there'll be some misfortunate men in New Jersey, but it can't be helped." He snorted, and then seemed to remember there was someone sitting beside him. "And that's nothing to ye, is it? Ye can go now, and we needn't set eyes on one another again."

Keller glanced at his wrist, where the garrote reposed, ready to be uncoiled and put to work. In a hot steamy room full of witnesses, against a man twice his size who'd yank it out of his hands and lash him with it.

Right.

SEVENTEEN

I felt like a worm," he told Dot. "I'm not sure, but I think he had me groveling."

"That's not how I picture you, Keller. Did you go to Catholic school?"

"No. I was in a Boy Scout troop that met in the parish hall of a Catholic church, but the scoutmaster wasn't a member of the clergy."

"So he just wore one of those silly little soldier suits."

"It was a Boy Scout uniform," he said, "and it never looked silly to me. Though I guess it might nowadays. You know, I don't think it was the religious aspect that got to me. He just plain assumed command of the situation."

"I guess he's used to it."

"Yesterday I thought maybe the robe had something to do with it, but this time all he had was a towel draped over his lap. Dot, the guy was sweating out yesterday's Scotch and he already had a good start on today's. His nose is red and his face is full of broken blood vessels. It's a shame the client can't wait for cirrhosis to take him off the board."

"We don't get paid for cirrhosis," she said, "and the client can't wait, not if he's made up his mind to testify. But I have to say I don't know how the hell you're gonna get to him. There's no way he'll take another meeting with you, is there?"

"No, I had my chance. If I'd just gone ahead and given it my best shot—"

"You'd be dead," she said, "or in jail. Say you brought it off. Then what? Dash out of the steam room with half a dozen witnesses in hot pursuit, pause to unlock your locker and put on your suit and tie your tie—"

"I wouldn't have bothered with the tie."

"Well, I hadn't realized that, Keller. That'd make all the difference, all right. Get dressed, rush past everybody, ring for the elevator—"

"I'd have taken the stairs. But I get the message, Dot. I know you're right. I just feel there should have been something I could do."

"The question," she said, "is what can you do now, and I have the feeling the answer is nothing. Say he keeps the same schedule every day as far as the steam room and massage are concerned. He walks what, ten or a dozen steps from his door to the limo? And if he's not escorted, at a minimum he's got the limo driver standing there holding the door."

"It wouldn't work."

"No, of course not. And what are your chances of getting inside the residence?"

"None, as far as I can see."

"Well, Keller, what does that leave?" She didn't wait for an answer. "Look," she said, "except for the money, what do we care if some of New Jersey's finest get a small fraction of what's coming to them? I'll give back the money. That's easy enough."

"You hate to give back money."

"I do," she said, "because once I have it in hand I think of it as my money, and giving it back is like spending it, and what am I getting for it? Well, in this case what we're both getting is piece of mind, and you could say we're paying for it with somebody else's money."

"Don't give it back just yet," he said. "Maybe I'll come up with something."

When he got out of the New York Athletic Club, Keller had had a fleeting thought of rushing to the auction gallery. But that was ridiculous; it was after eleven, and the most spirited bidding since the sale of the Ferrary collection couldn't have delayed the sale of British East Africa number 33. Besides, he'd already put in a high bid, which he'd second-guessed himself into raising after downing his croissant and coffee.

He'd rushed back to the hotel computer and upped his own bid from $4500 to $6000, and the instant he'd done so he began to have regrets. If he got the stamp for that bid, tax and buyer's premium would boost it to something like $7700, and that was far more than the stamp was worth to him.

Well, it was done. Before, he'd worried that he would miss out on the stamp, and now he was worried that he'd get it, and it was hard to say which was worse. It would work out however it worked out, and in the meantime he'd pushed it out of his mind and gone to his rendezvous with the Thessalonian abbot.

For all the good that did him.

Afterward, flushed from the steam bath and the ignominy

of it all, he returned to the Savoyard. He walked right past the business center and went to his room, and after he'd spoken with Dot he walked right past the business center again and continued four blocks uptown. He was a full half hour early for the afternoon session, and one of the assistants was happy to check on lot 77.

"Went for eighty-five hundred," the woman reported. "All of British Africa was going way over estimate. All the best stuff, that is. Well, that's the beauty of auctions. You never know."

"Like life itself," Keller said.

"Well, in my life," she said, "sometimes you know. But auctions, all it takes is two bidders who both really want the same lot. And this is just a stamp. With postal history, where every cover is essentially unique, well, there's no predicting. One piece will go for ten or twenty times estimate and another won't bring a single bid. You really never know."

She steered him to a refreshment table, where Keller joined a couple of other bidders who were drinking coffee and chipping away at a platter of sandwiches. Keller helped himself, and listened while one man told another how he'd been unable to interest his son in stamps, but his grandson was shaping up as an ardent young philatelist.

"Right now he likes first-day covers," the man said, "which is fine at his age, but I take him to shows, and he'll sit and go through boxes of covers, and you can see his imagination growing."

"So it skips a generation," his friend said.

"Exactly. Well, not to say what I shouldn't, but better he should take after his grandfather than his father in certain respects."

"And we'll leave it at that," the friend said, "before *I* say what I shouldn't."

The men walked off, laughing. Keller finished his sandwich and took his coffee into the auction room. He took a seat, paged through a catalog, and tried to get in the mood.

Without much success. The auction began at its appointed hour, and Keller couldn't get lot 77 out of his head. He was at once relieved not to have to pay the $6000 plus extras that his bid had committed him to, and disappointed to have missed out on the stamp. On the one hand he was a fool to have bid as much as he did; on the other, the high bidder had evidently seen something in the stamp that Keller had not, and maybe he knew something; maybe Keller should have been in there all the way.

He had, he realized, a severe case of the woulda-coulda-shouldas, and recognizing the syndrome wasn't enough to make it go away. Here he was, in a comfortable chair with a whole afternoon of worldwide stamps up for sale, and he couldn't concentrate on what was going on now because he was trying to rewrite what had already taken place hours ago.

The first lot he'd circled was a 1919 set of Albanian overprints, with a catalog value just under $500 and an estimate of $350. Keller had looked at the stamps, and figured he'd go $375, maybe $400. The bidding opened at $200, and there were no bids from the live online participants, no phone bids reported by either of the women manning the phones. Keller was one of a mere dozen bidders physically present in the room, and none of his companions showed any interest in the Albanian set.

Nor did Keller. He sat there as if mummified while the set was sold to the book bidder for $200.

Wonderful. That gave him something new to regret.

After an Egyptian lot got away from him, knocked down to an Internet bidder for less than he'd been prepared to pay,

Keller knew what he had to do. There was an exercise he'd developed to keep his work from exacting a psychic toll, and if it worked with dead people, why shouldn't it work with a stamp from a dead country?

First, he found the photo of lot 77 in his catalog and stared intently at it. Then he closed his eyes and held the image in his mind—the vivid color, the details of the design, the hand-stamped overprint, the handwritten initials. He brought the image in close, so that it was larger than its actual size.

And then he turned it over to the Photoshop of his mind. He let the colors go dim, the vermilion washing out, the black overprint fading to gray. He pushed the stamp away, letting it recede in the distance, growing smaller and smaller in his mind's eye. It became a distant colorless blur, and grew smaller and smaller until it vanished altogether.

By the time the lots from France and the French Colonies came up, he was back in the game.

EIGHTEEN

Back at his hotel room, Keller found another reason to be glad he'd missed the British East Africa stamp. The way things stood, it looked as though he wasn't going to be able to carry out his assignment. Dot would have to refund the advance payment, and he wouldn't be getting paid.

With nothing coming in, he'd have to pay attention to his expenses. He still had substantial funds in an offshore bank, but he'd been dipping into them just to cover ongoing household expenses, ever since the economic downturn flattened the business of rehabbing houses and flipping them. He could still afford to buy stamps, but he could spend more freely out of profits than out of capital.

He put away the stamps he'd just purchased, including a high value from Gabon that had eluded him for years. He was happy to have them, but maybe it was just as well he'd missed out on the stamps from Albania and Egypt.

Maybe he should skip tomorrow's afternoon session, with all of that outstanding German Colonial material. Maybe he should move up his departure. He could probably still get a seat on tonight's 8:59 flight to New Orleans. He wouldn't save anything on the hotel bill, it was hours past checkout time, but he'd be home a day earlier, and that had to be worth something.

Call Dot, tell her there was nothing for it but to give back the money.

Hell. Maybe he should have one last look at the monastery.

It looked as impregnable as ever.

Oh, he could get a foot in the door. All he had to do was bang away with the knocker, and some creature in a plain brown robe would open it. But it wouldn't be O'Herlihy, because when you were the abbot, you didn't have the job of opening up for visitors. Instead you kept busy telling everybody else what to do, or stayed in your room, sucking on the Scotch bottle.

Or did monks have cells? They seemed to in books, but then they weren't cloistered in Murray Hill town houses, not in the novels he'd read. O'Herlihy, he somehow knew, would have a large and well-appointed bedchamber all to himself, unless he managed to smuggle in one of those women he'd been bragging about.

Would that bedchamber front on the street? Could the man be standing at his window now, looking out at the passing scene? Looking out, perhaps, at the man he knew as Timothy Hannan?

Keller, on the north side of the street, drew back into the shadows.

If you knew which room was his, and if it did indeed look out on 36th Street, then what?

A bomb? Not a huge one to demolish the whole building, but something more along the lines of a hand grenade. Lob it through the window in the wee small hours of the morning, by which time O'Herlihy would have taken in enough Scotch to render him unconscious. Boom! The man would never know what hit him.

Of course you'd have to know which window belonged to his room. And you'd also have to know where to get your hands on a grenade.

Hmm. If he could just find another way into the building. A back door, say. So that he could contrive to be inside when all but a skeleton crew of monks had retired for the night, and their abbot along with them. Then, gliding down the corridors like a ninja, he could find O'Herlihy's room with the man passed out and snoring, his intimidation factor severely diminished. Keller, who could bring any weapon he wanted, might as easily dispatch his quarry with his bare hands.

He turned to his right, counting his steps as he walked to Madison Avenue, where he turned left and walked a block south. At 35th Street he turned left again, and counted his steps again, stopping when he reached the number he'd tallied earlier. Now, unless he'd screwed up somehow, the building in front of him was one that backed up on Thessalonian House.

And a handsome building it was, four stories tall, with a limestone facade and Greek Revival pillars. Like Thessalonian House, it had surely started life as a private home, and was just as surely something else now. There was a brass plaque alongside the door, but Keller couldn't make out what it said, and—

"Edward!"

The voice was familiar, even if the name was not. Keller

turned, and there was Irv Feldspar, the man who'd recognized him from years ago at Stampazine. He was wearing a tweed jacket and a checked shirt and a big smile, and he hurried along the sidewalk to where Keller was standing.

"Edward Nicholas," he said, panting from the effort. "Knew you right away. Never thought you'd be a member, living where you do. New Mexico, didn't you say?"

"New Orleans."

"Well, I was close. But of course we've got plenty of out-of-town members. We just don't get to see them so often. You're here for the presentation?"

"I was just walking down the street," Keller said. "And I'm afraid I'm not a member of anything, Mr. Feldspar."

"Please, make it Irv. And do you prefer Ed or Edward?"

"Well, I—"

"Or Eddie, even, for all I know."

"Actually," he said, "my name's Nicholas Edwards, so—"

"Well, I was close. Nick? Nicholas?"

"Either one, Irv."

"So you're not a member of the Connoisseurs? Your feet just brought you here? Well, I have to say you've got smart feet. We meet the first and third Wednesday of the month, drinks and hors d'oeuvres for an hour, then a one-hour presentation, and we're out by half past seven. Tonight we've got a visiting speaker from Milwaukee, an expert on the philately of the Civil War. Come on."

Feldspar had taken him by the arm and was urging him toward the door. Keller said again that he wasn't a member, but that didn't seem to matter. "You're my guest," he said. "You'll have a drink, you'll have something to eat, and you'll see some great philatelic material and listen to a terrific talk. And you'll meet some wonderful fellows. Franklin Roosevelt was a member of this club, FDR himself. Come on, Nick, you don't want to miss this."

"It was pretty interesting," he told Julia. "The place is the next thing to a mansion, and it belongs to the club. Someone gave it to them a hundred years ago, and there's no mortgage, and because they're nonprofit there are no taxes to pay. And they can afford to put out a spread of food and drinks before every meeting, and it's all free."

"And the people were nice?"

"Very pleasant fellows. And a couple of women, too. Irv kept introducing me to people, and he got a couple of names wrong, but they know him well enough to be used to him."

"Ass-Backward syndrome," she said. "How was the presentation?"

"That's what I wanted to tell you about. It was Civil War philately, which of course means the USA—"

"And the CSA, buster."

"Well, yeah. But it's an area I don't collect, so that made the material on display less interesting to me than it might have been otherwise. But the talk was fascinating, and I learned some things I never knew. Do you know what happened in 1861?"

"Well, I guess I do," she said. "Y'all started a damn war for no good reason."

"Besides that," he said. "See, someone in Washington realized that all those U.S. post offices in the southern states had large stocks of U.S. stamps on hand."

"So? They couldn't mail letters with them. They were a separate nation by then, even if nobody in Washington was willing to acknowledge it."

"Sometimes," he said, "you're more southern than usual.

This fellow in Washington was worried that those stamps constituted a danger to the Union. Confederate agents could smuggle them across the border and sell them at a discount to unscrupulous parties. On the one hand that would raise funds that could be used to aid the secessionist cause, and at the same time it could undermine the integrity of the United States mails."

"Would that work?"

"I don't see how. We're talking about stamps, for God's sake. But in order to nip such a scheme in the bud, the Post Office recalled all the current stamps and rushed a whole new series of stamps into production, with no end of complications that would only interest a stamp collector, and at a cost that had to be ten times what those mythical southern smugglers could have netted for their stamps."

"Yankees," she said. "Was it a southern boy who gave the presentation?"

"As a matter of fact he was from Milwaukee."

"Maybe his granddaddy moved north," she said, "though why he'd want to do that is beyond me. I'm just having fun, you know, when I get like this."

"I know."

"It sounds as though you had a good time. Are the dues very high?"

"Two hundred dollars a year."

"That's hardly anything. What, four dollars a week?"

"It's even less for out-of-town members. He offered to sponsor me."

"Who, Mr. Asperger?"

"Feldspar. I'd need references, but there are enough dealers I've done business with. And I'm a member of the American Philatelic Society."

"I think you should join."

"Well, I'll think about it. Who knows when I'll be back in New York?"

"But you feel okay there?"

"Pretty much." She hadn't asked about the job that had brought him there, nor had he volunteered anything. "But I'll be glad to get home."

"Me, too. Tomorrow night, you said? I'll pick you up at the airport."

"It'll be way past Jenny's bedtime. Anyway, I left the pickup in long-term parking."

"So what's there for me to do?"

"You could leave a light on."

"I could. And there'll be a fresh pot of coffee waiting for you. They don't make it with chicory up there, do they?"

"They don't."

"In that case," she said, "I guess you'll be glad to get home."

NINETEEN

The parlor floor of the Connoisseurs, half a flight up from street level, was given over to the club's offices, along with their extensive philatelic library. The meeting was held on the second floor, with food and drinks arrayed on a table in a room at the front of the building; a room for displays and lectures was at the rear. Keller made himself a light Dewar's and soda and helped himself to cheese and crackers and salted nuts while Feldspar introduced him to various members, all of whom seemed more than happy to have him in their midst.

"A general worldwide collector," said one man, whose name Keller recognized from articles in *Linn's*. "The wonderful thing about it is that there's always something to buy. And that's also the horrible thing about it—there's always something to buy."

Keller figured he'd remember that one. But he missed a lot

at first because his mind was largely occupied with figuring out how the club could provide access to Thessalonian House. There was a stairway leading to the upper floors, although a velvet rope indicated it was off-limits. Still, if he found a way to conceal himself in a men's room when the meeting broke up, the velvet rope would hardly stop him from ascending to the top floor, and from there he ought to be able to get onto the roof.

And then what? If all of these buildings were tenements, they might have been built right up against one another, enabling an adventurous fellow to spring from one roof to another. But that only worked if the buildings in question were the same height, and it seemed to him that the monastery was taller by a story. And both structures were on a block in Murray Hill that had never been given over to tenements, and the gap between this building and O'Herlihy's was almost certainly one that not even Nijinsky could span.

And if he somehow found himself on the monastery's roof? Then what?

No, forget the roof. The club surely had access to the rear courtyard, from the basement if not from the parlor floor, so that's where he could direct his efforts, if indeed he could hide out while everybody else went home. The club's rear exit would be locked, but fire laws assured that they could be opened from within. And there'd be a rear door for the monastery, and if he could work out a way to open it, why then he'd be in the basement of the monastery, surrounded by cellar-dwelling monks wondering who he was and what in hell he was doing there.

That was as far as he got before the formal meeting began. Then the guest speaker began talking and showing his PowerPoint presentation, and Keller had the good fortune to get caught up in it and, at least for the time being, forget all about Father Paul Vincent O'Herlihy and the impregnable fortress that kept the man out of harm's way.

Thursday morning, Keller woke up early. During his shower he realized that he felt good, and wondered why. He decided that somehow, during the night, he'd resigned himself to the failure of his assignment, and would be glad simply to be getting home.

He found the same food cart as yesterday, ordered the same breakfast of croissant and coffee, and told himself he'd just saved another $30. And yesterday, by God, he'd fed himself all day for the couple of dollars breakfast cost him. The coffee and sandwiches at Peachpit had been a satisfactory lunch, and he'd skipped supper after having enjoyed the food and drink at the Connoisseurs. And now, while he enjoyed feeding his trim body a light breakfast, the plump and stately P. V. O'Herlihy would already be pouring the first of today's whiskey down his throat while he prepared to sweat out yesterday's, and—

Wait a minute.

He dropped the remains of his croissant in the trash, followed it with his unfinished coffee. No time to waste. Things to do, people to see.

Alphabet City had already changed substantially when Keller was last there, its nasty tenements getting rehabbed left and right for young monied tenants. Now it was even harder to recall what a foul pit it had once been.

But he was comforted to see it was still a place to cop, if you could use your eyes and knew how to comport yourself. Keller, on East 5th Street between Avenues C and D, watched business being done, and got into character. He picked out the right man to approach and braced him.

"Got that," the fellow said. "Say you want a set of works, too? You sure 'bout that? Nobody shoots this shit, man. These downs, they ain't like lady or smack. You shoot up, you gone get abscesses."

"It's for a friend," Keller told him.

"The very best," the man said reverently. "It's not a single malt, mind you. Some of the special-batch single malts can get up there in price, but what we have here is a blend of several malt whiskeys, aged for an astonishing sixty years."

"And you say it's five hundred dollars?"

"A towering sum for a bottle of Scotch," the man admitted. He was wearing the vest and trousers of a three-piece gray suit, with a fresh white shirt and what Keller had to think was the tie of a good regiment. His hair was styled and his mustache trimmed, and he looked just right for his role behind the counter of a Madison Avenue purveyor of fine wines and spirits.

"The price," he continued, "is ten times that of any number of truly excellent Scotches. But to keep it in perspective, we've any number of bottles of wine for which we'd have to get three or four times as much, and some that are quite stratospheric in price. A Latour of the right vintage, a Lafite Rothschild—and to open such a bottle is to finish it. An hour or two and you've emptied it, whereas a liter of whiskey can be best enjoyed a dram at a time, over months or even years. And every time your man has his sip, he's reminded of the generosity of the giver."

"It certainly looks expensive," Keller said.

"At the very least, the packaging is equal to the contents.

Notice the bottle is sealed with lead over its twist-to-open cork stopper. Notice the wooden casket that holds the bottle, brass-bound and equipped with its own tiny brass key. It looks not only expensive but special. One glance and the recipient cannot fail to be aware of the high esteem in which you hold him."

"Well, that's important," Keller said, and drew out his wallet.

What was called for, Keller thought, was a Bunsen burner. And if he were back in his high school chemistry lab, he'd have the use of one. But he was in his room at the Savoyard, and had to make do with a candle.

He'd opened all fifteen of the purple-and-yellow capsules, and their contents pretty much filled the steel serving spoon. He'd bought it, and the little votive candle as well, at a housewares store. The spoon had been paired with a serving fork, which he'd discarded on the way back to the hotel. The candle came in a little glass container, and the Hebrew lettering on its paper label suggested it was some sort of Jewish memorial light.

He added a few drops of tap water to the grains of powder, then held the spoon in the candle's flame. A Bunsen burner couldn't have served him any better; the powder liquefied, and he was able to draw up almost all of it into the hypodermic syringe.

Now the bottle. Remove the lead seal? No, he'd never get it back just right. Easier to go right through the seal and the cork beneath it. Would it reach? Yes, easily, and he depressed the plunger all the way.

After he'd rinsed out both spoon and syringe, he had a look at the bottle. There was a visible pinhole in the lead seal. He could probably let it go, but could he fix it?

The lead extended almost two inches down the neck of the bottle. Keller helped himself to a small piece of the lowest portion, used the spoon and the candle to melt it, and used the softened lead to patch the top of the seal. The pinhole was gone.

He placed the bottle in its handsome wooden container, fastened the little lock. Reached for the wrapping paper.

TWENTY

Dear Father O'Herlihy,

First I must apologize for my intrusion into your life. I should never have bothered you, especially at a difficult time. Although my memory seemed real to me, you helped me to see that it was false, and I find myself wondering how many others have been unjustly smeared as a result of such false memories.

But I must thank you for removing the veil. I now understand what really happened, and that is the first step toward recovery. I feel much better already.

So I hope you will accept this gift as a token of apology and gratitude. I hope it brings you closure equal to mine.

Yours in Christ,
Timothy Michael Hannan

Keller looked over what he'd written out on a sheet of hotel stationery. He added a set of quotation marks around *memory* in the third sentence, and frowned at the last line. Closure? Oh, it was cute enough, but was cute what was wanted here? He crossed it out, and considered other last lines, and rejected them all. Was anything needed after *gratitude?* Not really.

On the front of the card he'd bought it said THANK YOU!, the words surrounded by unidentifiable flowers, and inside he copied his amended draft, using handwriting quite different from his own. The letters were small and carefully formed, and he felt they made a nice match with the voice and manner he'd given young Hannan.

Near the end, he hesitated. *Yours in Christ.* Was that too much?

Oh, the hell with it. He left it in.

Keller, carrying a shopping bag and wearing a brand-new short-sleeved shirt with a button-down collar, let the Savoyard's doorman flag a cab for him. In the cab he put on the plain dark blue tie he'd tucked in the bag, checking the rearview mirror to get the knot right.

Still in the bag, along with the gift-wrapped bottle of Scotch, was a billed cap the same medium blue as the shirt. The clerk who'd sold it to him had called it a Greek fisherman's cap, but to Keller it looked like something a messenger might wear.

The cab dropped him at the corner of 36th and Madison, and once it had driven off he put the cap on his head, tucked the package under his arm, and dropped the empty shopping bag in a trash basket. Then he walked straight to Thessalonian House, where he finally got the chance to use the brass knocker. It was satisfying, and enough time passed so that he was about to do it again, when the door opened to reveal a plump little monk in a nut-brown robe.

"Express rush delivery," said Keller, in Timothy Hannan's voice. "For Abbot Paul O'Herlihy. You'll make sure he gets it right away, won't you?"

Two blocks from the monastery, Keller ditched the Greek fisherman's cap and caught another cab back to his hotel. He took a quick shower, put on a clean shirt, finished packing, and went downstairs to check out. He shook off the doorman and walked, arriving at the Peachpit offices in plenty of time for a pre-session sandwich and coffee.

Before things got underway, he went to the men's room and locked himself in a stall, where he had a chance to count the cash in his money belt. He had a little over $12,000, and it was okay with him if he spent every cent of it.

Keller got to JFK hours before his flight. He remembered, finally, to buy a plush rabbit for Jenny, who collected stuffed animals as ardently as he collected stamps. He checked his bag, the rabbit snugly stowed inside it, and picked up his boarding pass, then found a bar with a TV tuned to local news. He ordered a Diet Coke, and of course the third news item reported a new link between sugar-free soft drinks and cancer. The barmaid evidently heard the item herself, and glanced at Keller even as he was looking her way.

Neither of them had to speak a word. She scooped up his glass, dumped its contents, rinsed it, and looked inquiringly at him. He pointed to a bottle of beer, which she uncapped and placed before him, along with the glass. He reached for his wallet, but she shook her head and walked off to serve somebody else.

The beer lasted Keller for most of an hour. He was waiting for a particular news item, not really expecting to hear it, but disappointed all the same.

Waiting was always the hardest part.

Around seven thirty he realized that a sandwich and the better part of a croissant didn't amount to a full day's rations. He moved from the bar to a nearby table, where he ordered a Caesar salad with grilled shrimp and a second beer. The salad wasn't bad. Neither was the beer, but half of it was plenty.

He could see and hear the bar's TV from where he was sitting, so he got another go-round with the sports and weather and various fires and traffic wrecks. And nothing much else.

Just as they were about to call his flight for boarding, he took out his cell phone and called Dot. "I'm heading home," he said.

"Well, I can't say I'm surprised. I don't know why I sent you in the first place. I'll send back the money."

"No, don't do that," he said.

"No?"

"Not just yet," he said. "Wait three days and see what happens."

"Three days?"

"Maybe four."

"Four days. I could do that. I mean, they don't know you're on your way home, do they?"

He ended the call, stopped in the men's room. Was the phone compromised? Even if it wasn't, what did he need with it now? He took it apart, snapped the chip in half, and did other things to render the thing inoperative. He dropped the different components in different trash receptacles and went to board his plane.

* * *

"She's going to love this," Julia said, brandishing the rabbit. "Not only is it wonderfully soft and squishy, it's from her daddy. Why don't you go put it in her bed and she'll find it when she wakes up?"

Was there anything more beautiful than Jenny sleeping? He tucked in the rabbit at her side and returned to the kitchen, where he looked at his wife and found an answer to his question.

"I'm a rotten husband," he said. "I didn't bring you anything."

"You came back in one piece," she said. "That's good enough. Did you bring a story to get me all excited?"

"Not quite yet."

That puzzled her, but she let it go. "Not a problem," she said. "Tonight you won't need a story. You know what they say about absence? Well, it's not just the heart that grows fonder."

"Now, here's a stamp I'm happy to have," Keller said, lifting Gabon number 48 with his stamp tongs. "If you just take a quick look, you'd think it was the same as this one here. Denomination's the same, five francs, colors are the same, and you've got the same picture. That's a woman of the Fang tribe, and isn't she pretty?"

"Pity," Jenny agreed.

"When I was a little boy, I had some of these stamps. Well, ones just like them. The low values. You see this stamp? It shows a warrior, also of the Fang tribe, and he's a man, and very fierce. But I saw the fancy headdress and always thought he was a woman. Funny, huh?"

"Funny."

"Now what makes this stamp different," Keller said, even as he slipped the stamp into the mount he'd cut for it, "is the inscription. It says 'Congo Français,' and the other one says 'Afrique Equatoriale,' so it belongs to the first of the two sets. It goes in the last blank space on the page, one I've been looking to fill for years now. There. Doesn't it look nice?"

"Nice 'tamp."

"Gabon was a French colony in West Africa," he told her. "It issued stamps until 1934, when it was merged into French Equatorial Africa. Now of course it's an independent country, but Daddy's collection only goes to 1940, so his Gabon stamps stop in 1933."

"Maybe Daddy'll take us to Gabon someday," Julia said. "You know what we ought to get? A globe, so you could show her where all the countries are. I can see how you thought the warrior was a woman. Though you might have noticed that he's holding a couple of spears."

"A fierce woman," he said. "A globe's a good idea. That's probably what I should have bought instead of the stuffed rabbit."

"Well, globe or no globe, don't try to take the rabbit away from her. She'll tear your arm off."

"Rabbit," Jenny said.

"A bunny rabbit," Keller agreed. "One of your better words, isn't it? Now, these stamps are interesting. They aren't very pretty, but there's a great story that goes with them. See, they're from German East Africa, which was a German colony before the First World War."

"Like Koochoo, which Daddy told you about, except even your mommy can tell where this one's located."

"Kiauchau."

"Gesundheit. I was close, wasn't I?"

"You were," Keller said. "But listen to this, will you? During the war, the post office in German East Africa couldn't get stamps from the fatherland, so they had these printed by the evangelical mission in Wuga—"

"Wuga," Jenny echoed.

"See, sweetie? Now Daddy's talking your language."

"—but before they were needed, new stamps did arrive from Germany. Then, with British troops advancing, the postal authorities buried all of the Wuga stamps—"

"Wuga. Wuga."

"—to keep the Brits from capturing them. Stamps! Why would they care if the enemy captured the stamps? They were overrunning the whole colony, for God's sake."

"Who thought that up, the same genius who ran your Yankee post office during the War of the Northern Aggression?"

"You'd almost think so," he said. "After the war, before the colony was taken away from Germany and parceled out to Britain and Belgium, the Germans dug up the stamps. Most of them were so damaged from being buried that they had to be destroyed, and the rest weren't exactly pristine, but they took them home and auctioned them off."

"And you've got a whole sheet of them."

"Of the seven and a half heller, yes. It's the least expensive of the three denominations, but an actual unbroken sheet—well, let's just say I wasn't the only person who wanted it."

No one actually present in the room had fought him for it, but there was competition online, and a phone bidder who just wouldn't quit. But here he was, trimming a large sheet of plastic mounting material to fit, and preparing a blank album page to receive it.

The sheet was fragile, and he handled it with great delicacy.

He'd have done so anyway, but having shelled out a small fortune for it made him especially careful with it.

Would he get the money back? He'd put on CNN at breakfast, behavior uncharacteristic enough to get a raised eyebrow from Julia, if not a question. He'd been hoping for a particular news item from New York, the same one he'd hoped for at the airport bar.

No luck. And there were so many things that could go wrong, the most likely of which being that O'Herlihy would decide to save this magnificent bottle for a special occasion, or even attempt to curry favor by passing it on to a bishop. Keller had an awful vision of the brass-bound casket ascending up the hierarchy, until it wound up carrying off the Holy Father himself.

Things to think about while affixing an extraordinary pane of stamps to an album page. And while Jenny was standing patiently at his side, waiting for him to tell her more about what he was doing. So he told her how the Belgian portion of German East Africa had been known as Ruanda-Urundi, but when it became independent it split into two countries, Rwanda and Burundi.

"Wanda," Jenny said. "Rundi."

TWENTY-ONE

"It's Dot."

He looked up. It was remarkable how stamps took him into another dimension. He hadn't been aware that Julia had left the room, hadn't heard the phone ring, hadn't heard her return, and here she was, handing him the phone.

"Well, congratulations," Dot said. "Your horse came in and paid a good price."

"Oh?"

"There's an online news feed that keeps you up to the minute," she said, "and the story's breaking right now. Respected religious leader, blah blah blah, extreme stress, blah blah blah, expected to provide invaluable testimony, blah blah blah."

"Sounds as though it's mostly blah blah blah."

"Well, isn't that always the way, Keller? Everything is mostly blah blah blah. What it boils down to, evidently the poor fellow got this special bottle of whiskey and it was so good he drank more than his usual amount."

"His usual amount," Keller said, "was enough to float a battleship."

"Oh, this is interesting. Preliminary examination suggests that the alcoholic intake was exacerbated by barbiturates. The man washed down sleeping pills with booze, and that's never a good idea, is it?"

"No."

"Death by misadventure," she said. "Now I have to wonder how you got him to take the pills. And if I had to guess, I'd say you dissolved them in the whiskey. Which would be good."

"Why?"

"Because once the lab works its magic on the leftover booze, they'll know what really happened. And that'll keep the client from whining that he doesn't want to pay us for something that happened all by itself. Not that I'd let him get away with that, but who needs the hassle?"

"Not us."

"You betcha. So I don't have to give the money back, and they have to send us some more. You happy?"

"Very."

"And New York was all right?"

"New York was fine."

"And I'll bet you brought home some stamps. Well, you must want to go play with them, so I'll let you go now. Now put Jenny on the phone so Aunt Dot can give her a big kiss."

"See?" Keller said. "I told you it wasn't exciting."

"It was a problem," Julia said, "and a complicated one, and you tried different things, and in the end you found the solution. How could that fail to be exciting?"

"Well..."

"Oh, because there was no action? No slam-bang adventure? The life of the mind is exciting enough, at least for those of us who have one."

It was evening, and Jenny had gone to bed, clutching her new rabbit. Julia and Keller were at the kitchen table, drinking coffee with chicory.

"I wasn't sure it would work," he said.

"But you came home anyway."

"Well, if it didn't work, what was I going to do about it? I didn't have anything else to try." He thought for a moment. "Besides, I was ready to come home. I had you and Jenny to come home to."

"Otherwise you'd have stayed there."

"Probably. But there wouldn't have been any real point to it."

"More coffee?"

"No, I'm good. Does it bother you that he was a priest?"

"No, why should it?"

"Well, it's your church."

"Only in the most tenuous way. I'm the child of lapsed Catholics. I was baptized, that was their sole concession to their own upbringing, but it was pretty much the extent of my own involvement with the Church."

"I never asked you if you wanted Jenny baptized."

"Don't you think I'd have said something? Do you even know what baptism is for?"

"Isn't it to make you a Catholic?"

"No, darling, guilt is what makes you a Catholic. What baptism does is rid you of original sin. Do you suppose our daughter is greatly weighed down by the burden of original sin?"

"I don't even know how you could go about finding an original sin these days."

"I suppose selling somebody else's kidney might qualify. And no, what do I care about some fat drunken priest whose greatest boast was that all his sins were strictly heterosexual? You want to know what's exciting?"

"What?"

"That you can tell me all this. That we can sit here drinking coffee—"

"Damn good coffee, too."

"—and either of us can tell the other anything about anything, and how many people have anything like that? God, though, I have to say I'm glad you're home."

"Me, too," Keller said.

KELLER AT SEA

TWENTY-TWO

When Julia and Jenny got home from day care, Keller was sitting in the kitchen with a cup of coffee and a magazine, *The American Stamp Dealer & Collector.* He'd picked it up after he got off the phone, but couldn't keep his mind on what he was reading. It was restless, darting all over the place. So he was more than happy to set it aside and ask his daughter what she'd learned in school that morning.

It wasn't a school, and the harried woman who ran it didn't try to teach her charges much; she was happy if she managed to keep them from hitting each other and screaming their little heads off. But Jenny, Julia had reported, called it school, and took the whole enterprise very seriously. As far as she was concerned, she went there to learn stuff, and it seemed to piss her off that they weren't teaching her to read.

So Julia had picked up a book on phonics, and Jenny was learning to sound words out. You couldn't always understand what she was saying, because there were words she couldn't yet get her tongue around, but damned if she wasn't reading.

She had her lunch and went in for her nap, and Keller asked Julia if she'd like to go on a cruise.

"A cruise," she said. "You mean like on a ship? Yes, of course that's what you mean. A cruise. You know, that sounds heavenly. When were you thinking? In the winter?"

"Actually," he said, "it would be sooner than that."

"Late fall?"

"A lot sooner."

"Oh. Can you get away?"

"There's no work," he said. "Getting away has never been less of a problem. Donny called me this morning, very apologetic. He's hired on with a contractor based over in Slidell. Says the pay's not much but he's sick of sitting in front of the TV while he runs through his savings. At least he'll have something to do and some money coming in."

"That part's good. But he must feel awful."

Donny Wallings had given Keller a job when he'd first moved in with Julia, and almost before Keller knew it he'd found himself a partner in an enterprise that bought distressed homes, patched them up, and flipped them. That worked well in the early post-Katrina days, but then the economy cratered and there was no money to be had for home renovation loans, no money to finance home sales. And, just like that, no business.

"He was concerned about us," Keller said. "But I told him we were okay."

"Are we? I mean I know we are, but can we afford to pick up and go on a cruise? You know, if we can it's actually the perfect kind of vacation. I bet Jenny'd love it, too. There are plenty of cruises out of New Orleans, and you can literally walk from here to the cruise port. Unless our ship uses the Poland Avenue terminal, and that's what, a ten-minute ride?"

"We'd be leaving from Fort Lauderdale," he said.

"In Florida?" She looked at him. "You've got a particular cruise in mind. Did somebody call this morning? Besides Donny?"

He'd just got off the phone with Donny when it rang again. He picked it up, and Dot said, "Keller, I can't help thinking you need a vacation. But before I go any further, there's something I have to ask you. Do you get seasick?"

"Seasick?"

"You know, rushing to the rail, tossing your cookies, feeding the fish? Seasick, Keller. What happens to you on the high seas?"

"I don't know," he said.

"You've never been on a boat? And the Staten Island Ferry doesn't count."

"I've been on the Gulf," he said. "I don't know if that counts. A friend of Julia's, well, he and his wife are actually friends of both of us by now—"

"Do I really need to know that part, Keller?"

"Probably not. I've been out a few times. Fishing, but I have to admit I never caught anything."

"But you didn't get seasick? Have they got waves there?"

"It's the Gulf of Mexico," he said, "so yes, there are waves, but they don't toss you around all that much. One time it was a little choppy, but I hardly noticed it."

"So you're a good sailor, Keller. And the cruise ships have stabilizers, and you can always take Dramamine, so I'm sure you'll do fine. Keller? Where'd you go?"

"I'm right here, waiting for you to tell me what you're talking about."

"Oh," she said, "I thought it was perfectly obvious. You're going on a cruise."

* * *

"Saturday," Julia said. "Monday, Tuesday, Wednesday, Thursday, Friday, Saturday. Why are you looking at me like that?"

"If you were Jenny," he said, "I'd congratulate you for getting your days right."

"My point is there's not much time."

"I know."

"I suppose we'd have to fly over there on Friday."

"The ship doesn't sail until late afternoon. We could get a flight Saturday morning and be there in plenty of time."

"It sails from Fort Lauderdale and returns to Fort Lauderdale. So you're back where you started. There's a pointlessness about it that's curiously appealing."

"There is?"

"Yet at the same time," she said, "it won't be entirely pointless, will it? You'll be working."

"That's right, and I can see where that might be a deal-breaker right there. There's something I'll have to do."

"Something you'll have to do. Some passenger for whom the cruise will have a surprise ending. Do they still bury people at sea?"

"I don't think so."

"There's probably an ecological argument against it, though I couldn't think why. People are biodegradable, aren't they?" She stepped behind him, put her hands on his shoulders, and began to knead the muscles. "You're all tense," she announced. "This feel good?"

"Very."

"I know what you do," she said, "and I don't entirely know how I feel about it, but I don't seem to mind. I honestly don't."

"I know."

"But I'm not there when it happens, am I? And in a sense I wouldn't be this time either, in that I wouldn't be in the room when—when what? When push came to shove?"

"When it goes down," he suggested.

"That works. I wouldn't be in the room, or I suppose you call it a cabin. Or is it a stateroom? Is there a difference between a cabin and a stateroom?"

"I have no idea."

"Does Dot know you're thinking about taking me along?"

"She suggested it."

"You're kidding."

"She apologized for the fact that it wasn't that long since New York, and I said I didn't really feel like being separated from you again so soon. 'It's a nice big cabin,' she said. 'Plenty of room for two.' And she went on to say I'd be a lot less conspicuous if I had a companion."

"That actually makes sense."

"I guess."

"'Look at that handsome gentleman all by himself. I wonder what his story might be.' But with me along you're far less interesting. I want to come."

"To make me less interesting?"

"Partly that. Partly because I've never been on a cruise. Partly because I don't feel like being home in New Orleans while you're island-hopping. And partly because it scares me."

"Then why—"

"'Do the thing you're afraid of.' I read that somewhere. Don't ask me where."

"I won't."

"But as for taking Jenny—"

"No."

"Even if I were deranged enough to think it was a good idea, we don't have time to get her a passport. She'd need one, wouldn't she?"

"It doesn't matter, because neither of us is nuts enough to take her. But yes, she'd have to have a passport."

"These days you just about need one to cross a state line. Well, this way she'll have her own vacation." She went to the phone, dialed a number she didn't have to look up. She said, "Claudia? Julia Edwards. Darlin', Nicholas told me how Donny's hired on with a crew, and I just want to say I was glad to hear it. Not that he had to but that he was able to, you know? And I know Nicholas already told Donny that we're fine here, but I wanted to say so myself, to you…"

Keller knew where the conversation was headed, but didn't feel the need to listen to it. He reached for his magazine and got lost in an article about a recently discovered cache of letters to and from a young Mississippian in Pemberton's army who'd been killed during Grant's siege of Vicksburg. He surfaced in time to hear Julia say she had a real big favor to ask, and Claudia should feel completely comfortable saying no. Then he went back to a letter filled with the youth's big plans for after the war was over. The letter was dated March 7, 1863, at which time its author had all of three months to live.

"…can't thank you enough," he heard, which wouldn't stop her from trying. Phone calls in New Orleans seemed to go on longer than in most places, especially if there was a woman on either end of the line. He tuned out again, and stayed lost in the magazine until Julia returned to the table.

"We're all set," she announced. "Claudia can't think of anything she and Donny'd rather have than Jenny's company for a week, not to mention her kids'll be over the moon about it. They place her somewhere between a baby sister and a house pet. And she loves going over there, so she'll just have a slightly longer visit than usual."

He got to his feet. "I'd better book our flight," he said.

"You've got the easy part, mister. I have to figure out what to pack."

TWENTY-THREE

Cruise ships out of Fort Lauderdale docked at Port Everglades, a six-mile cab ride from the airport. Keller paid the driver, who wished them both *buen viaje,* which was close enough to bon voyage for Keller to figure it out.

If packing for Julia had been a trial, she'd nevertheless managed to narrow down her choices to fit in a single medium-size suitcase. Keller's bag was smaller, and he carried his and wheeled hers through the cruise terminal and down the walkway to where their ship was receiving passengers.

Their ship, the *Carefree Nights,* looked large to Keller, but not after he'd seen the leviathans berthed on either side of her. Their cabin was on the second of five passenger decks, and once they were in it Keller excused himself and made his way back to the terminal.

He'd had an eye out for a man in a Hawaiian shirt and a New York Yankees baseball cap, and the guy had evidently had his eye out for Keller, too, because they'd exchanged nods and glances the first time through. Keller found him now, and, though it struck him as unnecessary, went through the prescribed ritual.

"Mr. Gallagher?"

"Absolutely," the man said. "Mr. Shean?"

"Positively."

"That fuckin' Dot," said the man, whose name was no more Gallagher than Keller's was Shean. "I swear the woman watches too much TV. Like we're not gonna be able to find each other." He took off his cap, set it on the floor under his seat. "There's some who look good in hats and some who don't, and we know which kind I am. And this fuckin' shirt." He glanced at the shirt Keller was wearing. "That one's her idea, too, right?"

The polo shirt, with narrow red horizontal stripes on a navy field, was one of Keller's favorites. He couldn't think of a response, and that turned out to be response enough.

"Actually," Gallagher said, "it's an okay shirt. Here, have a seat. I wish I could tell you to enjoy the boat ride, that it's all taken care of. Though how anybody could enjoy a boat ride's beyond me altogether."

"I guess it's not your thing."

"Let me put it this way, Shean. I take lots of showers. You know why?"

Keller could guess—guilt, a need to expunge the recent past. But that wasn't it.

"Because I don't even like bathtubs is why. They show *The Poseidon Adventure* on TV, I change the channel. The remote's on the fritz, I'll walk across the room to do it."

Keller, who couldn't help thinking of the man as Gallagher, felt that showed real commitment.

"What I like," Gallagher said, "is the long shot. I'm not talking gambling here, Shean. I'm talking riflery. I grew up in L.A., I never touched a gun my whole life, and I went in the service and they took me out to the rifle range, and I couldn't miss. Qualified as expert rifleman first time out, and the next thing I know I'm in sniper school. Join the army, learn a trade."

It would have been different, Keller thought, if he'd joined the navy.

"So I get a call. The subject's holed up in a house in Hallandale. That's a little ways south of here. Takes some doing, but I find a spot where I can set up. Minute he walks out the door, he's mine."

"But he never leaves the house."

"Oh, Dot told you? Maybe he leaves and maybe he don't, I couldn't tell you, because all I ever see is this black Lexus with tinted glass all around. Fuckin' car comes and goes, in and out of the attached garage. Is he ever inside it? Maybe yes, maybe no. When he's home, does he ever stand in front of the nice big picture window? Again, maybe yes, maybe no, because it's got curtains and they're never open. Two weeks I'm sitting on that house, and I never get a glimpse of the son of a bitch, let alone get to draw a bead on him. So let me ask you, Shean. What would you do?"

"I don't know. Maybe try to get into the house."

Gallagher shook his head. "What I didn't mention," he said, "is they got guards posted. There's a car just sits across the street twenty-four seven, three shifts, two men to a shift. UPS shows up, somebody pops out of the car, braces the driver, takes the package, and walks it up to the door. The newsboy knows the drill; he don't even throw the paper onto the porch, he brings it straight to the car and lets them deliver it for him. Nobody gets close to the house, let alone into it."

Keller thought of Thessalonian House, the phoned-in bomb threat, the meeting in the steam room. "You'd have to draw him out," he said.

"How?" Keller didn't have the answer, and Gallagher said, "Yeah, well, there you go. Then I get the word, they're so fuckin' proud of themselves, on account of they got him booked on a cruise, and there's a cabin just waiting for me. Yeah, right. So that's where you come in."

"He gets seasick," Dot had said. "Who knew? And even if I had known, nobody asked me. The client went ahead on his own and hooked him with a free cruise."

"How?"

"'Dear Mr. Dimwit, you've won a free all-expenses-paid cruise of the West Indies on the Good Ship Lollipop.'"

"And he fell for it?"

"Keller, how many times have the cops mailed out announcements to all the mopes with outstanding wants and warrants? 'You just won a free flat-panel plasma TV! Show up such and such a place, such and such a time, to claim your prize!' These are wanted criminals, Keller, and you'd think if they wanted a television set they'd go out and steal one, but year after year the cops throw a party like this, and year after year morons show up for it."

"Even so."

"I know, I know. Maybe he was going stir-crazy, cooped up and guarded around the clock. Maybe he just wanted to assert himself. 'Yes, I need your protection, but I still get to live my life.' And who knows if he'll actually wind up getting on the ship? He could come to his senses by Saturday, but let's hope he doesn't. Because he's a lot softer target on open water. As long as you're not stuck in your cabin, puking your guts out."

"No way I'm getting on a boat," Gallagher said. "Sitting here is as close as I want to get, and we're on a concrete floor on dry land, and I swear I can just about feel the motion. So I thought, okay, I got a couple of days, maybe I'll get a shot. Yeah, right. You know what I wanted to do? The garage door rolls up, the black Lexus comes out, and what I wanted to do was empty a clip into the fucking thing."

"That might work," Keller allowed.

"If he's in the vehicle, and if it's not reinforced and bulletproof six ways and backwards, and if I get lucky. Shean, getting lucky's not what I'm about. What I'm about is the subject's in the crosshairs and a single well-placed shot puts him forever in the past tense."

Keller thought that last phrase was a nice one. He had a feeling Gallagher must have heard it somewhere before making it his own.

"So I got no real complaints," Gallagher said, "on account of I get to keep the advance. It would have been nice to close the deal, but I got paid and I get to go home now, and that's not so bad. I thought they might get sloppy today, but the Lexus pulled out of the garage same as always, and I kept my finger off the trigger. I jumped in my ride and got here before they did, and if you were already here I'd a pointed him out to you, but I didn't see anybody fitting your description, and nobody approached me looking for Mr. Gallagher."

"I came straight from the airport."

"I found this seat," Gallagher said, "on account of the good view it gave me, and twenty minutes goes by, and thirty, and forty, and where is he? Did he get past me? Well, you're not here, so there's nobody to point him out to, but if I don't see him get on maybe he changed his mind, in which case my job's not done. You follow me?"

"Sure."

"Then he shows, and he's got this babe with him." Gallagher cupped his hands and held them in front of his chest. "Va-va-voom, right? Maybe she's old enough to vote, but not by much. Maybe Latina, maybe not, and what's the difference what she is? The woman is a total fox." He sighed. "Son of a bitch's got thirty-five, maybe forty years on her. Was she in the house all along? I never saw her, but I never saw him, neither, or anybody else but the guys sitting in the car across the street. My guess is that's where the forty minutes went, driving somewhere to pick her up, and she's still got packing to do, and makeup to freshen and all those things women find to do with time." He shook his head. "I'm talking too much. Sorry. I been sitting on my ass for two weeks, staring at nothing and doing less, and the only talking I've done's been to the weather guy on TV. 'Oh, yeah? Call that a perfect day, asshole? It's too fuckin' hot.'"

"Well," Keller said.

"Right. Here's the photo they sent me. He lost the beard since it was taken, and in my opinion he shoulda kept it, but otherwise he looks about the same. Don't ask me what name he's using."

"They booked his cabin under his own name," Keller said.

"Carmody, huh?"

"Michael Carmody. I'll check the passenger manifest. Anyway, he's got one of the premium cabins on the Sun Deck, and there are only four of them, so he won't be hard to find."

"Please," Gallagher said, holding a hand to his stomach.

"Stop it with the nautical terms, okay? I had lunch just three hours ago."

"Sorry."

"I been sitting here all along," Gallagher said. "And I been keeping one eye on the entrance and exit over there, and they haven't come back."

"Him and his girlfriend?"

"Why would they come back? If they weren't fixing to take their boat ride they wouldn't've come here in the first place. No, I'm talking about the muscle."

"Muscle."

"Security, bodyguards, whatever you want to call 'em. The two guys in suits who walked him and her through the door and up to where they look at your tickets and make sure you're getting on the right boat."

"He had escorts."

"Yeah, that's as good a word as any, though it's got a couple different meanings. I had an escort the other night, called a number in the phone book. Two hundred and fifty bucks and she had one eye on her watch the whole time. Nice tits, I got to admit. That's worth something, right?"

"Sure. Uh, his escorts—"

"Frick and Frack. I figure they're just seeing him to his room, checking out the basic situation. But they don't come back. No way anybody suckered them into thinking they won a cruise, so how do you figure that?"

Keller checked his watch. The escorts still had an hour before the scheduled departure time, but if they were still on the ship this late, they were probably there for the duration. The target's minders, unable to dissuade him from the cruise, had simply booked a cabin for a pair of their own men. If a private citizen like Dot had been able to get Keller on the ship, why couldn't the other side, with the full force of the law working for them, do as much themselves?

He asked Gallagher how he'd know them.

"You watch football? One's built like a tight end, the other's more of a running back. That give you a picture?"

"Sort of."

"Just look for two guys in suits. Not gonna get many of those on a fuckin' cruise, are you? And I know what you're gonna say."

"Oh?"

"'Suppose they change their clothes?' Which, granted, they might. So look for two guys who look like they're wearing casual clothes for the first time in twenty years. Hey, you'll spot 'em, Shean. They'll stick out like a couple of thumbs."

TWENTY-FOUR

A little after six, while Keller and Julia were in the Club Lounge for the Bon Voyage cocktail party, the *Carefree Nights* set sail for the Bahamas. Members of the dining room staff passed trays of drinks, and Keller picked off a pair of margaritas. He barely touched his, and offered it to Julia when she'd finished her own, but one was all she wanted.

She fell into conversation with an older woman who turned out to be from Mobile, and the two of them got caught up in a spirited game of Who Do You Know? That left Keller and the woman's husband to talk about sports or the stock market, say, but the fellow wasn't much of a talker, and the set of his face and the way he walked suggested that he might be recovering from a stroke. He seemed content to listen to the two women, or not listen, and that was fine with Keller, who was too busy scanning the room to pay much attention to anything else.

He didn't see Michael Anthony Carmody, whose photo was now in Keller's back pocket. Nor did he see any men in suits, or indeed anyone built like a football player, whether a tight end or a running back. Aside from the ship's staff, most of the people in the room looked as though they'd had their AARP cards long enough to forget where they'd put them. Carmody wouldn't stand out in their company, but his entourage would.

"Like thumbs," he said, not realizing he'd spoken out loud until Julia and her new friend shot him a glance. "Nothing," he said. "Just thinking out loud."

"Well, I'm not planning on thinking for the next seven nights," said the woman from Mobile. "Out loud or otherwise. I do enough of that back home. All I plan on doing is drinking and eating and laying out in the sun."

"And shopping," her husband said, proving he could speak after all.

"Well, maybe a little bit of that," she said. "Just to stay in practice."

After the lifeboat drill, Keller found his way to where they posted the names and cabin assignments. There was no Carmody listed, and Keller wasn't surprised. He figured it wouldn't be the trickiest thing in the world to get yourself listed under an alias, as long as you carried legitimate ID. Wasn't that what celebrities did? And didn't the people trying to keep Carmody alive have more than enough clout for that?

He went all the way through the list, and all four Sun Deck cabins were occupied, and none of the names meant anything to him.

There was an elevator—with the median age of this crowd, there would really have to be—but Keller took the stairs to the Sun Deck. There was a pool, which surprised him; he somehow hadn't imagined that you'd carry a pool of your own out into the middle of the ocean. Lounge chairs ranged around the pool, and there was what looked to be a health club, with a couple of treadmills and a Universal machine. And, toward the rear of the ship, he saw a little block of staterooms.

The stern, he thought. That was what they called the back end of the ship, and the front was the bow. And port and starboard were left and right.

Keller, wondering why you needed a whole new vocabulary the minute you left shore, felt the ship's motion. He hadn't really paid any attention to it until now. It didn't bother him, not as much as the new names for left and right and front and back and up and down. *Topside,* he thought. *Below*. Jesus.

He wasn't seasick, not at all, but all the same he found himself feeling a common bond with Gallagher.

At dinner, they shared a table with three other couples, and Keller didn't find out much about any of them. The conversation was mostly of other ships and past cruises, and that left him and Julia without much to contribute. It also made their company hugely useful to the others, who were able to tell them which ships they should avoid, which ones they were sure to love, and no end of other tips that demanded little more from Keller than a thoughtful nod, or the observation that he'd certainly have to keep that in mind.

Keller didn't see Carmody anywhere, or anybody who looked young enough to be his daughter, or to move Gallagher to cup his hands and say whatever it was he'd said. Va-va-voom?

Of course Carmody, like any of *Carefree Night*'s passengers, had the option of dining in his stateroom. And if his companion was indeed of the va-va-voom sort, and if this was a maiden voyage for the two of them, well, it stood to reason that the man might be reluctant to leave his cabin, at least for the first day or two. And there was also the chance that—

"Oh, my," Julia murmured.

Keller looked up, and saw where she was looking, and noted that half the people in the dining room were looking in the same direction.

Va-va-voom!

"I didn't know it would be like this," Julia said.

"What? The ship? Our cabin?"

They were back in their cabin now, and free at last to talk about the strawberry blonde knockout who'd stopped all dining room conversation in its tracks.

She shook her head. "Seeing him ahead of time. Oh, come on. That was him, wasn't it? The man playing Mr. December to her Miss May? Except that sweet young thing's barely made it into April. Is statutory rape legal in international waters?"

"I don't think anybody's going to arrest him."

"Still, he's got to be your assignment. Did you get a look at the two hoods keeping the charming couple company? A nice little table for four, and they all came in together and left together. I'm sure those two were carrying guns."

"The two younger men, you mean."

She gave him a look. "Just tell me I'm not spinning an elaborate story out of thin air. It's him, isn't it?"

"I wasn't going to say anything."

"No, and I wasn't going to try to coax it out of you, because I wasn't sure I wanted to know. Although it might be worse, having to be careful not to get too friendly with any of the women because one of their husbands might be the very man my husband was here to—do I want a euphemism? To nullify, to take off the board, what?"

"There's just the two of us here," he pointed out.

"You're right. To kill. Although I'm not sure you're going to have to kill anybody. She'll do it for you."

"Because she's young?"

"Darling, did you look at her? And don't tell me you didn't, because every man on the ship did, even the gay waiter. Her youth is just part of it. The woman oozes sex. It drips from her. Didn't you notice?"

"Well—"

"Of course you did, and why shouldn't you? Right now you'd love to be in bed with her, and don't deny it, because so would everybody else, and once again I'm including the gay waiter. Girls don't do a thing for me, darling, and even so *I'd* like to be in bed with her."

"Really?"

"I wouldn't literally *want* to, but I picture her with that pouty mouth and that hot body and those get-lost-in-here eyes and my mouth waters. Doesn't yours?"

She didn't wait for an answer. "But she's not here," she went on, "so neither one of us is going to get her tonight. But we're here in this lovely stateroom, and the two beds have an aisle between them, but I don't see why we'll need more than one bed anyway, at least for the next hour or so. There's a little movement to the ship, I think they call it a swell, and I can see where it might actually add something to the proceedings, can't you? And speaking of swells, what have we here? Hmm?"

A little later she said, "I got carried away there. I wonder how thick these walls are. Do you suppose people could hear me?"

"Only the ones in the Western Hemisphere."

"Was I really that loud?"

"You were a perfect southern gentlewoman."

"That sweet young thing got things started, but then she disappeared and it was just us, and wasn't it lovely? I was wondering. Do you figure she's a prostitute? Or just a talented amateur?"

"Probably somewhere in between, would be my guess. She's his girlfriend for the duration of the cruise, and when we dock in Fort Lauderdale there'll be a present for her."

"And by a present you mean—"

"Cash, I would think."

"But they wouldn't have set a price ahead of time."

"No, because it wouldn't be a price. It would be a week of sun and sea for her, with a present at the end of it. But she'd expect the present, and he'd know it was expected."

"How big a present?"

"No way to know. I would think it would have to be at least a thousand, and that seems a little low. Say two, three thousand."

"And it could be more."

"It could, but I wouldn't think it would be a whole lot more than that. Say five thousand tops—*if* he's rich, and if he likes to throw it around. What?"

"I didn't say anything."

"No, but you were about to."

"Well," she said. "The present comes at the end of the trip, right?"

"So?"

"So I was just thinking," she said, "that if all goes well from our point of view, she's essentially getting screwed, isn't she?"

TWENTY-FIVE

Keller woke up when the ship cut its engines. It was six thirty, and he figured that was Nassau he could see through the window. Or were you supposed to call it a porthole? It was large and square, not small and round, so that argued for window. And it was on the ship's starboard side—Keller had figured that out earlier. Could you call it a porthole if it was on the starboard side?

Julia was sleeping soundly. He showered and dressed and went to the dining room, where they were serving a buffet breakfast, with a happy chef on hand to make you whatever sort of omelet you wanted.

Keller wasn't sure he wanted that much human contact. He sat by himself at a table for two, nodded at the waiter's offer of orange juice, nodded a second time for coffee. He picked out a plateful of items from the buffet, and was agreeing to a second cup of coffee when Carmody's pair of bodyguards showed up.

It took him a moment to recognize them, because they'd finally embraced casual dress. At dinner their suits had given way to blue blazers and Dockers, and this morning they'd come all the way down to floral-patterned short-sleeve shirts. Something in their stance suggested they didn't feel entirely happy with their attire, but Keller wondered if maybe he was imagining that part.

He'd been giving the two some thought. Last night, before he drifted off, he'd wondered what he was going to do about them; this morning, in the shower, he'd had them on his mind.

Because, no question, they were a complication. They'd make it more difficult to get to Carmody, or even to do reconnaissance toward that end. But he had a week, and Carmody had already shown that he wasn't going to spend every minute in his stateroom, so Keller figured the opportunity would arise before the ship was back in Port Everglades.

So he could probably arrange some sort of accident. But with these two around, would it pass as an accident? Not likely. If they couldn't keep their charge safe, the least they could do was straighten things out after the fact. They'd turn the ship upside down looking for Carmody's killer, and if the net they cast didn't scoop up Keller, it still wouldn't make his life simpler, or the remainder of the cruise more comfortable.

Keller got to his feet, set his napkin beside his plate. "I'll be back," he told a passing waiter. "Don't clear the table."

Julia opened her eyes when he let himself into their stateroom. "Forgot something," he said. "Go back to sleep." He rummaged in his bag, found what he was looking for, and hurried back to the dining room.

His table was as he'd left it, and the waiter had refilled his coffee cup. More important, Carmody's minders were still at their table. They were in fact built like football players, though a little small for the pros. College, Keller decided, and not the NCAA top tier but one level below it. Appalachian State, University of Delaware—something like that.

What Keller hoped was that they'd have football-player appetites. They were both at the table now, with plates of food in front of them. Keller's best chance would have been right after they ordered their coffee and headed for the buffet, but he'd needed to get to the cabin first.

Packing for the cruise, Keller had made do with a small bag, but had managed to find room for more than his clothes. He knew he wouldn't have access to chain drugstores or neighborhood hardware stores or ghetto entrepreneurs, not aboard ship, so he'd brought along what he thought he might need. His toilet kit included some special pills and powders, besides the usual aspirin, and an improvised garrote, of the sort he'd made and discarded in New York, was wound into a coil and tucked into the toe of a spare shoe.

And he'd packed the HandyMan traveler's tool kit that had belonged to Julia's father. It was a sort of industrial-strength Swiss army knife, with a few implements Keller doubted he'd need. There was a little chrome-plated hammer, handy if he needed to check somebody's patellar reflex, and a pair of needle-nose pliers, and a belt punch. But there was also a knife blade long enough to be useful.

He sipped his coffee and set about watching the two men without being obvious about it. A waiter approached, filled their coffee cups. The running back took a sip, put his cup down, and got to his feet. He picked up his plate, and evidently the tight end reminded him that you were supposed to use a clean plate each time, because he returned his plate to the table and headed for the buffet.

A waiter appeared immediately and whisked away the abandoned plate. The tight end stayed seated and had a sip of coffee.

Come on, Keller urged him silently. *The bacon's crisp, the sausages are tangy. What the hell, let the guy make you an omelet.*

For a moment Keller thought his message had gotten through, because the man's hands fastened on the arms of his chair as if to brace himself for the hard work of standing up. But no, the son of a bitch stayed where he was, and all he did with his hands was reach for his coffee.

The running back took his time and came back with a plate piled high with enough food for both of them, and evidently the tight end thought it looked pretty good, because even as his friend was brandishing his fork, he was moving his hands again to the arms of his chair. And this time he followed through and got to his feet, plate in hand, and it was the running back's turn to remind him about the fresh plate requirement, and the tight end gave a laugh and put his plate back on the table.

Well, maybe they weren't terribly bright. Keller found that a hopeful sign.

But, bright or not, it seemed as though one of them was always going to be at the table. And if he waited any longer they'd leave the table together, and he wouldn't get another shot until breakfast the next day, if then—tomorrow morning might as easily find them at a table for four, with Carmody and his sexpot.

Keller took the little vial of pills from his pocket, uncapped the lid, shook two white tablets into his palm. Anyone watching would have seen him pop them into his mouth and chase them with a sip of water, but in fact the pills remained in his hand.

The ship had drawn up at the dock, and at nine its passengers would be able to disembark and spend the morning in Nassau. Keller's plan would work better, he knew, if they were in open waters with a lively sea under them. That would add verisimilitude, but at the same time it would add a degree of difficulty to his own moves.

Still, this was his chance, and he took it.

He got to his feet, walked down the aisle toward the table where the running back was plying his fork with enthusiasm. The deck was perfectly firm underfoot, no surprise given that the *Carefree Nights* lay at anchor, but Keller managed to teeter a bit as he walked, as if he might have equilibrium problems even on dry land.

He made sure not to overdo it, aiming for a diagnosis of *unsteady on his pins,* but when he reached their table he contrived to lose his balance big-time, lurching into the running back's chair and grabbing onto the man's shoulder for support.

While the fellow reacted, Keller reached with his left hand and dropped one of the pills in the man's coffee.

"Jesus! You all right, fellow? Here, let me give you a hand."

"Sorry, sorry. I was fine when the ship was rocking and rolling and now I can't—oops!"

And one more hearty lurch, this time into the now-standing running back, who had to work to keep his own balance now that Keller had assumed the role of loose cannon. But somehow both men stayed on their feet, even as somehow the second pill found its way into the other coffee cup.

Apologies from Keller, assurances from the running back. And then Keller was on his way back, passing his own table, and giving here a lurch and there a lurch, until he had made his stumbling way out of the dining room altogether.

* * *

As far as Keller could make out, everybody in Nassau had just disembarked from one of the cruise ships that thronged the docks. He figured there had to be other people around, but that they had the good sense to stay away from the harbor.

"Who buys all these T-shirts?" Julia wondered. "'Grandma and Grampa went to Nassau and all I got was this lousy shirt.' How stunningly original. Is there a tourist attraction on God's earth where they don't sell that shirt?"

"Auschwitz," Keller suggested.

"Were you ever here before?"

"Nassau? No. Were you?"

"Once," she said. "A man brought me here for a dirty weekend. I never heard the term before, and I gather it's English."

"He was English?"

"Welsh. His wife was English."

"Oh."

"Are you jealous?"

"It was before we met, wasn't it?"

"Oh, years ago."

"Then no," he said. "I'm not jealous."

Something in a shop window caught her eye, and they talked about that for a few minutes, while Keller glanced around to see if the two football types were around. He'd kept an eye out earlier, but hadn't seen either of them leave the ship, with or without Carmody and the girl.

Then Julia broke a silence to say, "It never happened."

"What never happened?"

"The married Englishman."

"Welsh," he said. "The wife was English."

"What difference does it make? I just told you it never happened. Neither of those two people ever existed, and I've never been to Nassau before."

"Oh."

"You really weren't jealous, were you?"

"Would you be happier if I said I was?"

"No, silly. I just didn't know if you would be or not, and I wanted to find out. Because you're a strange and unpredictable creature, Nicholas Edwards."

"I'm strange? You're the one who just dreamed up an adulterous affair with an English twit."

"Welsh," she said. "The wife was English."

They were heading back to the ship when they heard the siren. It was loud, and of a type familiar to Keller from films set in Europe—a long high note followed by a long note an octave lower, a sort of *ooh-gah-ooh-gah* effect. An ambulance roared past them, and it looked boxy and old-fashioned, but was unmistakably an ambulance.

Julia wondered if it was on its way to their ship. Keller hoped so.

They had lunch on the ship, and shared a table with two women, both of them retired schoolteachers from Crawfordsville, Indiana, along with a stockbroker and his wife who had retired to Florida from North or South Dakota, Keller wasn't sure which. The ambulance and its mission gave the six of them something to talk about.

"Now, I don't believe I met either of the two men," one of the schoolteachers said. "If I've got the names right, one was a Mr. Westin and the other was a Mr. Smith."

"Should have been Smith and Wesson," the stockbroker

said. "Way I heard it, after they took them off to the hospital, the cabin attendants packed up their bags, and they found a small arsenal there. A couple of guns, anyway, and ammunition to fit them."

"My goodness. On a cruise?"

"Oh, men and their guns," the second teacher said. She was taller and bulkier than her companion, and built not unlike a tight end herself, or maybe a linebacker. "I understand there are men who feel naked without their guns. But here we are having lunch, and not knowing what they ate that made them so ill."

"Nothing they ate," the broker said. "It was evidently an allergic reaction to some sort of drug. Analeptic shock, I think they call it."

"Anaphylactic," the first teacher said.

"Guns and drugs," the broker's wife said. "And it makes you wonder, doesn't it? Two men, traveling together, and sharing a cabin."

Her husband asked her what that was supposed to mean. She said it was just something to take into account.

In their own cabin, Julia said, "I'm still trying to figure it out. Was she suggesting they're gay? And what would that have to do with them both getting sick at the same time?"

Keller shrugged. "Beats me. AIDS, maybe?"

"I suppose. 'Two men sharing a cabin.' I don't know if you saw the look she got when she said that, but the schoolmarms didn't appreciate the implication. Given that they're two *women* sharing a cabin."

"And they're annoyed because they're lesbians?"

"Or they're not lesbians, and that's why they're annoyed. At the implication."

"The world's a complicated place," Keller said.

TWENTY-SIX

The lounge chair Keller selected gave him a good view of the block of four staterooms, one of which housed Carmody and his strawberry blonde. He sat down, put his legs up, and set about the business of anointing himself with suntan lotion. It boasted a high SPF number, and he found himself wondering if there was any point to the whole process. Wouldn't it be simpler to skip the lotion and stay in your cabin? Wouldn't you come out about the same?

Earlier, Keller had checked the listings, and found that Mr. Aldredge Smith and Mr. John Westin had occupied a cabin one flight below. That was unfortunate, because if their removal to a hospital in Nassau had left a Sun Deck stateroom vacant, Keller might have used it as a base of operations.

Keller hadn't thought to pack a bathing suit, but the shipboard shop had been happy to sell him one. It was black, and not too skimpily cut, but he still felt conspicuous in it, though less so than if he'd stretched out on the lounge chair in long pants and a shirt. And the sun felt good, and the ship had set sail shortly after lunch for Virgin Gorda, wherever that was, and Keller found its motion soothing. All he had to do was lie there and relax and keep his eyes open.

The third requirement turned out to be impossible. *Your eyes are closed,* he realized at one point, and told himself he'd have to do something about it, but by then it was too late. His mind had found a corridor to explore, and he drifted right off...

And came to abruptly. There was no sudden noise, and no one jostled his lounge chair or walked past it to block the sun. He wondered later if it might simply have been an unconscious awareness of her presence that did it, because when he opened his eyes there she was, not ten yards away from him, Ms. Va-va-voom herself, sitting sidesaddle on a lounge chair of her own, and applying coconut-scented suntan oil to those portions of her anatomy not covered by the scarlet bikini.

Which was to say almost all of her.

She took her time oiling her golden-brown skin, and it seemed to Keller that she was caressing herself as much as she was protecting it from the sun. He didn't want to stare at her, but seemed incapable of averting his eyes, and the next thing he knew she was looking right back at him.

He looked away, but it was as if he could see her no matter where his eyes were turned. He looked her way again, and she was still gazing at him, with an expression on her face that was not quite a smile, although it was definitely headed in that direction.

Then she turned her eyes from him, and swung her legs up onto the lounge chair, and worked the controls to lower the back into a horizontal position. She was still sitting up, and

Keller watched as she put her hands behind her back, uncoupled the bikini top, and removed it altogether.

She couldn't have exposed her breasts to him for more than a couple of seconds, but they were longer seconds than most. Then she was lying facedown on the lounge chair.

Had anyone else seen what Keller had seen? He looked around and saw no one who gave any evidence of having witnessed the performance. Had it been for his benefit? Or had he merely chanced to be present when a free-spirited creature displayed her charms without thinking twice about it?

Her head was turned to one side, resting on her arm, and facing toward Keller. Her eyes were closed. And she was smiling.

Go back to his cabin? Go to the bar for a drink, or the lounge for a cup of coffee? Find his way to the library and pick out something to read?

Or wait for her to give up on the sun and return to her cabin, so that he could see which one it was?

Keller closed his eyes to give the matter some thought, and once again the combination of sun and waves carried him off. He didn't doze for long, but when he opened his eyes he saw that the girl had changed position. She was lying on her back now, and was once again wearing the bikini top.

And she was no longer alone. On the lounge chair just beyond hers, wearing knee-length Bermuda shorts and a loose-fitting shirt with a palm tree on it, sat Carmody himself. His feet were bare—a pair of pink flip-flops rested at the foot of his chair—and from the knees down the man was fish-belly white, while from the knees up he was pretty much invisible, with the shirt and the shorts and his sunglasses and his pink cotton sun hat covering up most of him.

The contrast between the two of them, dramatic enough in

the dining room, was far greater beneath the sun. Earlier he'd looked old enough to be her father, or perhaps her father's older brother; now you'd be more apt to cast him as her dead grandfather.

She was lying down. Carmody's chair was in what the airlines call the full upright position, and he sat there looking like a man waiting for his number to be called. Then, after a few moments, he reached out and rested a hand on his companion's shoulder. Keller thought that was a tender gesture until the hand moved lower and slipped inside a cup of the bikini halter.

Keller looked away, willing the old goat to keep his hands to himself, and when he looked their way again it was as if his wish had been Carmody's command. Both the man's hands were now resting on the arms of his own lounge chair.

Well, that was better. On the other hand, a little more touchy-feely and they might get up and return to their cabin, and Keller could note its number. And he wished that would happen sooner rather than later, as there was a limit to how much sun he could handle.

But how much sun could Carmody take? Not too much on those pale white legs, so…

Hell. Keller watched as Carmody picked up his towel and draped it carefully over his feet and lower legs. Taking the sun without taking the sun, he thought. Wonderful.

Time to give up and get out of the sun himself? Wait, Carmody was saying something.

"Carina? You don't want to get too much sun, honey."

"Feels so good," she replied, so softly that Keller could barely make out the words.

"I can think of something else that'll feel good. Time to go inside, Carina."

"Give me a few more minutes, Mickey. You go. I'll be there by the time you're out of the shower."

"You and the sun," Carmody said.

"Makes me warm. You like me warm, don't you, Mickey?"

The man answered by leaning over to cop another feel, and Carina contrived to show her appreciation by squirming a little on the lounge chair. Then Carmody slipped his feet into his flip-flops, told her not to be too long, and stood up.

Keller gave him a head start. He got to his feet, and out of the corner of his eye he thought he saw Carina glancing at him. He didn't turn to check, but took off in Carmody's wake.

He followed the man around the pool and over to the four cabins. Carmody led him to one of two on the far side, so if he'd stayed where he was he'd only have been able to halve the possibilities from four to two, but now he was half a dozen steps behind the man by the time he'd used his key card to let himself into number 501.

The door closed, and Keller moved in front of it. His immediate mission had been one of reconnaissance, and it had paid off, but did he have to stop there? If he knocked, Carmody would open the door. And once he did, he was there to be taken.

Keller's swimsuit had a pocket, but all it held was his own key card. No garrote, no HandyMan, no pills or powders. All he had were his two hands, but if he needed more than that to cope with Michael Carmody he was in the wrong business.

He looked in both directions, and there was nobody around. How soon would the girl come back? Could he dispatch Carmody in time to be out of the room before she made her appearance?

If not, well, that would be bad luck all around, especially for her. Keller preferred to avoid that sort of situation, but sometimes you couldn't, and he had learned to do what had to be done.

He knocked on the door, listened for footsteps.

And didn't hear any. No, of course not, the son of a bitch was taking his shower. He wouldn't be able to hear Keller knocking, or if he did he wouldn't feel the need to cut short his shower to go see who it was.

Knock again? He was about to, but now there was someone in view, a maid pushing a service cart. And when she passed there would be somebody else, and sooner or later the girl would show up, and Keller would have to wait for a better time.

Maybe it was time to check out the library, see if he could find something to read. First, though, he'd get his own shower.

Mickey, he thought. Mickey and Carina. Well, the afternoon hadn't been a total loss. He now knew which cabin they occupied. And, though he couldn't see what good it did him, he knew what they called each other.

TWENTY-SEVEN

Julia had made a new friend during the afternoon, and worked things out so that the two couples could share a table for four at dinner. They were Atlantans, though both had grown up in the Midwest. The husband, Roy, said he had the perfect job. He worked for an insurance company, but he didn't sell anything, or weasel out of paying claims, or sit at a desk and crunch numbers. Instead he flew around the country and met with groups of insurance agents, explaining why they should push his company's policies instead of the competition's.

"I buy the pizza, I buy the doughnuts, I've always got the latest jokes, and whenever I show up everybody's glad to see me. I swear it never feels like I'm working."

"He works very hard," said his wife, who was called Myrt, which Keller figured had to be short for Myrtle. "On and off planes all the time."

"The planes are fine," Roy said. "It's the blankety-blank airports. But don't get me started."

Nobody did, and the subject shifted to the two men who'd left the ship, and whom everybody had taken to calling Smith and Wesson, and who were assumed to be very dangerous men. Mafia torpedoes, the consensus seemed to be, no doubt dispatched to kill one of the passengers, or even a crew member.

"It could be anyone," Myrt said darkly. "The captain looks perfectly decent, but he could have gambling debts."

"Are we playing Pick the Victim?" her husband wondered. "My candidate's Foxy Grandpa. Oh, you know who I mean. The dirty old man with the hot redhead."

"Gambling debts, Roy?"

"Hell, who needs a motive? I'd kill him myself if I thought it'd get me a shot at her."

"Oh, Roy," Myrt said, and swatted him with her napkin. "Am I gonna have to keep you on a leash?"

"Arf arf," Roy said.

"I swear, men are terrible creatures. Still, I have to say this is more interesting than our last cruise."

"You had a good time."

"Well, I did, but the conversation! Perforations, inverted underprints—"

"Overprints," Roy said.

"Like it matters? Roy," she announced, "took me on a cruise for stamp collectors. Can you imagine? Every time we landed and the wives went shopping, all of the men rushed to the nearest post office."

Roy said it wasn't quite like that, and Myrt said it was close enough, and Roy said only thirty-some passengers were stamp collectors, it was just a small portion of the whole, and Myrt said yes, but those were the people they had to sit with every night at dinner, and finally Keller was able to get a word in edgewise.

"You're a collector," he said.

"Guilty as charged, but I never would have brought it up, because there's nothing less interesting than someone else's hobby."

Was that true? Keller didn't think so, and had found most people to be at their best when talking about their hobby or pastime. But what he said was, "Well, I wouldn't be bored. I'm a philatelist myself."

"I guess you just might be, if you can pronounce it correctly. Myrt still has trouble after all these years. What do you collect, Nick?"

Keller told him, and Roy nodded respectfully. "Classic general worldwide," he said. "Got to admire that. Myself, well, nothing quite that ambitious, but I've got a batch of collections going. My main interest is stamps of Turkey, and don't ask me why. No Turkish ancestors, no connection of any sort, and I've never been to the country and don't expect I'll ever get there. I just like the stamps, for some reason."

It made perfect sense to Keller.

"And of course along with Turkey I collect a batch of dead countries connected to Turkey, like Hatay and Latakia."

"And Eastern Rumelia," Keller offered.

"You bet. And, let's see, besides Turkey I have one topical collection. I collect fish."

"That's fish on stamps," Myrt said, as if otherwise Julia might think Roy had a collection of actual fishes.

"Now, I like fish," Roy said, "though I wouldn't want it served to me every night. And when I was a kid I had an aquarium and I used to like watching the fish, until they all died and I emptied the fish tank and gave it to my mother to grow ferns in. And I've been fishing, but only a couple of times in my life, and I don't care if I never waste time again in that particular fashion. But I do like stamps with fish on them. I just like the way they look, all the different species."

That made sense to Keller, too.

Keller, stretched out on his bunk, turned at the sound of Julia's key card in the lock. She entered, holding the plastic rectangle aloft like a Plains Indian brandishing a scalp.

"That's the key to 501?"

She shook her head. "It's a spare key to our cabin. I just let myself in with it."

"Oh."

"Silly me, locking myself out. In a minute I'll take the key back." She tapped it with her thumbnail. "There's no way she'll give me a key to Carmody's cabin. You need to show ID and sign for it. But I saw where she keeps the keys, and how they're sorted. Now if somebody could get her to come away from the desk for a minute or two, someone else could slip away with the key to 501."

"Last time I passed the desk," Keller said, "there were two girls behind it. They looked enough alike to be Xerox copies, but there were two of them."

"Two to a shift," Julia agreed. "Two on duty from eight in the morning till four in the afternoon, and two others from four to midnight."

"And only one after midnight?"

"Pilar is so glad she does not have the graveyard shift this week. She had it last week, and you get so lonely."

"You got friendly with her."

"It never hurts to be friendly," she said. "She's from the Philippines."

"I think they all are."

"Uh-huh. All the dining room and housekeeping staff, and the ones on the desk. The cruise director and his staff are American, except for the ones who aren't. And the crew's a mini United Nations, with a lot of Eastern Europeans. The chef is Swiss. Pilar doesn't like the Ukrainians."

"Why not?"

"She says they're not nice. I was thinking if we waited until one o'clock, and then you found a way to lure the attendant out from behind the desk, all I'd need is a couple of minutes to get the key to their cabin."

"Maybe you should do the luring."

"No," she said, "because I saw where the keys are. You can play helpless confused man in need of help. Besides, if anybody happens to see me behind the desk, it'll be less unsettling than if they were to see you."

"Because you look more like a Filipina?"

"Because I'm a girl, silly. Women are less threatening. How could you not know that?"

He didn't say anything, and she asked him if something was bothering him.

"I'm just wondering," he said, "if this is really something you want to do."

"The key will help, won't it?"

"It might. It certainly wouldn't hurt."

"Well," she said, "I want to help."

He made one change to Julia's plan, delaying the starting time an hour to give the girl on the desk a little more time to appreciate the loneliness of her situation. At a couple of minutes past two, Keller approached the desk, where the attendant met him with a big smile.

"I was wondering if you could help me," he said. "The only thing is, I don't know if it's okay for you to leave the desk."

"It's not rush hour here," she said. "How can I help?"

There was a notice on the board he couldn't understand, he said, and he led her down a corridor to where notices were posted, and pointed to one he'd scouted out earlier. Its message, some drivel about evacuation in the event of fire or shipwreck, was pretty clear, but she was evidently willing to believe he was somewhere in the early stages of cognitive decline, and worried about drowning, and so she explained it all very clearly and carefully.

Keller asked if there were many shipboard fires, and after she'd reassured him on that score he raised the subject of piracy. That was pretty much limited to the Indian Ocean, she said, and the only real pirates in the Caribbean these days were running gift shops. He laughed at that, and found a joke to tell her in return, and she was polite enough to pretend it was funny.

She went back to her post and Keller returned to his cabin, where Julia showed him a key card. "What did I tell you?" she said. "Nothing to it."

In the morning they left the ship with Roy and Myrt, whose last names turned out to be Huysendahl. The wives had shopping to do, and Roy suggested a visit to the post office. "You won't find anything," Roy said. "Not if your collection's got a 1940 cutoff date. And I probably won't find anything, either."

"Not much from Turkey," Keller said.

"Doesn't seem likely, does it? But they might have some fish stamps. It's a popular topic, and easier to justify for a Caribbean island than some landlocked African dictatorship that gets three drops of rain every two years."

The post office had a special philatelic window, and a display showing just what stamps were still available for purchase. There was a very attractive set of stamps showing brilliantly colored reef fish, along with a six-stamp souvenir sheet; they'd just come out, and Roy picked up four sets, sheets included. "One for me and the others for some guys I know'll want them. Cheaper at the post office than from a new-issues dealer."

Back on the ship, Julia showed off a blouse she'd bought. "I don't know that I'll ever wear it," she said, "but it was cheap, and Myrt bought one, so I picked it up in the interest of female bonding. Did you find any stamps to buy?"

He showed her the two souvenir sheets he'd bought, one with fish, another showing the various islands that comprised the British Virgins. "They're souvenir sheets," he said, "so I bought them for a souvenir."

"And in the interest of male bonding?"

"I suppose. He's a nice fellow."

"Myrt thinks the four of us should make *dîner à quatre* a regular thing. Could you stand sharing a table with them every night? Just the four of us?"

"Saves trying to find things to say to new people."

"That was my thought. The British Virgins. You know what a British virgin is? A ten-year-old girl who can run faster than her brothers. Actually, that's an old joke about Cajuns. But I'm not sure it really works to adapt it. The British don't have that reputation."

"Quite the reverse," he said. "'Dead? Sacre bleu, Monsieur, I thought she was English!'"

"Oh, I heard that joke years and years ago," she said. "And it's still awful."

TWENTY-EIGHT

At dinner that night, Keller waited until he'd finished his main course, a nice piece of fish that had been swimming not too many hours ago. If it had been on a stamp, he thought, Roy would have snatched it away from him.

He put his fork down, patted his pockets, said, "Hell," and got to his feet. "Something I forgot," he said. "I'm not interested in dessert, so please go ahead without me. I'll join y'all for coffee if I get done in time."

The elevator might have been faster, but he didn't even think of it until he'd already climbed the first flight and started on the second. He was breathing hard when he reached the Sun Deck, but caught his breath by the time he was slipping the key card into the door of the Carmody stateroom. The lock turned and he was inside.

The maids serviced everybody's cabin during dinner, turning down beds, turning on lights, drawing curtains, and leaving a square of foil-wrapped chocolate on the pillow. The Sun Deck staterooms were essentially two-room suites, and Keller moved around the place looking at things and wondering what he was doing here. It put him in position for an ambush, but that would only work if Carmody turned up alone. And he might: he had a lot of years on his bladder and prostate, and could well feel the need for a quick pee before catching up with the lovely Carina in the lounge, where tonight's scheduled entertainment included a comedian and a torch singer.

But there was at least as good a chance that they'd return together, and then what did Keller do? He'd have the advantage of surprise, and he was a skilled professional up against two amateurs, one an out-of-shape older man and the other a woman. He was confident in his ability to take out both of them, and could probably do so before either one made enough noise to attract attention. And if they did get out a cry, so what? She'd sound as though she was feigning passion, while he'd come off as a self-styled Tarzan, pounding his chest and yowling in triumph.

If he was alone, that was how he'd want to do it. The girl was collateral damage. It was safer and easier to do two for the price of one, and while Carina was a good example of what Mother Nature could do when inspired, she was unlikely to find a cure for cancer or bring about a lasting peace in the Middle East. She'd assumed a certain risk when she agreed to share a cabin with a man like Carmody, and if her luck was bad, well, that was just bad luck. Killing her would bother Keller for a while, but he knew how to deal with that sort of thing, and he'd get over it.

That's if he was alone. But he wasn't, he had Julia along, and it was hard to know how Julia would take one death, let alone two. She knew that his assignments occasionally included women—Dot had more than once called him an equal-opportunity killer—but this was a woman she'd seen up close, and that made it different.

Well, maybe both he and Carina would be lucky this time, and Carmody would come back all by himself. But then what? Carina would return sooner or later and find the body, and just how much of a flap that raised would depend on whether or not he could make it look like natural causes. If he couldn't, there'd be cops on board the next time they made port, and he could probably handle the questioning until he had a chance to get off the ship and disappear, but once again, dammit, he wasn't alone, he had Julia along.

He paced the floor—the Sun Deck cabins provided ample room for pacing—and his mind kept working, trying to find a way, and then he stopped pacing and stopped thinking and froze in his tracks.

There was a key in the lock. So soon? How could they be done with dinner already?

He braced himself. Let it be Carmody, he thought, and the door flew open.

It was Carina.

His hands were out in front of him, ready to stifle her cries of alarm. But there were no cries, nor did she seem at all alarmed.

"Thank God!" she said.

Huh?

"The way you look at me," she said, moving closer to him, kicking the door shut. "And I know you saw the looks I gave you in return. But you have not approached me, and I saw you leave the dining room, and I thought maybe he's going to my cabin, and I made some excuse, and—"

She really was quite beautiful.

"But there's no time," she said. "Not now, he'll be here any minute. Oh, I want to be alone with you! What shall we do?"

"Uh..."

"Later tonight," she said. "One o'clock. No, one thirty, he'll definitely be asleep by then. I'll meet you on Deck Two out on the afterdeck."

"Uh, port or starboard?"

"All the way at the back," she said. "Behind the library. At the rail, at one thirty. Can you be there? Oh, I hope you can. Oh, God, there's no time, but kiss me. You have to kiss me."

And she pressed her mouth to his.

"I don't get it," he told Julia. "I wonder what she wants."

"Your fair white body, if I had to guess."

"Not unless she thinks I'm a Hollywood casting director," he said. "And it's just as well I'm not, because she wouldn't get the part. She's not that good an actress."

"It was an act?"

"'Oh, I want to be alone with you! What shall we do?' Yes, I'd say it was an act."

"I don't know," she said. "I frequently want to be alone with you. *What shall we do?* I ask myself that all the time."

"You usually come up with something."

"I asked myself just before you got back, and what I came up with was that we should call Donny and Claudia's. It's early, they'll be up, and with any luck so will Jenny."

Everyone was still awake at the Wallings house, and everybody talked to everybody else, until Donny Wallings took the phone and said, "This is costing y'all a fortune, and y'all are having fun and so's Jenny, so I'm gonna say good-bye now."

They ended the call, and Julia said, "She's having a wonderful time."

"That's great."

"She'll probably want to stay there forever. With her new family, that she now likes ever so much better than her old one."

"Maybe we can rent out her room."

"Go ahead, make fun of a mother's tears. Did you enjoy it? Was it hot?"

"Was what hot?"

"Kissing her. It must have been, that woman's one of the chief causes of global warming."

"It was just…I don't know. Dumb."

"Dumb?"

"I knew it had to be an act, and that she had an agenda. And even if it wasn't, I didn't want to be there."

"Poor baby. Was she at least a good kisser? Did she use her tongue?"

"Julia—"

"And press her tits against you? I'm sorry. I'm embarrassing you, aren't I?"

"I don't know. Yeah, sort of."

"If she doesn't want your body—"

"She doesn't. It was an act, pure and simple."

"Pure? Simple?"

"Well—"

"What do you suppose she wants?"

"I'll find out in a couple of hours."

"Well, I guess you will. One thirty, did you say?" She started to say something more, than stopped herself.

"What?"

"No, it's nothing. Well. What I was going to say was we could fool around a little first, to take some of the pressure off, but you're not in the mood, are you?"

"Not really, no."

"I'm as bad as she is, trying to make this about sex, and it's not about that, is it? And I at least should know better. Have you got something to read? I'll let you alone."

When Keller left their cabin, it was a little after one and most of the ship's passengers had retired for the night. There were still some holdouts in the bars and lounges, making up in volume what they'd lost in number, and a few passengers hung around on deck, looking out at the stars or thinking deep thoughts at the rail.

He got to the spot designated for their rendezvous a good ten minutes ahead of schedule, and found a vantage point nearby where he could observe Carina's approach and assure himself that she didn't have anyone trailing her. He'd changed to dark clothing, and found a dark spot to lurk, and evidently succeeded in rendering himself invisible; a couple passed within a few feet of him, pausing to kiss with surprising passion, and then walked on, never aware that he was almost close enough to reach out and touch them.

One thirty came and went. Keller stayed where he was, half hoping she'd stand him up. But then, seven minutes late by his watch, she hurried by without seeing him, positioned herself at the rail, and looked around in what looked like genuine concern.

"Right here," Keller said softly, and came out where she could see him.

"Oh, thank God. I thought that you weren't coming, or that you came and left when I was not here. I had to wait until he was sleeping. But come here, come kiss me."

She moved toward him, stopped when he held up a hand. "No kisses," he said. "You've got an agenda, and I want to know what it is."

"Agenda?"

"Tell me what you want."

"The same thing you want," she said. "I saw you looking at me."

"Lots of men were looking at you."

"Yes, and women, too. But there was something about the way you looked at me." She frowned, the original act shelved for now. "You don't want to fuck me?"

"You're a very attractive young woman," he said, "but I'm married, and no, I don't want to have sex with you."

She said something in a language he didn't recognize, frowned again, then looked up to meet his eyes as recognition dawned in hers. "Then what were you doing in my cabin?"

His hands were at his sides, and he raised them to waist level. There was no one around, and all he had to do was break her neck and fling her overboard. If she managed to cry out first, it might pass for a scream she'd uttered on the way down.

"Maybe we want the same thing," she said.

Oh? "Tell me what you want."

"What do I want?" She said the foreign word again. "What do you think I want? I want you to kill my husband."

TWENTY-NINE

Julia had been awake at one o'clock, reading what she'd called a novel of magnolias and miscegenation, but she was sleeping soundly when he let himself into the cabin. He didn't think he'd be able to sleep himself, but a hot shower took some of the tension out of him, and he went right out.

In the morning he told her what happened. "Apparently they're married," he said. "That's why it took as long as it did for them to get to the ship Saturday afternoon. They went through a quickie wedding ceremony first."

"Why? To make the cruise line happy?"

He shook his head. "Not the cruise line. The Witness Protection Program. After he testifies, they'll set him up in some little town somewhere out west, but the only way she can be part of the deal is if she's his wife. And I guess he didn't think the local talent in East Frogskin would be up to his standards, so he bit the bullet and proposed."

"How romantic. But why did she go along? And why change her mind and want him dead?"

"Two questions with one answer."

"Money?"

He nodded. "He's got a lot of money, or at least she thinks he does. And she's living the life we figured, going on dates and getting presents, and the life's not that great and neither are the presents, and these are her peak years."

"She's got a lot of her youth left."

"But she can see what's coming. And here's this rich guy who wants to marry her."

"But that means living in, what did you call it? East Frogskin? And that's more than she signed on for?"

"Actually," he said, "I think it's exactly what she signed on for, but that was before she had a chance to think it through."

"And now she wants to tear up the contract. Can't she divorce him? Get an annulment? Oh, but she wants the money."

"She also would like him to be dead."

"Oh, it's personal?"

"He takes a lot of Viagra," he said, "and he has certain preferences in bed that she doesn't care for."

"Like what?"

"She didn't get specific."

"What a tease. I bet I can guess, and I'd like to sit her down and explain that once you get used to it it's actually quite enjoyable. Are you blushing?"

"No. It's not just what he likes to do, it's apparently that now that they're married she finds everything about him objectionable."

"And if he dies she's a rich widow."

"She was pitching one of the minders, the shorter of the two."

"The running back."

"Right. I guess he didn't push her away when she made her move."

"I guess he didn't have a wife along."

"I don't know if he was stringing her along, or if she'd even made her pitch about how they could be together forever if only something happened to her husband. I can't think he'd have actually followed through with it. But when he and the tight end went off in the ambulance, her whole plan fell apart."

"And that's when she started giving you the eye."

"Along with a peek at what she had under her bikini top."

"And she thought it worked, because there you were waiting for her in her cabin. And when she found out she was wrong, she just went and made another plan. Except it's the same plan, isn't it? But with a different prize instead of her body. What's she offering? It would almost have to be money."

"An unspecified amount, payable after the estate's settled."

"Lord, who wouldn't rush to commit murder for terms like that?"

"She's given up the idea that I'm blinded by lust, but she evidently still thinks I'm pretty stupid. I agreed, and the first thing I explained was that we couldn't see each other again. No more secret meetings, no kisses, no long looks. And I told her what we'd do for now was nothing at all, not until the last night of the cruise."

"So that we'll be off the ship by the time they find him."

"And so will everybody else. She'll be unable to rouse him, and they'll haul him off to a Fort Lauderdale hospital and pronounce him dead, and once the estate clears probate I'll get my very generous payment from an extremely grateful widow."

"So what's the next step?"

"Breakfast," he said. "I'm starving."

"I mean—"

"I know what you mean. There's no next step until the night before we dock in Fort Lauderdale. All you and I have to do between now and then is enjoy the cruise."

"My God," she said. "What a concept."

"And another little collection I've got," Roy said, "is mourning covers. You probably know what those are."

"With the black bands?"

"That's right. They've been around about as long as stamps, since sometime in the mid-nineteenth century. Stationers made up envelopes with the black bands printed on 'em, and that's what you bought for notes of condolence. They got a lot of use, mostly in Europe and America, and then right around 1940 the whole custom pretty much died out. Which is ironic, considering how people were dying faster than ever once the war started."

"Interesting thing to collect," Keller said.

"Morbid, you mean? That's what Myrt says, but it's no more about death than my other collections are about Turkey and fish."

"I meant interesting because of the variety. Different stamps, different dates, different countries."

"And sometimes the letter's still in the envelope," Roy said, "and like as not it barely mentions the deceased. Just a nice newsy letter, who's getting married, who just had a baby, who got a new job. And oh, by the way, I'm sorry for your loss. Now that's interesting, don't you think?"

"Very."

"Well, different times. Now what would they send, text

messages? 'Heard N8 dead. Bummer. R U OK?'" He sighed. "The covers, I must have close to two hundred of 'em. They're not high priority, but when I see one that's a little different, or that I like, well, I pick it up. But I've got to figure out what to do with the damn things. I've got a Scott Specialized album for my Turkish, and I print out my own pages for the fish, but all I've managed to do so far with my mourning covers is heave 'em in a box. Sometimes I haul 'em out and look at 'em, and then I just toss 'em right back in the box."

And did Keller collect any postal history, or just stamps? As a matter of fact, Keller said, he'd begun picking up covers mailed in Martinique, if they were interesting and attractive and reasonably priced. Martinique wasn't exactly a specialty, but he had all of the country's stamps through 1940, and had begun acquiring minor varieties, and somebody gave him a cover once, and—

"Say no more, Nick. I can see the same thing happening with Turkey, when I run out of stamps to buy. Ah, here come the ladies. I wonder what they found to buy this time."

The cruise was an unalloyed pleasure once he was free of the need to do anything. The Huysendahls continued to provide good company, and the shore visits weren't limited to shopping for the wives and postal expeditions for him and Roy. Twice they signed up for shore excursions, and got to see some wildlife and swim beneath a waterfall, or at least look at it.

As he'd noted the first night, one of the chief activities of people on a cruise seemed to be talking about other cruises they'd taken, and Keller, who'd never thought much about cruises, began to see what a world of possibilities they presented.

A smaller ship would be nice. *Carefree Nights* was comfortable and luxurious enough, but cruising on it was like being a guest in a huge floating hotel. In one port, they'd been berthed next to an actual sailing ship, carrying just over a hundred passengers. It had engines, so they could make good time when they had to and never worry about getting becalmed, but the ship was really beautiful with its sails flying, or whatever it was that they did.

A more interesting itinerary would be a plus, too. Cruising the Baltic, cruising the South Pacific—there were some genuinely exotic routes available to cruise ships, going places he'd like to see.

Places he'd like to take Jenny. She was sure to love life aboard ship, and there were plenty of activities for kids if he and Julia wanted some private time.

Plenty to think about. And he'd much rather keep his mind busy with that sort of thing than with their final hours aboard the *Carefree Nights*. Which didn't promise to be all that carefree.

THIRTY

The fish on the dinner menu that last night was marlin, lightly grilled and served with a brown butter sauce. The two women ordered it, as did Roy. Keller asked for the filet mignon, medium rare.

"Well, that's a switch," Roy said. "This must be the first time I've seen you have anything but fish. I was beginning to wonder if you shouldn't be the one collecting fish stamps."

When you ordered fish, the waiter took away your ordinary table knife and gave you an oddly shaped fish knife. No one ever seemed to use it, and Keller figured any piece of fish he couldn't cut with the side of his fork was one he didn't much want to eat.

When you ordered steak, they brought you a steak knife.

At one thirty, Keller scanned the Sun Deck. All was quiet, and he couldn't see anyone around. At dinner they'd requested that all bags be placed out in the corridor by three a.m., so that crew members could collect them prior to departure, and the occupants of all four Sun Deck cabins had already complied.

Keller positioned himself in front of the door to stateroom 501. Several pieces of luggage were on the deck to his right. There was music playing within the cabin, barely audible through the heavy door, and the DO NOT DISTURB sign was suspended from the knob.

He had the key in his pocket, the one Julia had picked up for him, but he left it there and knocked. Carina opened it at once, wearing a pale yellow nightgown to which he supposed the word *diaphanous* might apply. He got a whiff of her perfume and a sense of her body heat as she reached to embrace him, then stopped herself when she realized that wasn't in the script anymore.

Instead she made do with stating the obvious: "You're here."

He was, and so was Carmody, stretched out on the bed on his back, naked to the world but for a pair of boxer shorts and an arresting amount of body hair. The man's mouth was hanging open and he was breathing slowly and heavily through it. The music Keller had heard through the door was still low in volume. Soft jazz, and Keller recognized the song but couldn't put a name to it.

"I put the powder in his nightcap," she said. "He drank it."

No kidding, Keller thought.

"He wanted to fuck me," she said, "but he passed out instead. You know where I can get some more of that powder?"

Keller had obtained it by crushing two capsules, collecting the powder in a folded-up slip of paper. As arranged, he'd met Carina that afternoon and passed it to her, along with instructions for its use. If he'd given it to her earlier she might have rushed things, and he hadn't wanted that.

"Out like a light," she said. "Look at him, hairy like an ape. You know what I almost did?"

"What?"

"Put a pillow over his face. I thought, what if he wakes up? But he wouldn't wake up. He's dead to the world, and a few minutes with a pillow over his face and he'd stay that way forever. Save you the trouble, huh?"

Satin Doll, Duke Ellington and his orchestra. That's what was playing.

He said, "It's good you restrained yourself."

"Why? I would have paid you all the same. You're the one gave me the magic powder."

"You want it to look like death by natural causes."

"So? He stops breathing, his heart stops beating, he's dead. What's more natural than that?"

"He'd have these pinpoint hemorrhages in his eyeballs."

"So his eyes bleed, what do I care? What's it gonna hurt him if he's dead?"

"They'd see the hemorrhages," he said patiently, "and they'd know immediately that he'd been smothered."

"Oh, fuck," she said. "Like *CSI*?"

"Something like that. And who do you think they just might suspect of smothering him?"

"Fuck. Good I didn't do it."

"I'd say."

"So," she said. "How you gonna make it look natural?"

He moved quickly to the side of the bed, drew the steak knife from his pocket, and sank it between two of Michael Carmody's ribs and into his heart. The body shook with a brief tremor, the hands raised up an inch or so from the bed, and then all was still.

"Holy fuck!"

"Well," Keller said.

"You just killed him. Just like that."

"You're a rich widow. That's what you wanted, isn't it?"

"But you stabbed him! The knife's right there sticking out of him!"

"Good point," Keller said, and removed the knife. There was hardly any blood on it.

"But won't they see the wound? How's that gonna look like natural causes?"

"Now, that's a good question," he said, and reached for her.

THIRTY-ONE

The ship docked in Port Everglades before breakfast, and at nine o'clock passengers were allowed to disembark. Keller collected their bags in the cruise terminal, and a cab had them at the airport three hours before their flight home.

They found a place to have coffee, and Julia said, "You didn't say, and I didn't ask, but I'll ask now. It's done, isn't it?"

"It's done."

"I want to hear, but I don't want to hear now. Okay?"

"Sure."

"I miss Jenny. I miss her like crazy. I've been sort of holding that off to one side, how much I miss her, but now we're on dry land and we'll be home in a couple of hours and it's okay to let myself feel it. I miss her something fierce."

"So do I."

"They were nice, weren't they? Roy and Myrt."

"Very."

"And there was a lot to him besides the stamps. That opened the door, but he's an interesting person in other respects, don't you think?"

"Definitely."

"I wouldn't mind seeing them again. I wonder if we ever will."

"We have their email."

"And they have ours, but did you see all the people exchanging email addresses last night? How many of them do you think will ever get in touch?"

"We could make a point of it," he said. "Maybe go on a cruise with them again sometime."

"With Jenny, though."

"Absolutely."

"And with no—"

"Work connected to it. Again, absolutely."

"That might be fun. Okay, I think I'll read the paper now. There won't be anything in the paper, will there? No, of course there won't, it's far too soon. Honey? We'll talk later."

"Okay."

"When I'm ready."

"Right."

Keller always liked the New Orleans airport, not least of all because it was named for Louis Armstrong. He didn't know who O'Hare was, but doubted he ever amounted to much as a horn player. Neither did JFK or LaGuardia. Orange County had named an airport after John Wayne, and that was pretty good, and there was Bob Hope Airport in Burbank, but Keller figured New Orleans had them all topped.

They drove straight from the airport to the Wallings house. Donny wasn't home from work yet, but Claudia and the kids were there, and something unwound in Keller the second he saw his daughter, something he hadn't even known was coiled tight. He picked her up and nodded happily as she told him a million things, some of which he could even understand.

Claudia poured coffee and put out a plate of cookies, and Julia unzipped her bag and played Lady Bountiful, passing out presents for everybody. Claudia got a blouse, which she professed to love, and for Donny Julia'd picked out a Hawaiian-style sport shirt with a desert island motif.

"I don't know if he'll ever wear it," she said.

Claudia said, "Are you kidding? He'll love it, and you know it's something he'd never pick out and buy for himself. The hard part'll be getting that man to take it off."

The kids got what they got, and seemed content. And, as soon as they decently could, they packed up Jenny and headed for home.

He'd found a spare moment to call Dot from the Fort Lauderdale airport, reporting success in an ambiguous sentence or two, ringing off after she'd expressed congratulations. Now he busied himself with the week's worth of mail. There was a new list from one of his favorite dealers, ten pages of Portugal and Colonies, and while it was hardly a priority, he'd been a week away from his stamps and couldn't resist.

He was circling an 1899 set of four Lourenço Marques overprints when Julia came into the room. He looked up and saw her face.

"I found the story online," she said.

"And?"

"It was simple and straightforward. An American couple, Mr. and Mrs. Michael Carmody, were found in their cabin, the victims of a double homicide. He'd been stabbed once, she'd been stabbed multiple times. The cabin was ransacked, and the apparent motive was robbery. The killer left behind an extra key card for the cabin, and one seems to have gone missing from the desk."

Keller nodded. That was the connection they were supposed to make.

"The murder weapon was also left behind. It was a steak knife, suggesting that a member of the kitchen or dining room staff might have been responsible."

"I can see how they might think that."

"Yes." She was sitting down now. Her hands were loosely clasped on the table in front of her, and she was looking down at them. "I knew you had to do it that way. Not the knife, I didn't even think about how, but I knew you were going to kill them both."

"I didn't really have much choice."

"No."

"The minute she walked in on me in their cabin, it was pretty much settled. When I met her out on deck in the middle of the night—"

"Two a.m., wasn't it?"

"Something like that. When she said what she wanted, I thought about doing her right then and there. Put her down fast and fling her overboard."

"And take care of him later?"

"If I could figure out a way. What I decided was the best thing to do was wait until the last night."

"And do them both."

"Yes."

She thought about this. "If you did what she thought you were going to do, made his death look like a heart attack—could you have done that?"

"I could have tried. But a good medical examiner wouldn't

be fooled. And the guy was going to be a star witness, and his two bodyguards had gone down the first day out of port."

"One of them died."

"I didn't know that."

"It was in the article. And the other one's still in the hospital in Nassau. Just a coincidence, as far as the early story is concerned, just a sign that this was a hard-luck cruise, because they don't know there's a connection between those two men and the Carmodys."

"They will."

"If he died and she didn't, they'd question her."

"Right."

"And she'd fall apart."

"Within a couple of hours, would be my guess."

"Even if it passed for a heart attack—but it wouldn't, would it?"

"If it was a genuine bona fide heart attack," he said, "and she's the just-married younger wife, who's pretty much of a semipro hooker, they'd still grill her six ways and backwards."

"Yes, of course they would. And she'd give you up in a New York minute, so there's no question, you had to do them both. Multiple stab wounds?"

"The first one killed her," he said. "The others were for show."

"So at least it was fast. For whatever that's worth." She looked up. "Oh, what am I going on about? She was trash to the bone, she was trying to get her husband killed, so why should her dying bother me? 'Cause she was a woman? Like that makes a difference? Please."

He didn't say anything.

"They were both horrible people, and the two bodyguards

were a pair of thugs, and what do I care about any of them? You know what it is?"

"You were there."

"That's exactly right. I was there. If I stayed home and you flew off somewhere and came back and told me the story, I wouldn't be able to wait to get you in bed. Now all I am is slightly sick to my stomach. And I wasn't just there, darling. I was a participant. I got you the card key."

"That's true."

"Doesn't that make me an accessory? Of course it does. I don't mean legally, I don't care about that. I mean the way I feel. Is there something I can do? So I don't feel like this?"

"Take a shower."

"Seriously?"

"Seriously."

She went off to do so, and he returned to his price list, but had trouble staying focused. He was still sitting there when she came back wearing a robe with her hair wrapped up in a white towel.

She said, "I couldn't see what good a shower would do, but I have to say I feel a little better. Isn't there something you do afterward to get over it?"

He'd performed the exercise the previous evening, before he fell asleep, and he talked her through it now: picturing the victim, concentrating hard on the image, and then turning it over to the Photoshop of the mind: shrinking it, fading it, pushing it off into the distance, until it was an undefined gray dot that ultimately vanished altogether.

"It's hard to do," she said.

"It gets easier with practice."

"I suppose it must. I'll work with it. And I may take more

showers than usual over the next week or so. But I don't want to have to do this again."

"No."

"I'm not sorry I was there. This is something you do, and I'm fine that you do it, and I even like it a lot more than I don't. And I should know what it's like, what it feels like. I didn't, and now I do."

"But once is enough."

"Once is plenty. Oh, a price list. 'Portugal and Colonies.' Are you finding stamps that you need?"

"A few."

"That's good," she said. "What and where is Lourenço Marques?"

"It's part of Mozambique."

"Well, I know where that is. And they have their own stamps?"

"Not since 1920."

"I guess nothing lasts forever. You know what I'm going to do now? Besides making the mental picture shrink and turn gray? I'm going to email Myrt Huysendahl to make sure we don't lose touch. Do you think Jenny would like a small-ship cruise of the Turkish Riviera?"

"You know, I'll bet that's what she was saying earlier."

"Must have been. I think you and I would like it, and Roy could see where his stamps come from. I'm going to be fine, you know."

"I know," he said.

KELLER'S SIDELINE

THIRTY-TWO

I'll tell you what's annoying," Dot said. "I was in Denver myself this past weekend."

"What's the matter with Denver?"

"Nothing," she said, "aside from the fact that I had a perfectly nice room for two nights at the Brown Palace, and I didn't get to sleep in it."

"Insomnia?"

"I never have insomnia, Keller. Nothing keeps me awake. That's one of the benefits of leading a blameless life. I slept fine, but not in my room. And don't ask."

"I won't."

"I had a dirty weekend. Flew up to Denver and slept with a strange man."

"Oh."

"That's it? 'Oh?' That's all you've got to say on the subject?"

"You said not to ask."

"It's an expression, Keller. If I really didn't want you to ask I wouldn't have brought it up in the first place."

"Oh."

"You're just insisting on hearing it all, aren't you? All right. I met this man on JDate. You know what that is?"

"I've heard of it," he said. "It's an online dating site. But isn't it for Jewish people?"

"So?"

"I never knew you were Jewish."

"Look at it this way, Keller," she said. "I'm a lot closer to being Jewish than Stuart Lichtblau is to being sixty-two."

"Oh."

"He's a widower," she said, "and I gather he was sixty-one when his wife died, but that must have been fifteen years ago. He spent a few months mourning her and a few more searching for a replacement, and then he discovered he liked being single, and ever since he's been spending his golden years screwing his brains out."

He couldn't say *Oh* again, but what else was there to say? He asked her if she'd had a good time.

"Yes," she said, "and no. He's retired, he had a chain of record stores that he sold back when people still bought records, and he's got this town house in a gated community in Aurora. His bed's the size of a tennis court, and I bet he spends more on Viagra than you spend on stamps. I have to say he taught me some new tricks, though I can't say my life's fuller for having learned them. And I had good food to eat and pricey wine to drink, and he treated me like a lady, and you know what? I couldn't wait to go home."

He thought about it. Then he said, "What's annoying?"

"Annoying?"

"You said what's annoying is you were in Denver this past weekend, but..."

"Right, right. I could have done it while I was there. Except of course for the fact that it's your line of work, not mine. But, you know, call it irony. I made a trip to Denver, and now you have to make a trip to Denver. Assuming you feel like taking the job."

"You have a job for me."

"Well, of course," she said. "Why else would I be calling? Just to tell you I got laid by a foxy old Jewish guy?"

He dialed the number, and when the woman answered he said, "Mrs. Soderling? This is Nicholas Edwards in New Orleans. We spoke last week."

"Yes, Mr. Edwards."

"I hope you still have the stamps."

"Why, of course I do. And I hope you're still interested. I believe I was to expect you sometime the middle of next month."

"I was wondering if we could move it up," he said. "I'm going to be making a trip to your part of the country early next week, and I hoped to come see you as early as this Friday, if that's convenient."

He listened for a few minutes, made notes, exchanged pleasantries. He found Julia in the kitchen, stirring something that smelled wonderful. "Friday's fine," he told her. "Her husband's collection is still intact, and she's happy I'm still interested."

"And she's in Denver?"

"Cheyenne. Well, outside of it. She gave me directions, and anyway I'm sure the rental car'll have GPS."

"So you'll fly to Denver and drive up to Cheyenne."

He shook his head. "I'll fly to Cheyenne," he said, "although I'll probably have to change planes in Denver. I'll drive from Cheyenne to Denver, and then I'll drive back to Cheyenne, and I'll fly home from there."

"Even though you'll once again have to change planes in Denver."

"Right."

"Because if anybody asks, you flew out to Cheyenne to buy a stamp collection and flew straight home afterward. Denver? You were only in Denver to change planes."

"That's the idea."

"Is the collection worth the trip?"

"I won't know until I see it," he said, "but I was going to take the chance anyway."

"Before you heard from Dot."

He nodded. "The husband collected for years," he said. "He subscribed to a couple of publications, and he was a life member of the American Philatelic Society, and he was sitting on the sofa reading the latest issue of *Linn's* when he had a heart attack and died."

"I suppose that's not a bad way to go."

"She watched it happen. That part couldn't have been much fun. Anyway, by the time the body was in the ground she started getting letters. 'So sorry at your hour of grief, but we'll make sure you get the best price for your husband's stamps.'"

"Vultures," she said.

"When the first letter came she was pleased, because she figured she'd deal with these people and be done with it. But when all the other letters flooded in she began worrying that she'd make a mistake and deal with the wrong person. They were all in such a rush to send a buyer to her home that she got a little suspicious."

"So she picked someone she hadn't heard from at all."

"Me," he agreed. "Remember Mrs. Ricks?"

"Was that the one near Audubon Park?"

"That's her."

"This woman in Cheyenne is a friend of Mrs. Ricks?"

"No, never met her."

"But she's from New Orleans?"

"Never even visited."

"Then—"

"You know that kids' game, Telephone? Where a message passes all around the room, and gets garbled along the way?"

"I played it as a child," she said. "But as I remember, it never worked out the way it was supposed to. The message didn't get garbled. It just made its way around the room."

"Well," he said, "the same thing happened with Mrs. Ricks's message, which was that there was a young man in New Orleans who bought stamps, and you could trust him all the way."

"I remember now," Julia said. "You bought her stamps, and then they turned out to be worth more than you thought. And you handed her an extra check out of the blue."

"Well, it just seemed like the right thing to do," he said. "It never occurred to me she'd run around telling everybody."

"I know they're very valuable," Edith Ricks had said.

She perched on the edge of a ladder-back chair and fixed her clear blue eyes on Keller. On the coffee table between them were three stacks of albums designed to hold sheets of mint postage stamps.

There was coffee as well, in two bone china cups, and shortbread cookies on a matching plate. The coffee was strong, and flavored with chicory, and he was fairly sure she'd baked the cookies herself.

"When my husband was a young boy," she said, "his father realized that there was a foolproof way to invest. You didn't have to pay a commission to a broker, and your money was safe, because it was guaranteed by the government."

Keller had seen this coming. "He bought stamps at the post office," he said.

"Exactly! He bought full sheets, and put them in these folders with this special paper to keep them in perfect condition—"

Glassine interleaving, Keller thought.

"—and he tucked them away for safekeeping. And for quite a few years he continued his regular visits to the post office. Then he got out of the habit, but now and then he'd show me some of the stamps. They go all the way back to 1948, when his father first got started."

That figured, Keller thought. It was in the years right after the Second World War that the whole country discovered the can't-lose investment potential of mint U.S. postage stamps.

"And now he's gone," she said.

"I'm sorry."

"It's been almost five years since he passed," she said. "And, you know, I've thought about the stamps. If we'd had children, I wouldn't even consider selling them now. I'd pass them on."

"That would be ideal," Keller said.

"But I lost one baby, and then I could never have another. I have a niece and nephews, but we're not close. And I don't really *need* the money, but I'm not *doing* anything with the stamps, and who knows what would become of them if anything happened to me?"

A clock chimed. They were in the parlor of a substantial three-story house on Hurst Street, just east of Audubon Park.

Keller could have had a look at one of the albums, but felt he ought to wait for an invitation. Besides, he was in no hurry. He knew what he would find, and what the ensuing conversation would be like.

"I know there are people who deal in postage stamps," she said, "and I did look in the Yellow Pages once, but that's as far as I went. Because it's very difficult to know whom to trust."

"Your husband never did any business with stamp dealers?"

"Oh, no. He and his father dealt only with the post office. So I really didn't know how to avoid being cheated, and then I was talking to a friend, and she mentioned that someone had told her that the young man who married the Roussard girl had an interest in buying old stamp collections, and..."

She'd gone to school with Julia's mother, who had herself died many years ago, but that was enough of a connection to suggest that he was the sort of person she could admit to her house, and entertain with coffee and cookies. He'd be well-mannered and soft-spoken, and wouldn't try to cheat her out of her inheritance.

Nor would he. But he was going to have to break her heart.

THIRTY-THREE

The stamp business was Julia's idea.

He'd come home from a day on a construction crew, his muscles sore from ten hours of installing Sheetrock, his head throbbing from ten hours of salsa music pouring out of one crew member's boom box. He'd been paid in cash at the day's end, and he put three twenties and a five on the kitchen table and stood there for a moment staring at his earnings.

"Let me draw you a bath," Julia said. "You must be exhausted."

The bath helped. He returned to the kitchen, where the four bills were still on the table, along with a welcome cup of coffee. "I must be out of shape," he told Julia. "Used to be Donny and I'd work dawn to dusk and I'd feel fine at the end of it. Tired after a long day, but not like I'd just had a beating."

"You're not used to it."

"No," he said, and thought for a moment. "And it's different. We had a business, we were working to accomplish something. Now all I'm working for is six fifty an hour."

"Which you don't really need in the first place."

"Donny got the guy to take me on. I didn't really know how to turn it down. Donny's doing me a favor, I can't throw it back in his face."

"There ought to be a way," she said. "You don't want to keep on doing this. Or do you?"

"I suppose my body would get used to it before too long. But what's the point? We don't need the money."

"No."

"And even if my body gets used to it, I'm not sure my head will. They're mostly Hispanic, which is fine, except that the opportunity for conversation is limited. But the music they like, and the volume they play it at—"

"I can imagine."

"What am I going to tell Donny? 'Thanks all the same, but I've got a ton of money in an offshore account.'"

"No."

"'And now and then I get a phone call and...' Well, obviously I can't tell him that part, either."

They talked about it, and the following afternoon Julia followed Jenny into the den while he was working with his stamps. She stood there silent while he was cutting a mount. When he looked up she said, "I was thinking."

"Oh?"

"You need a business."

"I do?"

"Something," she said. "So that there's something that you do, so it'll make sense to Donny that you don't need to swing a hammer."

"That'd be nice," he allowed. "And it's not just Donny. There must be a lot of people who wonder just what it is I do."

"Not so much in this town. New Orleans is full of people who don't seem to do much of anything. But it wouldn't hurt if you had some visible source of income."

"I've had that thought myself," he said. "But there's nothing I know all that much about."

"You know a lot about stamps, don't you?"

"So I could go into the business?" He thought about it, frowned. "The dealers I know," he said, "work all the time. And they're constantly making little sales and filling orders and doing all this detail work. I don't think I'd be good at it. I enjoy buying stamps, but if you're going to make a business out of it, the part you have to enjoy is selling them."

"If the buying part's what you like, couldn't you make a business out of that?"

He extended a hand, indicating first the album on the desk in front of him, then the double row of albums in the bookcase. "I'm already doing that part," he said, "and it keeps me busy, but it's hard to call it a business."

"Did you ever meet my friend Celia Cutrone? She was a year behind me at Ursuline. Skinny little creature then, but she filled out. Yes, you did meet her, she was at Donny and Claudia's cookout."

"If you say so."

"She brought her big old dog, and the two of you were talking about dogs."

He remembered now, an owlish woman with a wonderfully well-behaved Great Pyrenees, and he'd found himself remembering Nelson, the Australian cattle dog he'd had for a while, until the dog walker walked off with him.

"We didn't talk about stamps," he said. "Did we?"

"Probably not. She's not a stamp collector."

"Oh."

"She's in the antiques business, but she doesn't have a shop or list things on eBay. She's what they call a picker."

He'd heard the term. A picker went around and scooped up items at garage sales and junk shops and wholesaled them to retailers.

"I could do that," he said. "I guess the way to get started is run standing ads in all the neighborhood papers. The ones they give away."

"Shoppers, they call them. And you wouldn't want to forget Craigslist."

"Craigslist is free, isn't it? Running ads in it, I mean. And ads in the shoppers can't cost the earth."

"And then there'd be word of mouth," she said. "'You know those old stamps Henry had all those years? Well, the nicest young man came over and paid me decent money for them.'"

"'The one who married the Roussard girl, and he's surprisingly polite for a Yankee.'"

"Word of mouth," she said, "New Orleans–style. You can run all the ads you want, but once you get them talking about you, you're in business."

He thought about it. Low start-up costs, nothing like opening a store. Even so…

"I don't know," he said.

"Whether you'd enjoy it?"

"Oh, I'd like it well enough. What I don't know is if there's any way to do it and come out ahead. I wouldn't want to cheat anybody, and I wouldn't get big prices from the dealers I sold to, and I could see myself putting in a lot of hours and barely breaking even."

"Hours doing what?"

"Well, driving around and looking at people's stamps," he said. "And then looking at them some more afterward, and figuring out just what I bought and what it's worth and who's the best buyer for it."

"And you might spend hours doing these things and make chump change for your troubles."

"Chump change," he said.

"Isn't that the expression?"

"It sounded funny," he said, "coming out of your mouth. But yes, that's the expression, and it's probably what I could expect to earn."

"So?"

He looked up at her, and got it.

"I don't have to make money," he said. "Do I?"

"No. We've got plenty of money. And every once in a while you get a call from Dot, and we get more money."

"All I need," he said, "is something that looks like a business. I need a sideline, but it doesn't have to be a profitable one. It could even lose money and that would be all right. In fact, we could declare a net profit whether we actually earned one or not. Pay a few dollars in taxes and keep everybody happy."

"You've got that quick Yankee mind," she said. "I do admire that in a man."

THIRTY-FOUR

Keller, in the parlor of the house on Hurst Street, spent as much time as he could leafing through the stack of mint sheet albums. The contents were what he'd anticipated, panes of commemorative stamps ranging from 1948 to sometime in the early 1960s, when James Houghton Ricks had stopped paying regular visits to the post office.

That was the collector's name, Keller had discovered, even as he'd learned that his hostess's name was Edith Vass Ricks, and that her husband was actually James Houghton Ricks, Jr., and was called Houghty to distinguish him from his father, although there was nothing remotely haughty about Houghty.

Mrs. Ricks spoke softly and expressively, and Keller found her words soothing without having to pay very much attention to them. All these stamps, he thought. All commemoratives, all three-centers for years, until the first-class rate went up to four cents.

"The condition's good," he said.

"They were placed in those books," she said, "and never touched."

That was no guarantee, Keller knew, not in the New Orleans climate. Mold and mildew could find their way into a sealed trunk, and even between the glassine interleaving of a mint sheet album.

"It must have seemed like such a good idea at the time," he said gently. He kept his eyes on the panes of stamps. "But there was something people didn't realize."

"Oh?"

"You can't sell stamps back to the post office," he said. "They're not like money. All you can do with them is mail letters."

He glanced at her, and she did not look happy, but neither did she appear to be taken entirely by surprise. He explained, not for the first time, how it worked. A stamp, while indeed issued by the government, was not currency. It represented the government's obligation to provide a service, and in that respect it never expired. The stamp you bought in 1948 was still valid as postage sixty-some years later.

"Of course there's inflation," he said. "Postal rates go up."

"Every year, it seems like."

It wasn't quite that often, but Keller agreed that it did seem that way. He pointed to a sheet of red stamps showing a young man's face with a flag on either side, one with only a scattering of stars, the other with considerably more.

"Francis Scott Key," he said. "The flag on the left flew over Fort McHenry during the War of 1812, and when it survived the bombardment, he's the one who wrote a song about it."

"'The Star-Spangled Banner,'" she said.

"It only had fifteen stars," he said, "because we only had fifteen states at the time. And this other flag has forty-eight, because Alaska and Hawaii weren't admitted to the union until 1959. I suppose that's another sort of inflation. But when this three-cent stamp came out it would carry a letter, and now it would take fifteen of them to do that job."

"That many?"

Well, fourteen, Keller thought, plus a two-cent stamp to make up the deficit. But her question didn't seem to require an answer.

"You'd cover both sides of the envelope," she said. "And all those stamps would add weight, and you'd wind up needing another stamp, wouldn't you?"

"You might."

She'd been to the post office, she told Keller, just to establish a baseline value for the stamps, and the postal clerk had told her essentially the same thing. But he'd been brusque with her, and she'd thought he might be shading the truth in order to keep the line moving. She'd taken it as an article of faith that, if all else failed, the post office would buy the stamps back from you.

But if that wasn't true, and she could see now that it wasn't, and if the stamps were too common for collectors to be interested in them, then what was she going to do with them?

"I don't mail ten letters a month," she said. "I pay bills, and I write a note if somebody dies or a baby's born, but you couldn't put fifteen stamps on one of those little envelopes, and how would it look if you did? If the post office won't take the stamps back, would they at least let me trade them in for the new ones?"

"I'm afraid not."

"You buy it, it's yours. No refunds and no exchanges. That's about it, then?"

"That's their policy."

"So these are worthless, then. Is that about the size of it? I can just put them out with the trash?"

Not quite, he told her. And he explained that there were brokers who sold stamps at a discount, somewhere around 90 percent of face value, to volume mailers looking to trim their costs. These brokers replenished their stock by buying holdings like that of Mrs. Ricks, paying 70 to 75 percent of face value for them. He'd be happy to give her contact information for one or two brokers and she could deal directly with them.

Or, if she wanted, he'd buy the stamps himself. He could only pay half their face value, but it would save her negotiating with the brokers, along with the nuisance of packing the stamps for shipment.

"And taking them to the post office," she said darkly. "And paying the postage!"

"Now, if there's anyone you know who might enjoy having the stamps," he said. "Church youth groups always welcome donations. Or a Boy Scout troop, or—"

But she was shaking her head. "Add them up," she said. "See what they come to, and what you can pay me. I just want them out of here."

The total face value of the lot ran to $1838, and he divided the sum in half and counted out nine $100 bills and added a twenty. She said she owed him a dollar, and insisted on paying it. As he was packing up what he'd bought and wondering if he'd come out ahead by the time he was done shipping it, she asked him if there was anything else he could use. She had books that she wouldn't mind selling, and some of them were pretty old. Did he have any interest in books?

Just stamps, he told her. If she happened to have any old envelopes with stamps on them, he'd be glad to take a look at them and let her know if they were something he could use.

She snapped her fingers, which was something you didn't see often. "In that trunk," she said. "You know, I've been meaning to get rid of that, but it's way up in the attic and I don't go there if I can help it. But there's a little stack of envelopes there. People in the family used to save letters, you know, and in Houghty's family as well, and some of them go all the way back to the war."

He knew which war she meant.

"A few times," she said, "I thought some of those stamps might be worth something, and what I ought to do was soak them off the envelopes, but—"

"No, never do that."

"Well, I guess I'm glad I never got around to it, from the tone of your voice! But isn't that what collectors do?"

"Not with old envelopes. No, you don't want to do anything of the sort. There are people who collect the whole envelope—covers, they call them—and they like them even better with the letters intact."

"That's what's in the attic. Envelopes with letters in them. And then there's some that don't even have any stamps on them, though how they got through the mail without them is beyond me. You probably won't want those, will you?"

"Maybe we should see what's up there," he said.

There were forty-one envelopes, and they fit quite comfortably in a box that had once held fifty Garcia y Vega cigars. "I don't think there are any outstanding rarities here," he told Mrs. Ricks, "but I can pay you twelve hundred dollars for these."

"That much for those old letters?"

"I'm pretty sure I'll come out okay at that figure," he told her. "And if I don't, well, I'll just add them to my own collection."

But he didn't collect U.S.—or Confederate, either, for that matter—and he knew just where to send the material he'd purchased. He'd met a fellow at an auction in Dallas, a dealer-collector hybrid from Montgomery who specialized in the postal history of the Confederacy, and when he got home he was able to put his hands on the man's business card.

He picked up the phone in his stamp room, dialed the number. "I've got a few pieces that might interest you," he said. "Can I send them for your offer?"

The offer came by return mail, in the form of a check for an even $15,000. There was a note along with it, allowing that one particular item alone might bring almost that much at auction. "But we'll never know," the fellow said, "because it's found a permanent home in my personal collection. You come up with any more goodies like this, you know where to send them."

He put the check in the bank, and added another a few days later, from the gentleman in Connecticut who bought and sold discounted postage; the mint stamps he'd paid $919 for had returned $1286. That was no more of a profit than he deserved, considering his time and shipping costs, but the $15,000 from the Alabaman, welcome though it was, left a sour taste in his mouth.

He spent a few days thinking about it, and then he made a phone call and showed up at the Hurst Street address with a check for $3500. "Those covers were better than I realized," he told Edith Ricks. "And it seems only fair that you should share in the profits."

She was astonished, and tried to get him to come in for another round of coffee and cookies, but he pleaded another appointment and went home. "It's not as though she needed the money," he told Julia, "but she was certainly happy to have it."

"That's the way it is with money," she said. "It's welcome wherever it goes. You didn't have to pay her extra."

"No."

"She'd never have known what you got for those covers."

"No, of course not."

"Conscience money."

"Is that what it was? It just seemed, oh, I don't know. Appropriate?"

"I'll tell you what it is, even though you didn't mean it that way. But that's how it'll turn out."

"What's that?"

"Bread upon the waters," she said. "You'll see."

And he did get a few nibbles over the next month or so, though none of them amounted to much. He told a woman in Metairie that her late husband's boyhood stamp collection, housed, as Keller's own had been, in a *Modern Postage Stamp Album,* would be best donated to charity—a church rummage sale, perhaps, to save the cost of shipping it to one of the stamp charities.

Another woman had a soldier's letters home, or in any event the envelopes they'd come in. The letters themselves had disappeared, and she had no idea who the sender might be, or the recipient, either; they'd turned up, carefully wrapped in oilcloth, when her husband had taken down a wall to enlarge their kitchen.

The letters, an even dozen of them, had been posted from Germany in the immediate aftermath of World War II, and bore stamps issued by the Allied Military Government. The stamps were common, but the covers were interesting, and Keller's offer of $20 for the lot was accepted.

It was also high, as he found out when he emailed a couple

of scans to an eBay dealer who did a lot with covers. The man's offer was $1.50 a cover, $2 less than Keller had paid for the material, and he'd have the trouble and expense of mailing them to upstate New York.

He mailed them off, took the loss. He could have kept them, but this way he'd recorded another transaction for his sideline.

Bread upon the waters, but nothing much to show for it, and when the calls stopped coming he more or less forgot about Edith Vass Ricks.

And then he heard from the woman in Cheyenne.

THIRTY-FIVE

Keller packed everything he needed in a wheeled case that was well within the airline's limits for a carry-on. He checked it anyway, because he didn't want some zealous security officer to confiscate his stamp tongs.

Which seemed unlikely, but Keller had known it to happen. A perfin and precancel collector he'd met at a show had told him about it, how the woman from Homeland Security had glared at his tongs as if they were an AK-47. "Look at this," she'd said, holding them aloft. "Five, six inches long! Made of steel! You could put somebody's eye out with these!"

"I extended my index finger," the man told Keller, "and I was just about to point out how easily I could use it to gouge her eye out, but something stopped me."

"Just as well, I'd say."

"Oh, I know. I'd be awaiting trial even as we speak. But can you imagine taking a man's tongs from him? That particular pair didn't even have pointed tips, I want you to know. Rounded, so you couldn't stab yourself by accident."

Or even on purpose, Keller thought, packing two pairs of tongs (one with rounded tips, the other with tips just made for stabbing) and two magnifiers and, of course, his catalog. He checked his bag straight through to Cheyenne, and boarded his flight to Denver with his laptop in a padded briefcase and his cash in a money belt around his waist.

The airport in Denver had a free wi-fi connection, so he logged on and checked his email. He'd been outbid in an eBay auction, and the email invited him to raise his bid and win the lot after all. But of course the other bidder had waited until the last minute to top him, so the auction was over by the time Keller received the invitation.

Not that he'd have bothered anyway. He always bid his maximum at the beginning, and if someone else was willing to outbid him, then that person wanted it more than he did. He'd explained as much to Julia once, and she'd told him his attitude was remarkably mature. He still hadn't decided whether she was being ironic.

He thought of killing time at a couple of favorite sites, but decided to save his battery instead. He logged off and carried his briefcase to the men's room, where he locked himself in a stall and took out the envelope Dot had sent. It held a pink ruled index card with one side blank and a name and address and phone number on the other.

He'd memorized that information earlier, and had considered destroying the index card afterward, but dismissed the notion as stupid. He'd also considered copying the data into a computer file, and decided that would be even stupider. For now the man whose name was on the card was alive and well, and that meant there was no risk in having the card in his possession. If something happened to the fellow, then something would happen to the card as well. You could get rid of an index card, you could burn it or shred it or chew it up and swallow it, but once it was on a computer it had eternal life.

The envelope also contained two small photographs, which Keller could only assume were of the same man. One was taken from the side, and showed him walking along a street, with a shoe repair shop behind him. The other was full-face, and had probably been taken at fairly close range and with a flash, because it had caught the subject blinking. If the subject had any strong features, neither photograph had managed to capture them. You couldn't use them to make an ID, just to rule out other fish that might turn up in the net.

Keller, who hadn't needed to use the toilet, flushed it anyway in the interests of verisimilitude. The rushing water proved a stimulus, and he used the toilet after all, and then flushed it again, which was rather more verisimilitude than the occasion would seem to require. Way more, he found upon exiting the stall, as he seemed to be the only person in the restroom.

He walked away, frowning.

His Cheyenne flight was on a regional carrier, and the plane was a small one, with minimal capacity for overhead luggage storage. Most of the passengers had to check their putative carry-ons at the gate, and Keller, who'd checked his all the way through, felt he was ahead of the game.

The pilot spent most of the hour apologizing for the rough air, which didn't seem all that rough to Keller. The landing was certainly smooth enough. He collected his bag, picked up the car Hertz had waiting for him. It was a perky little Toyota, slate blue in color, and it had a GPS system, but Keller didn't have an address to program into it, so he just followed the signs to the motel strip on West Lincolnway. Ten or a dozen of them huddled there, like cattle bracing against a storm, and he passed three for no particular reason before pulling into a La Quinta.

It seemed to him he'd stayed at a La Quinta not too long ago, but he couldn't remember where, or whether he'd liked it. He tried phrases in his mind: *Oh, La Quinta, that was the nice clean one. Oh, La Quinta, with the moldy carpet.* One seemed as likely as the other, and what difference did it make? If this one had a moldy carpet, or a flickering TV, or a bad smell, well, he'd go to the one next door.

The woman behind the desk had an easy manner that inspired confidence, and the room she gave him was perfectly acceptable. He unpacked, shifting his stamp tongs to his breast pocket.

His cell phone got a signal right away. His first call was to Julia, just to let her know he'd survived a couple of hours in the air. She didn't offer to put Jenny on, nor did he ask. He was working, and that part of his life could wait until the job was done.

He made a second call, to Denia Soderling, who immediately invited him to dinner. There was enough for two, she said, if he hadn't eaten. He said he was tired, which was true enough, and that it would be better to start fresh in the morning. He wrote down the directions she gave him, and they agreed that he'd show up around nine thirty or ten.

He ate across the street, at a family restaurant that proclaimed itself locally owned and operated. He had shrimp in a basket, which didn't strike him as all that local, and a small garden salad, and drank a glass of iced tea. The menu promised him unlimited refills on the iced tea, but one glass was plenty.

Back in his room, he took a shower and decided his shave could wait until morning. The TV had a satellite connection, and got what seemed to be an infinite number of channels. He put on CNN while he booted up his laptop and checked his email. No email of note, and no news he cared about. He turned everything off and went to bed.

Ten hours later he was eating breakfast down the street at Denny's. An hour and a half after that he was looking at stamps.

THIRTY-SIX

The first thing that struck Keller, when Denia Soderling showed him into her husband's den, was that no one could have designed a better room for a stamp collector. Walls paneled in knotty cedar, half a dozen rifles and shotguns in a glass-fronted cabinet, a pair of swords crossed on one wall, a matched pair of dueling pistols to their right. A picture window opened onto a rail-fenced paddock, where a pair of horses as well matched as the pistols stood enjoying the morning sun. And the window faced north, Keller saw, so the sun wouldn't come into the room and cause trouble.

One of a pair of glass-fronted bookcases held books unrelated to stamp collecting, most of them history, along with a dictionary of quotations and a few volumes of poetry. The other case contained the owner's philatelic library. There was a full set of the Scott catalogs, each volume two or three years old, and there were other catalogs as well, Michel and Yvert and Gibbons and more. And the shelves were filled with books and pamphlets on one stamp-related subject or another. The majority dealt with European nations and their colonies, but Keller spotted Michael Laurence's study of the ten-cent covers of 1869. He'd almost bought the book himself, even though he didn't collect U.S. issues and had no real interest in the subject. J. S. Soderling had evidently had the same impulse, and acted on it.

The second thing Keller realized, and he did so even as he was looking around and taking everything in, was that it shouldn't have been necessary for him to check his carry-on bag. Bringing his own tongs to a room like this had to be right up there with carrying coals to Newcastle.

He confirmed this when he opened the bookcases where the stamp albums were housed. One shelf held the tools of the well-equipped philatelist, and Soderling had equipped himself fully. There were magnifiers and watermark detectors and guillotine-style mount cutters and, not surprisingly, an even dozen pairs of tongs. There were tongs with pointed tips, with blunt tips, with spade-shaped tips, with rounded tips. There were tongs with angled tips, for getting at otherwise inaccessible stamps, and tongs with their arms angled in the middle, which no doubt made them particularly well suited for some special purpose, although Keller couldn't think what it might be.

And then there were the stamps. The albums stood up in rows—France and Colonies, Portugal and Colonies, Italy and Colonies, Germany and Colonies. Russia. Eastern Europe. No U.S. that he could see, and no British Empire, and no Latin America, either. No Asia or Africa, aside from the colonial issues. But all of continental Europe was there, from Iceland

and Denmark clear across to Russia and Turkey, and the albums filled two large bookcases. Most of them were from the Scott Specialized series, but there were leather-bound stock books as well, and blank albums.

"It's overwhelming," Denia Soderling said, and Keller was surprised to realize she was in the room with him. They'd entered it together, but he'd been so transported by the room and its contents that he'd lost track of her. But there she was, a tall and slender woman with just a touch of gray in her dark hair.

"It's quite a room," Keller said.

"Jeb loved it. If he wasn't at the desk working on his stamps he'd be in the leather chair with his feet up, reading about some battle in the Thirty Years' War. Or the Hundred Years' War, I'm afraid I can never keep them straight."

"One was longer."

"Once a war lasts thirty years," she said, "I can't see that another seventy would make much of a difference. I can't tell you how many times I've come into this room since Jeb passed. I can't keep from coming in, and I can't make myself stay for more than a few minutes. Do you know what I mean?"

He nodded.

"I tried to look at the stamps. And I thought he might have left a letter for me, telling me what to do with them. I couldn't find anything. And of course there were all those letters from all those dealers. Overwhelming, all of it."

"I can imagine."

"Now you're going to want to spend some time just looking, aren't you? And you don't need me watching over your shoulder, and frankly I'd just as soon not spend any more time in this room than I have to. In fact, I think I'll go out and ride for an hour. I try to ride every day. I think it's good for me, physically and emotionally, and I know it's good for the horses."

Keller voiced his agreement without being at all certain what he was agreeing with. Her words had washed over him without entirely registering. Something was evidently good for the horses, and it seemed safe to be in favor of it.

He carried the first volume of Portugal and Colonies to the desk and opened it.

At one point the door opened, although he never heard it. Then she was at his side, announcing that she'd brought him a cup of coffee. It was black, she said, but if he took cream or sugar—

He told her black was fine. She told him to let her know when he was ready for a lunch break, and he said he would.

She withdrew, leaving the coffee where he could reach it but far enough away so he'd be unlikely to knock it over. Well, she'd probably brought coffee to her husband in similar circumstances. She'd had plenty of time to work out just where to put the cup.

And coffee was just the ticket. He could use a cup of coffee, no question about it.

First, though—

By the time he reached for the coffee, it was cold.

"Are you sure you won't have another sandwich, Mr. Edwards?"

"No, I'm fine," he said.

She'd served him lunch at a glass-topped table on the back patio, where the view was the same as the one from the stamp room's window. The two horses were keeping each other company in the paddock. Both were chestnut geldings, and wonderfully gentle, she'd told him, and added that she'd been out for an hour on the one with the star on his forehead. And did he ride, by any chance?

He shook his head. "Stamps keep me busy," he said.

"They certainly kept Jeb busy," she said, "although he was always eager to spend plenty of time in the saddle." The double entendre was clearly unintentional, and she colored when she realized what she'd said. Keller, who'd been about to suggest she call him Nicholas, decided they'd be better off staying with Mr. Edwards and Mrs. Soderling for the time being.

He said, "About the stamps."

"Yes."

"Do you have any sense of what you'd like to get for them?"

"Well, as much as I can."

"Of course."

"I know Jeb put a good deal of money into his collections. His line of business was quite volatile, he had interests in oil and cattle and real estate, so we'd be rich one day and broke the next and rich again the day after. When there was plenty of money he'd buy stamps, and when his cash flow tightened up he'd bide his time."

"Did he keep records of what he spent?"

"I don't believe so. He got a lot of his income in the form of cash, so he preferred to pay for his stamps that way. Something to do with taxes, I suppose."

And the nonpayment thereof, Keller thought.

"He said stamps were an investment, that the better ones would go up in value. But he also said it wasn't like the stock market, that you couldn't expect to get close to retail when you sold. And there was one time when he talked about selling."

"Oh?"

"When the market crashed a few years ago. 'Maybe I'll sell

the stamps,' he said. 'That'd keep us going a while, anyway.' But I don't think he was serious, and nothing ever came of it. You asked me if I had any idea what they're worth. I don't, not really, but I would think it would come to six figures, wouldn't you?"

He took a moment before answering. Then he said, "I could make a phone call right now, and move some money into my checking account. And then I could write you a check for a quarter of a million dollars. I'd be running a certain risk, because there are rare stamps that haven't been authenticated by experts, and they might or might not turn out to be genuine. It's a chance I'm prepared to take. But I don't think it would be the best deal for you."

"Because it might be worth more."

"Possibly a great deal more," he said. "I only collect stamps up to 1940, and your husband's collections go all the way to the present. The modern material's out of my area of expertise. And in some of his collections, Russia in particular, there's a ton of specialized material, imperfs and errors and other varieties."

"He had no use for the Russians," she said, "but he liked their stamps."

"Well," he said. "The point is I can make you that offer, but I'd advise you to turn it down. If this were a much smaller collection I'd take it on consignment, giving you an advance and a share in whatever I received over a certain figure. But that's not really good, either."

There was still some iced tea in his glass, and he took a drink of it. "Here's what I'd propose," he said. "I'll act as your agent, and I'll call the three dealers most likely to be ideal purchasers of your husband's stamps. I'll make appointments for them each to send a representative within the next week.

Ideally we'll have them here on three consecutive days, and we'll get sealed bids from each of them, and the high bidder gets the collection."

"And they'll all be able to get someone here on the day you specify?"

"If any of them can't," he said, "I'll call the next name on the list."

"And you think one of them will pay significantly more than a quarter of a million dollars."

"Yes."

"As to how much more—"

"I'd be guessing."

"I understand. But that guess would be at least a half a million?"

"Probably more."

She thought for a moment. "And if their offers turn out to be lower than you expect—"

"That won't happen. But if it does, yes, I'll still pay you the quarter million."

"And you'll be here when they come?"

"To protect your interests. Yes."

"And what about your own interest, Mr. Edwards? You'll be stuck in Cheyenne for a week, and of course you'll be entitled to a portion of the price I receive, but do you have a figure in mind?"

THIRTY-SEVEN

Getting from Cheyenne to Denver was simple enough. You got on I-25 and drove south for a hundred miles, and if it took you more than an hour and a half you weren't keeping up with the light Saturday morning traffic. He held the Toyota steady at four or five miles over the posted speed limit, thus inviting neither the attention of a highway patrolman nor the scorn of his fellow motorists.

He'd programmed the GPS with the address from the pink index card, and its soothing ladylike voice didn't have much to say for most of the way on the interstate. She perked up as they got close to Denver, and guided him southwest on I-76 to where that highway ran into I-70. There he let her talk him through a complicated cloverleaf ("Prepare to keep to the left, followed by a keep to the left...") that left him heading south on Wadsworth Boulevard.

He went on doing as instructed, until he made a turn into

Otis Drive and she told him, not without a measure of self-satisfaction, "You have arrived."

He hadn't quite, though. Not yet, because the street number of the house to his right, conveniently painted on the curb, was 4101, and the number he'd punched into the GPS was 4132. That would put it halfway up the block and on the left-hand side.

Where there were a couple of cars parked, two of them with flashing lights mounted on their roofs. And where all those people were standing.

And where the house, on the other hand, was not.

"You hear about houses burning to the ground," he told Dot, "but I always thought it was a figure of speech, because they never do. They burn, all right, and the property winds up being a total loss, but you still have walls standing."

"But not this time?"

"Burned to the foundation," he said, "which extended maybe a foot and a half above the ground, but that's it. Don't ask me how it happened."

"Keller, who else am I gonna ask?"

He and Dot had cell phones that they used only to call each other, and even then only when it was important that no record of the call exist. He'd had that phone with him, but waited until he'd driven a mile or so from what used to be 4132 Otis Drive. He pulled into a strip mall and parked in front of a furniture store that had closed for the night, if not forever, and he called the one number the phone was programmed to call, and she picked up midway through the second ring.

And now he held the phone in his hand and stared at it.

"Keller? Where'd you go?"

"You thought I did it," he said.

"Well, sure. I gave you a name and an address."

"And a picture and a phone number."

"Let's just stick to the name and the address, okay? I gave them to you, and sometime last night the address ceased to exist and the name wound up in the hospital."

"And you assumed I was responsible."

"Put yourself in my place, Keller. What would you have thought?"

"But to burn down a whole house?"

"I know, it's like that essay everybody had to read in high school, burning down the house to roast the pig. I forget who wrote it."

"Charles Lamb."

"Now how would you happen to know that, Keller? Don't tell me, I'll bet he's on a stamp. Do you suppose there's an alternate universe where Charles Pigg wrote a famous essay about lamb chops?"

"Uh..."

"Never mind. I thought it was pretty heavy-handed for you, not your usual style. Collateral damage and all that. Though the collateral damage could have been a lot worse. Two kids, and thank God it was Friday."

"Friday?"

"No school on Saturday, so they were both away from the house on sleepovers. Keller, you're right there in Denver and I'm filling you in from what I skimmed off the Internet. Here's a radical idea. Why don't you pick up a newspaper and call me back when you're up to speed?"

He bought the *Denver Post* from a convenience store clerk who seemed anxious that Keller was about to hold her up, and relieved when he didn't. The story wasn't hard to find, and he read it through twice and called Dot.

"Severe injuries," he said. "But he's expected to live."

"For now," Dot said.

"He had fish tanks," he said. "Aquariums, except I guess the plural is aquaria."

"Thanks for pointing that out."

"All destroyed, of course. His wife was away when it happened."

"That'd be Joanne."

"Joanne Hudepohl, right. She's described as distraught."

"There's a surprise. Your house is gone, fish tanks and all, and your husband's in the hospital with tubes coming out of his toes. Wouldn't you be distraught?"

"I suppose."

"Unless she did it," Dot said. "That's what you're thinking, isn't it? And it's what I'd have been thinking myself if I hadn't pretty much taken it for granted that you were the one who did it. She was out chauffeuring the kids to their sleepovers, wasn't she?"

"She dropped off her son first," he said, "and when she delivered her daughter, the other mommy invited her in. And there were two other mommies on hand, as it was a four-girl sleepover."

"How old were the daughters?"

"I don't know," he said. "What difference does it make?"

"None," she said, "only it's beginning to sound like a movie they were showing on cable the other night. Except those girls were college age, and they should have been ashamed of themselves. What did the four mommies do, break out the gin bottle?"

"I think it was wine. At some point she called her husband,

and he told her to stay as long as she wanted because he was busy with his fish."

"I suppose he was pasting them in an album," she said, "like you and your stamps."

"She called home before she left," he said, "but when he didn't answer she assumed he was asleep. Then she drove home in time to watch the firemen at work. They'd taken him to the hospital by then."

"So her alibi's solid."

"It looks that way."

"Just good luck that she wasn't home herself when everything went pear-shaped."

"Pear-shaped?"

"I've been watching English mysteries on the BBC," she said. "And once in a while an expression creeps into my speech. She wasn't home, and neither were the kids. Just her husband."

"And the fish."

"Collateral damage," she said. "Innocent byswimmers. It's awfully damn convenient for her, isn't it?"

"It does look that way."

"Not that she did it, but that she had it done. I suppose the same possibility might occur to the cops."

"You'd think so."

"And they'll ask her a couple of questions, and she'll fall apart."

"Amateurs generally do."

"Is she our client, Dot?"

"I think she's got to be somebody's client," she said, "but I don't know if she's ours or not. The job came from a broker who got it from a cutout, and there are too many levels for anybody to get through. There's no way she can implicate us, in case that's what you were wondering."

"The question did come to mind."

"We're clear," she said, "and why shouldn't we be? You didn't do it."

"No."

"So what you can do now," she said, "is catch the next plane back to Julia and Jenny. If the Fish Whisperer recovers, I'll tell my guy that we're keeping the advance payment and washing our hands of the whole business."

"And if he dies?"

"Then I ask for the second payment. Why not? Who's gonna prove you didn't do it, or sub it out to somebody?"

"So there's nothing I have to do?"

"Like what? Put on a white coat and hang a stethoscope around your neck? And sneak past hospital security so you can punch the guy's ticket? He ceased to be our problem when his house went up in flames."

"I guess you're right."

"Of course I'm right. Go home, Keller."

"Well," he said, "I can't. Not for a while."

Back in his room at La Quinta, Keller took a long hot shower. When he was done drying off, he tossed his towel on the floor of the shower stall.

That's what the little card told you to do, but it was hard for Keller to get used to it. If you returned your towels to the rack, that meant you wanted to use them again. If you felt fresh towels might be a good idea, you were supposed to throw them on the floor. This would save water, the management explained, and fight global warming, so Keller figured it was the least he could do.

But he couldn't throw a towel on the floor without imagining the look on his mother's face.

He got into bed, letting his mind conjure up a conversation with his long-gone mother. They hadn't had many conversations during her lifetime, and Keller had since wondered if the woman might not have been suffering from some degree of mental illness or impairment, but on balance she'd certainly been a good mother to him, and there were times when he regretted the talks they hadn't had. So he had them now occasionally, when he waited for sleep to overtake him.

They began by talking about the towel, and why he'd thrown it on the floor. *Well, if that's what they want you to do,* she said, *that's a different story. But I didn't bring you up that way.*

And then they were talking about Denia Soderling and her husband's stamps. He'd be in Cheyenne for most of the week, he told his mother, because he'd booked appointments with three dealers who'd be sending buyers to the Soderling home on three successive days, starting Monday. That gave him all day tomorrow to go through the albums and pick out the stamps he wanted as his commission.

My stars, Johnny. You've gone clear across the country to spend a week in the middle of nowhere, and all you're getting for your trouble is some stamps?

He tried to explain, but his mother wasn't having any. *If I sent you to town to sell our cow,* she said, *I swear you'd come home with a handful of magic beans. You remember that story? You used to love that story, and I used to love telling it to you, but I never for a moment thought you'd take it as gospel.*

It had struck Denia Soderling as a perfectly reasonable solution, and it even seemed to make sense to Dot, although she'd have been just as happy to see him back home in Louisiana. But why couldn't his mother seem to grasp it? He marshaled his facts and restated his arguments, and the next thing he knew it was morning.

THIRTY-EIGHT

Denia Soderling must have heard him pull into the drive, because she met him at the front door with a cup of coffee. "I know you want to get right to work on the stamps," she told him.

He set himself up in the stamp room, with a pad and pencil close at hand, along with his tongs and a box of small glassine envelopes. And he'd brought his own Scott Classic catalog along; he used it not only as a price guide but as a checklist, circling the number of each new acquisition, so that it served as a full inventory of his collection.

The bookcase full of albums was daunting, but you had to start somewhere, and he began with Italy and Colonies. He opened it to the Italian Aegean Islands. But for stamp collecting, Keller figured he wouldn't know a thing about the Turco-Italian War of 1911–12, which ended with Italy in control of three provinces in Libya and thirteen islands in the

Aegean Sea. The largest island was Rhodes, which he figured most people had probably heard of, though they might have trouble finding it on a map. The others were Calchi, Calino, Caso, and Coo, Lero, Lisso, and Nisiro, Patmo and Piscopi, and Scarpanto, Simi, and Stampalia, and it had taken many hours at his desk to enable Keller to reel them off like that.

Turkey officially ceded the islands to Italy in 1924, under the Treaty of Lausanne, but as early as 1912 the Italians had begun overprinting stamps for use there, and each island had its own stamps. One island's stamps looked rather like another's, the overprints constituting the only difference, but Keller liked them, and some of the early issues, though priced at only a few dollars apiece, were virtually impossible to find.

They were well represented in Jeb Soderling's collection. Keller, tongs in hand, went to work, selecting a stamp, slipping it into a glassine envelope, noting its catalog number and price. Calchi 5, $3.25. Calino 4–5, $6.50. Caso, same numbers, same value, and Soderling also had the Caso Garibaldi issue, the only Garibaldi set Keller still needed. Caso 17–26, unused, lightly hinged: $170.

And so on.

There was a moment when he sensed Denia Soderling's presence in the room, but by the time he looked up she was gone, and a fresh cup of coffee had replaced the empty one. He was working his way through French Colonial issues by then, and got all the way to an early overprinted issue from Gabon, when she returned to ask if he'd like to break for lunch.

"In a few minutes," he said, without raising his eyes from the stamp. Then he forgot about her, and about lunch, and the next thing he knew the door had opened and closed again, just barely registering on his consciousness, and there was a tray at the far end of the desk holding a plate of sandwiches and a glass of iced tea.

He forced himself to take a break, ate the sandwiches, drank the iced tea. Away from the stamps, even for the short time he spent eating his lunch, his mind returned to the burned-out suburban home a hundred miles to the south. He'd caught a Denver newscast on the motel's TV before breakfast, read a morning paper while he ate his breakfast, and as far as he could make out the situation was essentially unchanged. Richard Hudepohl remained in critical condition, a fire department spokesman attributed the fire's rapid devastation to the use of "multiple accelerants strategically deployed," and Joanne Hudepohl, having released a statement through an attorney, seemed to have lawyered up.

No concern of his, Keller assured himself. It was impossible to keep from thinking about it, but there was nothing to do about it, and it vanished from his mind the moment he returned to the stamps.

It was hard to know when to stop. Jeb Soderling's collection had no end of stamps lacking in Keller's, but it wasn't his intention to go through it like locusts through a field of barley. He worked diligently, keeping a running tally as he went along.

At one point he looked over at the window and was surprised to note that day had apparently turned to night. He hadn't glanced at his watch, and didn't do so now. He told himself it was time he got out of there, but first there was one more album he ought to have a look at…

By the time he emerged from the stamp room, it was almost ten o'clock. He was pretty sure Denny's would be open, not that he felt much like eating.

But the dining room table was set for two, and before he knew it she had steered him to a chair and suggested he pour the wine. While he filled their glasses from the opened bottle of California Cabernet, she brought their dinner to the table—a tossed salad in a large wooden bowl, a pot of chili.

He'd been ready to apologize for his lack of appetite, but once he got a whiff of the chili he had nothing to apologize for. He polished off one bowl and let himself be talked into another.

"I know beer's the natural accompaniment to chili," she said, "but my husband preferred wine. He said a full-bodied red transported the dish from a West Texas juke joint to a three-star restaurant."

"It's great chili," Keller said.

"The secret's the cumin," she said, "except it's not much of a secret, because you can smell it, can't you? But there is a secret. Would you like to know what it is?"

"Sure."

"Coffee. Leftover coffee, although I suppose you could make a pot for the occasion if you didn't have any left over. You simmer the beans in it. You can't taste it, can you? I can't, not even if I know it's there. But it *is* there, and it makes all the difference."

Over coffee—in china cups, not in their chili—he told her that he'd finished selecting the stamps that would constitute his commission on the sale. He estimated the fair market value of what he'd picked out at around $50,000, though of course the book value was a good deal higher than that.

The stamps, he added, were in the shoe box she'd given him that morning. And the box would remain in the stamp room until it was time for him to take it back to New Orleans.

"Of course," she said. "It wouldn't be safe to leave it in your motel room."

Keller supposed that was true enough, although he hadn't even thought of that aspect of it. The stamps weren't his yet, and wouldn't be until the rest of the collection was sold.

"And that brings up another question," she said. "We'll have a stamp dealer here on each of the next three days, and I don't suppose they'll breeze in, flip through albums for half an hour, and breeze out again."

Keller agreed that it would take each dealer the better part of a day.

"And you'll be here while they are? Not that I wouldn't be safe, but—"

"Whenever somebody's looking at the stamps," he said, "I'll be in the room with him."

"Today's Sunday, so Monday Tuesday Wednesday, and then you'd fly back on Thursday."

He nodded. He'd booked his flight as soon as he'd confirmed the appointments with the three dealers.

"Well, isn't it a nuisance having to drive back and forth each day? Not to mention the waste of money? I'm sure the guest-room bed is at least as comfortable as you'd get in a motel room, and the coffee's better. I would think you'd get more rest without the traffic noise, too. You could stay here tonight, as late as it is, and tomorrow you could fetch your things and check out of your room. Doesn't that make sense?"

THIRTY-NINE

Keller, back at La Quinta, heard the phone ring once as he emerged from the shower. When it didn't ring a second time, he reached for a towel and dried off, then found his cell phone on the dresser. It was turned off, so he turned it on to find out who'd called. There weren't any calls, and even if there had been, how could he have heard the ring if the phone was turned off?

He picked up the room phone and rang the front desk, where a man who sounded as though he had better things to do informed him there had been no calls to his room. Keller hung up and worked on the puzzle for a moment before he remembered he had another phone, the one he used only for conversations with Dot.

But that phone often went unused for weeks on end, and he kept it turned off unless he was expecting a call or had one to make. Where was it, anyway?

He couldn't seem to find it, and decided that was ridiculous, because he knew it was here, in this small room. Hadn't he just heard it ring?

If it rang once, it could ring again, and couldn't he make that happen? All he had to do was use his other phone to call his own number.

But he couldn't do that, he realized when he had his regular phone in hand, his thumb poised over the numbers. Because, of course, he didn't know his own number, and had never added it to his speed dial. Why would he? He never had occasion to call it himself, or to give it out to others. Only Dot used it, and only for calls that had to be kept private.

So much for that shortcut. He had a phone he couldn't locate, and it was somewhere within earshot, but he couldn't make the damn thing ring. All he could do was keep looking for it, knowing it was there, drawing precious little joy from the knowledge, and wishing it would ring.

It rang.

And, of course, there it was on the desk, invisible beneath a complimentary copy of *Cheyenne This Week,* which he'd picked up and paged through and tossed aside earlier. Evidently he'd tossed it right on top of his phone, but it had landed in such a way that it looked to be lying flat, an illusion that the ringtone instantly dispelled.

"Hello," he said.

"Well, hello yourself," Dot said. "Are you all right? You sound as though you just ran up three flights of stairs."

"I'm fine."

"Whatever you say, Pablo."

Pablo?

"You're still there, right? Counting stamps?"

"I'm here, but I'm not counting anything."

"Not even your blessings? Well, whatever you do with stamps. I don't suppose you lick them, but then neither does anybody else these days, not since the Post Office switched from lick-and-stick to whatever they call the new ones."

"Self-adhesive."

"Catchy. When's the last time you actually licked a stamp, Pablo?"

He did so whenever he had a letter to mail, but Dot didn't need to hear about discount postage. "It's been a while," he said, "but why are you calling me Pablo?"

"To keep from calling you by name."

"Oh."

"It's reflexive," she said. "I have this habit of calling you by name, using your name the way other people use commas. Not your new name. The old one, the one that's one silly little vowel away from your occupation."

Huh?

"I guess there's nobody who calls you that anymore, is there?"

Julia did, sometimes. She'd known him before he'd picked the name Nicholas Edwards off a child's tombstone, and like everyone else she'd called him by his last name, Keller. She never slipped and called him Keller in front of other people, and he didn't think Jenny had ever heard the name spoken, but when they were making love, or when she was in the mood to make love, all at once he was Keller again.

But less so lately. Subtly, gradually, Nicholas was displacing Keller in the romance department, edging him out in the bedroom...

"Hence Pablo," Dot said. "If you hate it I can probably come up with something else. I just always liked the name."

"Pablo."

"You hate it, don't you?"

"It's fine. Is that why you called? To see if I liked being called Pablo?"

"No, I just wanted to check in. I guess you've been keeping busy with stamps."

"Pretty much."

"Well, it's not as though you missed anything. Richard Hudepohl's still got a pulse, and nobody knows who burned his house down with him in it."

"The wife hasn't talked?"

"She hasn't," Dot said, "and I have to say I don't blame her. I've been thinking about her."

"Oh?"

"I think she's our client."

"Isn't that what we said the other day?"

"Not exactly, because at the time I thought she'd set it all up. Took the kids, left the house, and made sure she stayed away until the deed was done."

"Makes sense."

"It does," she said, "except it doesn't. Pablo, she hasn't got a thing to wear."

"Huh?"

"What woman gets someone to burn down her house with all her clothes in it? That might seem like a good idea to Charles Lamb, but I bet Mrs. Lamb would see it differently. Mrs. Hudepohl, the good news is that your husband is dead. The bad news is your fifty pairs of shoes are history."

"She had fifty pairs of shoes?"

"If she did, Pablo, she doesn't anymore. And her husband's not even dead."

He thought about it. "All right," he said. "She hired us, but while I was taking my time, somebody else went ahead and did the job. Who?"

"Suppose we just call him the other guy."

"Okay. Who hired the other guy?"

"I don't know," she said. "I know the wife didn't, and she's pissed."

"Pissed."

"Royally. I got a call from somebody who got a call from somebody who got a call from her. I know, it sounds like a bad song. The way she sees it, whoever burned her house down has to be the stupidest, craziest, most amateurish moron in the business."

"Well," Keller said, "I have to say I agree with her on that one."

"It's a pretty good description of our friend the other guy, isn't it? I passed the word that it wasn't us, so either one of the sub-brokers made more than one phone call—"

"Or someone else had the same idea she did. Are we sure she didn't make arrangements with some joker she met in a bar, then call in a pro when she figured he wouldn't go through with it?"

Dot was silent.

"And he went through with it after all? Except burning down the house that way called for some expert knowledge, wouldn't you say? I certainly wouldn't have known how to do it."

"You wouldn't have done it in the first place."

"Well, there's that. Still, does it sound like the work of some tattooed joker that you'd find on the Internet and meet in a bar?"

"Or find in a bar," she said, "and meet on the Internet. I've got some calls in, Pablo, and I think I might make a few more.

On the one hand, what do we care? Nobody's asking us to give back the first payment, and there's no way to earn the balance, so for us the war is over. Even so…"

"It'd be good to know."

"It would," she agreed. "I'll be in touch. You're with the Stamp Widow tomorrow? Keep your phone handy."

FORTY

The first stamp buyer was due at ten thirty, so Keller had a quick breakfast at Denny's, read the Denver paper's coverage of the Hudepohl case, and got to the Soderling house a little before ten. He wanted to make sure the fellow didn't get there first.

The previous evening, when Mrs. Soderling proposed he stay the night and check out of his motel in the morning, he'd invented a reason why that wasn't a good idea, some work he needed to do that very night on his computer. This morning, after his shower and shave, he packed up everything and stowed his bag in the Toyota's trunk.

But he kept the room, and even left the DO NOT DISTURB sign on the knob so the maid wouldn't assume he'd left early. Just keeping his options open, he told himself.

"I was up early," he told Denia Soderling. "I'm afraid I've already had my breakfast."

"But I'll bet you can manage another cup of coffee," she said. And he agreed that he could.

They sat together at an outdoor table, and quite out of the blue she began talking about the Hudepohl case. Had he been following it? He said he hadn't, which eliminated the possibility that he might disclose something that hadn't made the papers, but led her to furnish a full account of everything that had.

"That poor woman," she said. "She's lucky to be alive."

"If she'd been home—"

"Exactly! And her children. They seem quite certain it's arson, but you have to wonder."

"I guess you do."

"He kept tropical fish, didn't he? I wonder if there might have been chemicals involved. Spontaneous combustion, you know."

She topped up his cup of coffee, and when she put the pot down her hand brushed his. It might have been accidental, he told himself. Just like the fire on Otis Drive.

The stamp buyer, whose name was either Griffin or Griffith, was a short and slender man who wore a red-and-black striped vest with a black pinstripe suit. He had a narrow face, a sharp nose and sharper chin, and a full head of lustrous auburn hair, so full and so lustrous Keller was reasonably certain it was a wig. He looked as though he ought to be dealing blackjack in a casino, or touting horses at a track, and he bolstered this image when he hung his suit jacket over the back of his chair. The more you saw of his vest, the more it held your attention.

Then, as he seated himself at Jeb Soderling's stamp table, he completed the picture with a green eyeshade. He'd turned down the offered coffee, shook off the suggestion of tea or water, and drew a pair of tongs from one vest pocket and a magnifier from another.

"Europe," he said.

His voice was soft, and if he'd been a stage actor he'd have been inaudible past the first row. Keller, sitting just across the table from him, had to work to hear him.

"From Iceland to Turkey," Keller said.

"Actually," the man said, "there's some question as to whether Iceland is in fact a part of Europe. There's a geological fault line that runs right through the country. One side's Europe, other's North America. Philatelically, of course, it's grouped with the Scandinavian countries. I don't remember your name."

"Edwards."

"Edwards. Are you planning on sitting here the whole time? Because once I begin I won't want to talk, and I won't want to be talked to, either. I assure you I'm perfectly comfortable sitting alone with the collection."

"I'll stay," Keller told him.

The man didn't say anything. Neither did Keller, and eventually the man let himself be outwaited. He drew a breath and let it out without quite sighing.

"There are approximately a third of a million Icelanders," he said, as softly as he said everything, "and they are all descended from five Viking men and four Irish women. If you're going to stay here, you might as well bring me some albums."

Keller got to his feet.

"Not Iceland," the man said, answering a question Keller had not been about to ask. "France. I'll begin with France."

* * *

When he left his motel that morning, he'd set his phone—the one reserved for calls to and from Dot, the one he was already thinking of as the Pablo phone—on vibrate. He'd never done that before, and when a call actually came in it took him a moment to realize what it was. A strange sensation, really, as if a large centipede were dancing around in his breast pocket.

He withdrew to a corner of the room, pushed the appropriate button, but didn't say anything. Neither did Dot at first, but then she said, "Pablo?"

"Yes," he said, very softly.

"There are people around," Dot said.

"Yes."

"Dangerous people? Or just ears that don't need to hear our conversation?"

"Ears."

"Well, don't put me on speakerphone, okay? I got past a few middlemen. You can forget the moron with the tattoos. Her father was a magazine distributor, dealt with some people who knew some people. Died some years ago, but a while back he introduced her to a guy, then told her he was the man if she needed some heavy lifting done. Long story short, she called the guy. Remember me? I'm Benny's little girl, di dah di dah di dah, and he told her who to call and what to say, and she did and she did. Pablo? Are you still there?"

"Yes."

"Thought I lost you. Did you get all that?"

"Yes."

"I'd love to know what you think about it, but it's hard to get much from a man who never says anything but *yes* and *ears*. But if the other guy wasn't somebody that she found, that opens things up."

"All," Keller said.

"It opens it all up?"

It was frustrating, having to talk like this. The little man with the eyeshade seemed entirely caught up in the task at hand, which had him paging through the Benelux countries. Had he even noticed that Keller was on the phone, and could he possibly be giving any attention to the conversation?

It seemed unlikely, as softly as Keller was talking, and as preoccupied as the man was with the stamps. But anyone who spoke so softly was apt to have acute hearing, Keller figured, and along with his sharp nose and chin the guy had ears like a bat, so how could you be sure?

"Pablo? Where'd you go?"

"Why?"

"Why does it open it up? That's obvious, isn't it? But that's not your question. Why, why, why. Why did she want him hit? Is that it?"

"Yes."

"Good question," she said. "I'll get back to you."

The little man's name turned out to be neither Griffin nor Griffith, but was in fact Griffey, E. J. Griffey. He had shown up at ten thirty on the dot, and was in the stamp room murmuring about Iceland well before eleven. When Denia came into the room around twelve thirty to suggest lunch, he said politely that he'd had a large breakfast and would prefer to work straight through. Then he returned to the album he was examining, and made a note in his little notebook.

Keller stayed in the stamp room and ate the sandwich she brought him. A little before two, Griffey stood up and said something Keller didn't quite catch. He asked him to repeat it, and it turned out to be "bathroom." Keller walked him to the door, pointed him to the room he wanted. Griffey left, and took his notebook with him.

When the door closed behind him, Keller whipped out his phone and called Dot. As soon as she answered he said, "The fire was supposed to kill them both. Maybe the whole family, but let's say the other guy knew about the Friday night sleepovers. What he didn't know was it was going to turn into Girls' Night Out. He thought he'd get Mr. and Mrs. H. Gave her plenty of time to get home, spread his accelerant, set a timer, took off."

"Right."

"You figured all that."

"Pretty much. She hired you, and somebody else hired the other guy. If you'd gotten there first, what do you suppose the other guy would have done?"

"What I'll do," he said. "Go home. Why should we care who did what and why, Dot?"

"We shouldn't."

"And yet we do," he said.

"So it appears. I've got an idea, I'll talk to you—"

"Later," he said, and rang off even as Griffey opened the door.

"A sealed bid," E. J. Griffey said, brandishing an envelope with his firm's name and address in its upper left corner. Collectors of commercial covers called that sort of printed return address a *corner card,* a term that had always struck Keller as curious, a bit of philatelic whimsy, an insistence on employing a vocabulary that was as esoteric as thieves' argot. Covers, corner cards…

"Now I have a suggestion," the little man was saying, his voice a little more forceful though still low in volume. He and Keller had joined Denia Soderling in the parlor, where the three glasses of red wine she'd poured remained untouched. "What I recommend is that you open this envelope now. You'll see a figure which I think will please you, and which I suspect is higher than any other bid you're likely to receive. But if you open the envelope now and accept the bid on the spot as a preemptive offer, thus enabling me to make immediate arrangements for packing and shipping, I'll raise my own bid by ten percent."

He expanded on the subject, countering their objections. The other bidders would be disappointed? Why, this sort of thing happened all the time. They'd get over it.

Keller took the envelope from him, weighed it in his hand as if to assess its contents. "I think we'll stay with the original plan," he said. "Three sealed bids, and we'll open them all at the same time, and the high bid gets the collection."

Griffey started to offer an objection, then took another direction. "Suit yourselves," he said. "I'm confident my bid will turn out to be the high one. When that comes to pass, just remember you could have had ten percent more."

"My turn to make a suggestion," Keller said, and noted with satisfaction the quick flash of surprise on Griffey's face. "Raise your own bid."

"I beg your pardon?"

"You've just established that you're willing to pay ten percent more than the sum you wrote down. That was a nice tactic, but now that it hasn't worked, do you want to risk losing the collection because you didn't submit your highest offer?"

Griffey stared at him for a long moment, and all that

showed on his face was the effort it took to keep it expressionless. Then he snatched the envelope out of Keller's hand and marched into the stamp room with it.

He returned, envelope in hand. "My card's in here," he announced, "along with my firm's bid. I think... well, never mind what I think. I assume you'll open all the bids the day after tomorrow. Please call right away to let us know that our bid was high."

Or that it wasn't, Keller thought, as his hostess showed E. J. Griffey to the door.

FORTY-ONE

Keller's room was on the second floor, just to the left of the staircase. Even as the sound of Griffey's rented car was dying in the distance, she'd said that he'd probably want to freshen up before dinner, and suggested he get his bag from the Toyota. Had he even mentioned that he'd packed and left the motel? Or had she just assumed it?

Either way, here he was in a guest room, with a large four-poster topped by a patchwork quilt. The design, squarely geometric, looked Amish to him, but he didn't know much about quilts. Nor, he supposed, did he know much about stamps, not in comparison to a fellow like E. J. Griffey, who could flip through a few dozen albums in a matter of hours and come up with a professional assessment of their value.

On the other hand, what did E. J. Griffey know about fashioning a length of picture-hanging wire into a garrote?

* * *

After a shower and a change of clothes, Keller got his regular cell phone from his suitcase and called Julia. The brief conversation was ordinary enough, but he felt oddly detached from it. Should he mention that he'd relocated to the Soderling home? It wasn't information she needed, he hadn't bothered to tell her the name of his motel in the first place, but even so...

He called Dot on the Pablo phone. No answer, and after the fourth ring a male voice, computer-generated, invited him to leave a message. He rang off.

"I didn't know what to do while the two of you were in the stamp room," she said. "I would have gone for a ride, but somehow I felt I ought to be here, although I can't think why. So I cooked."

She'd prepared coq au vin. The *coq,* she told him, had grown up a mile and a half away, where he and his flock mates ranged free and enjoyed an organic diet. The *vin* was the same Pommard they were drinking. Jeb had enjoyed establishing a wine cellar, and ordered cases from a wine merchant on New York's Madison Avenue.

She'd changed for dinner. She'd changed the blouse and slacks for a simple black dress that showed a hint of décolletage.

And she was wearing perfume. He caught the scent when she came around behind him to pour his coffee.

"That Mr. Griffey," she said. "There was something very forbidding about that little man. I'd have been at a loss, trying to deal with him on my own. But you handled him brilliantly. You could see it in his face, that he'd been outmaneuvered and didn't know how to respond. And he sat right down and raised his own bid."

"Or didn't," Keller said. "For all we know he came back with the same envelope and never opened it."

"Do you think that's what he did?"

He shook his head. "I nicked the original envelope with my thumbnail," he said, "and the envelope he came back with didn't have the nick."

"How on earth did you think to do that?"

"I don't know," he said, "and I'm not sure it made any difference, but he must have changed his bid, and he certainly wouldn't have lowered it. I wonder how much he raised it."

"What figure do you think he wrote down?"

"I couldn't even guess."

"More than a quarter of a million?"

He nodded.

"So you won't get to buy Jeb's stamps."

"I'm afraid not."

"Should we open the envelope? We could steam it open and reseal it. No one would ever know."

"We could cut it open," he said, "because no one but the two of us will ever see the bids anyway. And they're your stamps, so you get to decide, but I'd rather stick to the script."

"And open them all at once," she said. "Like kids on Christmas? So as not to spoil the surprise?"

He thought about it. "That might be some of it," he admitted, "but I have the sense that we're in a stronger position if we don't know. I can't explain why, but—"

"No one can read our minds," she said, "if there's nothing in them. It's fine with me, Nicholas. I'd rather go with your instincts than mine."

Nicholas.

A few sentences later, almost to make a point, he managed to use her name in conversation. Mrs. Soderling.

"Denia," she said at once. "You're my houseguest now, and my negotiating partner. You can't go on calling me Mrs. Soderling."

"Denia."

"It's an unusual name, I know, but it's better than the one given me at birth. Can you guess?"

He couldn't.

"Gardenia," she said. "Flower names are all right, but some are better than others. Rose and Iris, for instance, are less of a burden than Pansy or, I don't know, Forsythia?"

"I don't think I've ever known a Forsythia."

"Neither have I, but I did know a girl named Dahlia, and that wasn't too bad. My mother wore this overbearing scent called Jungle Gardenia, and evidently it had a profound visceral effect on my father, who bought it for her by the half gallon. And insisted on it for my name. I hated it, and as soon as I was old enough I had it changed legally."

"To Denia."

"Yes, which I like, except for the nuisance of having to explain its derivation. I have a complicated relationship with the scent. I can't imagine wearing it, and I find it slightly sick-making, but at the same time it smells like Mommy, and that means warmth and comfort, doesn't it?"

"It sounds complicated."

"It might be," she said, "but how often do I encounter it? Not once a year, I wouldn't think. Generally speaking, I find things don't have to be all that complicated, Nicholas."

Oh?

"Some more wine? We really ought to finish the bottle."

He covered his glass. "I'm already having trouble keeping my eyes open. It was oddly exhausting, sitting across the table from Mr. E. J. Griffey."

"I can imagine."

"And there's a call I have to make before I turn in."

"To New Orleans?"

To Sedona, but she didn't need to know that. "I spoke to her earlier," he said, "but I like to check in before I call it a day."

"He was having an affair," Dot said. "Why won't you boys learn to keep it in your pants?"

Keller, sitting on the edge of the bed in the guest room, felt the rush of blood to his face.

"Pablo? You there?"

"I'm here."

"Can you talk?"

"I'm the one who called," he reminded her. "I'm in the client's house, but I'm alone."

"You're in the client's—oh, the stamp lady. Not the *client* client."

"Who doesn't have a house in the first place."

"Not anymore. Well, he was having an affair, he had a tootsie on the side, and he wanted a divorce. And he was talking about a custody fight, and bringing up a lot of dirt on her, because she'd had an affair of her own a few years ago, which she regretted and thought they'd gotten past, and now he threw it in her face, and she just wanted him dead, the son of a bitch, and she remembered the man her father introduced her to, and—well, the rest is pretty much the way we figured it."

"Jesus," he said. "You got all this from the broker? From one of the cutout men?"

"No, of course not. She wouldn't spew all of this to some guy, and if she did he'd never pass it on to me."

"Then—"

"She told me. But can we cut to the chase, Pablo? She wants to call it off."

"The client."

"Right."

"Wants to call off—"

"The contract. She wanted us to do something, remember? And now she's changed her mind."

"When did this happen?"

"In his hospital room, seeing him all helpless there with tubes coming out of him. Do you want to know exactly what passed through her mind?"

"Uh—"

"Okay, she's in his room, he's unconscious, nobody's around, and it occurs to her that she can finish the job and no one will be the wiser. Pinch a tube shut, pull one out, pour something in his IV—there's a dozen ways to do it, and she realizes she loves him and she wants him to pull through. I'll spare you the emotional part, that comes under the heading of girl talk, but the bottom line is she loves him again and just wants him to live and be hers."

"Dot—"

"You know, same reason you're Pablo, I ought to be somebody else. You're not as addicted to saying names as I am, but now and then it slips out. How's Hilda?"

"Hilda?"

"If you have to call me something, Pablo, well, Hilda'll do. No, come to think of it, it won't. It's too close to my official name these days. Make it Flora, okay?"

"If you say so. How did she get in touch with you?"

"She didn't, Pablo. I got in touch with her. How? I picked up the phone and called her."

"Who gave out her number?"

"Nobody, but how many Joanne Hudepohls are there? Her cell phone's listed, so I dialed it, and she answered on the first ring. You'd have thought she was waiting for my call."

"What phone did you—"

"Easy there, Pablo. A new phone, bought for cash and unregistered. Same as this one, but just for her. And I got her number via a Google search, and I used a computer in a Kinko's in Flagstaff. There won't be any trail, paper or electronic, and as soon as all of this is over the Joanne phone goes in a storm drain."

"Maybe you should ditch it now."

"I might need to talk to her some more."

He frowned. "Why, for God's sake?"

"Once she got that we didn't burn her house down—"

"She knew somebody else did. And she only made that one call to her father's buddy."

"Right."

"So she knows about the other guy, and that somebody else hired him." He thought for a moment. "The girlfriend?"

"Gotta be. Or the girlfriend's jealous husband."

"The girlfriend's married?"

"That I couldn't tell you. But the girlfriend has to be the connection."

"And the girlfriend, and thus the other guy, might not feel the game is over."

"Right. They might try again. She's hired people from a security agency to protect her husband in the hospital, and she'll keep them on after he's released."

"Assuming he pulls through," he said. "But why do we care?"

"Pablo, that sounds so cold. 'Why do we care?' A man's life

hangs in the balance, and his wife is in peril, and you ask a question like that."

"And if I wait long enough," he said, "maybe you'll answer it."

"Opportunity," she said. "I hear it knocking. Pablo, get some rest. I'll get back to you."

FORTY-TWO

He spent a restless night, got up early, and found coffee poured and breakfast ready when he got downstairs. She said she hoped he liked huevos rancheros, and told him the eggs were from the same organic poultry farm that had supplied last night's free-range cockerel.

"One-stop shopping," she said. "I'd call it a Mexican breakfast, but according to Jeb, a Mexican breakfast is a cigarette and a glass of water. Do you suppose that's an ethnic slur? I suppose I could ask Rosita."

"Rosita?"

"That's right, you haven't met her. She stays out of sight, and she's straightening your room even as we speak. More coffee?"

No perfume this morning, and no décolletage. There'd been something on offer during the dinner hour, and he'd found a way to let it go without giving offense, and he had every reason to feel relieved.

But was it relief that he felt? Not entirely. He'd dodged a bullet, but what he felt was the skimpy self-satisfaction of a dieter who'd passed up dessert.

Martin Rombaugh struck Keller as a man who'd never passed up a dessert in his life, and there was nothing skimpy about his self-satisfaction, or his satisfaction with life in general. He was a big man with a hearty laugh, and he showed up fifteen minutes early for his ten thirty appointment.

"Afraid I'd have trouble finding the place," he said, "and then I didn't. Your directions turned out to be foolproof. Marty Rombaugh, representing Colliard and Bowden, and Lou Colliard specifically asked me to convey his sympathies, Mrs. Soderling. He'd met your husband on several occasions, he'd valued him as a customer, and..."

There was more, but Keller tuned it out. Soon enough they were seated across from each other in the stamp room, but Rombaugh had said yes to coffee, and hadn't protested when a plate of cookies accompanied it. "Homemade," he announced, after a bite. "Have one?"

Once again, Keller passed up dessert.

The hours went more quickly in Rombaugh's company than in Griffey's. The big man paged through albums as rapidly, made notes as cryptically, but kept up a running conversation throughout. He'd been ten when he started collecting stamps, joined a local stamp club where he could trade off his duplicates, decided to specialize in U.S. and took a table at a stamp show to sell off his foreign, spent so much time at a downtown stamp shop that they gave him a job, and had explored many facets of the hobby and business ever since, all of which he was apparently eager to share with his new friend Nicholas.

It could have been tiring for Keller, but he realized early on that he wasn't required to comment. When he did, Rombaugh was happy to engage in the back-and-forth of dialogue, but when Keller remained silent, Rombaugh was just as content to keep up the conversation on his own.

Keller found most of it interesting, and even informative. And, when his attention flagged, he could safely let his mind go elsewhere.

When his phone vibrated, Keller excused himself and took the call in the far corner of the stamp room. Rombaugh closed one stamp album and reached for another, clearly wrapped up in his task.

Should he leave the room? Rombaugh wouldn't hear anything, he decided, and wouldn't know what he was listening to even if he did.

He said, "Yes?"

"There's someone in the room."

"Sort of."

"How can someone be sort of in the room? Never mind, you can't talk freely, and I don't need to know. You got a pencil handy?"

"A pen."

"That'll do. If there's anything you need to erase just cross it out. Meanwhile, write this down."

She read out an address and he dutifully jotted it down on the back of Martin Rombaugh's business card.

"The girlfriend," she went on. "Her name is Trish Heaney, which I suppose must be short for Patricia. The Trish part, I mean. I don't think the Heaney part is short for anything."

"Right."

"Though I suppose it could be short for Heaniapopoulos. You don't think that's funny, do you?"

"Right."

"The girlfriend's got a boyfriend. Not the one we know about, with the tubes coming out of him. This guy's more of an ex-boyfriend, the kind of old pal a gal might call on in a pinch. His name's Tyler Crowe. He's younger than Hudepohl, but prison ages a man, and you'll never guess what he did that got him three years in Cañon City."

He could guess, but didn't want to say the word.

"Arson. You see where this is going, Pablo?"

Like Griffey, Marty Rombaugh didn't want to interrupt his work for lunch. But neither did he care to miss a meal, and polished off the sandwiches Denia provided.

A little after three he pushed back his chair and heaved a sigh. "Stamps," he said. "Just little pieces of paper, but they're more than that, aren't they?"

"They are."

"You didn't know Soderling, did you?"

"No."

"Neither did I, but you can tell a lot about a man from his collection. This was an orderly and systematic gentleman, but there was a lot of romance there as well, a little dash, a certain flair. I can't tell you how I know that, but I do."

"I know what you mean."

"You're not from around here."

"My wife and I live in New Orleans."

He'd mentioned his wife to keep the man from jumping to a certain conclusion, and he saw the word register. "You're basically a friend of a friend," Rombaugh said, "advising the lady on the disposal of her husband's holdings."

"I buy and sell some," Keller said. "Someone recommended me, but when I saw the extent of the collection—"

"You figured deeper pockets were required. I suppose the lady will be compensating you for your trouble."

The sentence didn't have a question mark at its end, but invited a response. Keller didn't supply one.

"Who'd they send yesterday, if you don't mind my asking? I bet it was the Griff, wasn't it?"

"If you mean Mr. Griffey—"

"Yeah, the little guy. He and I spend our lives tagging each other all around the country. All those Russian locals, the zemstvo issues, they might as well be from Uranus for all he knows about them." He paused, frowned. "That's the planet Uranus, but when you just say it, well, it comes out off-color. I should have said Jupiter. It's less open to misinterpretation."

"Well," Keller said.

"He'd lowball you on the Russian stamps. Other hand, he'd go high on some of the Czech and Polish overprints, on account of there's forgeries there that he probably wouldn't spot. Including one or two that Kasimir Bileski signed off on."

"Really."

"Just for curiosity, what did the Griff offer you?"

"He gave us a sealed bid."

"So? Come on, don't tell me you didn't sneak a peek."

"We didn't."

"Playing it absolutely straight, eh? Well, cards on the table. This is a very sweet little collection, and not even all that little, and my own compensation is tied to what I bring in to my employers. So what can you and I do just between ourselves to make that happen?"

Keller thought it over. "There is one thing," he said at length.

"I'm all ears."

No, he thought. Griffey was all ears, and might have flown

if he'd been able to flap them. As for Rombaugh—well, never mind.

"Figure out the absolute maximum the collection is worth to you," he told the man. "The most you can pay and still make your employers happy."

"And?"

"And that's your bid," Keller said. "Write it down and seal the envelope. If it's higher than either of the others, you win."

The address Dot had furnished was on Arapahoe Street, in that part of downtown Denver known as LoDo. Keller wasn't clear on where the term came from, but if he had to guess he'd have opted for LOwer DOwntown, the same way New York's SoHo and NoHo were NOrth and SOuth of HOuston Street.

He programmed the GPS accordingly, and halfway to Denver he thought about Dot, and how she'd driven all the way to Flagstaff to use a rental computer to chase down Joanne Hudepohl's phone listing. Because if she used her own computer, there'd be an electronic trail you couldn't rub out.

Well, what about his GPS? He'd already punched in the address on Otis Drive, including the precise number of the house that had burned to the foundation. And now he'd added another address, the LoDo loft that was home to Trish Heaney, and it didn't have to go up in smoke to draw attention from the authorities. All the trouble he'd gone to, flying in and out of Cheyenne, and he'd be returning his Cheyenne rental car with a GPS showing just where he'd been in Denver.

He took the next exit off the interstate, found a place to park, thought the whole thing over. The simplest thing, he realized, was to take out the Pablo phone, call Dot, and tell her he wanted to scrap the whole thing. They had the first payment, and that was plenty. Then he could turn the car around and have a romantic dinner with Denia Soderling.

"I'm going to have to go to Denver this evening," he'd told Denia, after Marty Rombaugh had delivered his sealed envelope and taken his leave.

She'd offered to hold dinner, and he said he wasn't sure how long his business might take. "Here's a house key," she said. "In case you're very late. But I'll probably be up, and if you're back before ten we can dine together."

And if he went back now? The sun wasn't even down yet, and he'd have to explain how his urgent business engagement had wrapped itself up in no time at all. Various possibilities suggested themselves—a medical emergency, a canceled flight—and he told himself he was overthinking the situation.

He could delete the Arapahoe Street address, but wouldn't it still be recorded somewhere in the gadget's history? Probably, and he'd only saddle himself with the difficulty of finding Tricia Heaney's loft without the patient guidance of the nice GPS lady.

He started the car, got back on the road. "Recalculating route," the voice said, infinitely patient, and only the slightest bit judgmental. He beamed the invisible woman a silent apology for deviating from the script, and followed her instructions all the way to LoDo.

"You have arrived," she said, and there was the address he wanted, a squat six-story brick building with big industrial-type windows.

Keller was glad he wasn't contemplating arson. The building looked like a hard structure to burn down.

FORTY-THREE

Keller, returning to Arapahoe Street from where he'd parked the car, reminded himself that he didn't have to do anything. He was simply a private citizen, paying a call on a woman at her residence. If she wasn't home, or if she wouldn't let him in, or if the right opportunity failed to arise, he'd go back to Cheyenne and eat a good dinner.

And there was Trish Heaney's building, right where he'd left it, with a row of buttons next to the windowless red door. Helpful little cards marked each button, and he pressed the one that said HEANEY.

Waiting, he reminded himself that he'd committed himself to nothing. That he'd neither misrepresented himself nor broken any laws.

"Yes?"

Just a citizen, ringing a doorbell.

"Hello? Who is it?"

"Officer Griffey," he said. "Police."

There was a lengthy pause.

Well, he'd just broken a law. It shouldn't take too long to drive back to Cheyenne. He wouldn't even need the GPS, although it would probably be simpler to use it. The Soderling address was already programmed into the system, and the woman with the soothing and infinitely patient voice was waiting to guide him home, and get him there in plenty of time for dinner. And Denia was a good cook, no question about it, and—

The buzzer sounded. He pushed the door open and went on in.

The elevator was industrial, but it had been converted to self-service when the building turned residential. There'd been a 4 next to the bell marked HEANEY, so he pushed the appropriate button and rode to the fourth floor. The elevator door glided open, and there she was, holding a drink in one hand and a cigarette in the other.

While he hadn't formed a mental picture of her in advance, it would have been hard to improve on reality. Trish Heaney was no more than five foot four, but she made an impression. She wore wheat-colored jeans and a fuzzy pink sweater, both garments skintight. The jeans would have been tight on anyone who wasn't severely anorexic, but most women who could have squeezed themselves into the jeans would have found the sweater a loose fit.

And that might have been true of this woman, he thought, before some obliging nip-and-tuck artist had put her in competition with Dolly Parton. The result was impressive, he had to admit, but no more convincing than the vivid red hue of her upswept hair. She had a butterfly tattoo on her neck, and the Geico gecko inked onto the back of one hand, and enough piercings to put a metal detector on tilt, and God knows what else she had underneath the sweater and jeans.

"You're a cop," she said. "You don't look like a cop."

"You don't look like a kindergarten teacher."

"Who said I was—" She broke off, frowned, took a deep drag on her cigarette. "That supposed to be a joke? You want to show me some ID?"

"I could," he said.

Or, he thought, he could cut to the chase. One hand cupping her chin, one hand grabbing that mop of red hair. Be over before she knew it.

"So?"

"But once I do," he said, "this becomes official. You sure that's what you want?"

"I don't know what you're talking about."

"There's a guy in the hospital, touch and go whether he lives or dies. I won't mention his name, but you wouldn't be living here if he wasn't paying for it."

"This is my place," she said. "The deed's in my name. And I still don't know what you're talking about."

Was this working? Keller wasn't sure. The cigarette smoke was bothering him, and so was her perfume, an overpowering floral scent redolent with musk.

He said, "Sure you do, Trish. You were all set to get Richard Hudepohl away from his wife, and then you realized he'd be broke after the divorce. But suppose he didn't have to go through a divorce? Suppose something happened to his wife and kids?"

"Not the kids," she said, and put her hand to her mouth.

"Not the wife, either," Keller said, "because old Tyler burned the house down with the wrong person in it."

"She took his car," she said, "and all Tyler saw was the car, and the kids in the backseat. He couldn't see who was driving it. If you're wearing a wire, that's too fucking bad. You never did read me my rights."

"Or show you my ID," he reminded her. "Because this isn't official. Trish, there'd be nothing easier than hanging this on Tyler, and if he's in it then you're in it, and having your rights read to you isn't going to help you. But I'm the only person who made the connection, and why would I want to see you go to prison?"

She looked at him, breathed in, breathed out. Really a bad idea, that perfume she was wearing. He could see how it might work on a primitive level, but it was so blatant, and so unpleasant—

"What do you want?"

"Your boyfriend's professional services, Trish. I got property that's underwater."

She frowned. "How can it burn if it's underwater?"

"It's an expression," he said. "It means I owe more money on it than it's worth. The bank's set to foreclose on the mortgage, and when that happens, my investment goes up in smoke."

"Unless—"

"Unless the property goes up in smoke first. Call him, get him to come over here. You'll both make a few dollars, and I'll forget what I happen to know about you and a man named Hudepohl. And Trish? Have you got a gun in the house?"

"Why?"

That was as good as a yes. "Get it for me," he said.

FORTY-FOUR

Halfway to Cheyenne, he spotted a sign for a country-style chain restaurant and found it at the next exit. The menu ran heavily to quaint—*Grampa Gussie's Crispy Taters, hand-cut wif his own Bowie knife*—but the food was what you'd get pretty much anywhere. He ate half of a grilled cheese sandwich and drank a few sips of his iced tea and let it go at that.

He stopped at La Quinta and caught the late local news on the CBS affiliate in Denver. A jeweler on Colfax Avenue had been robbed, apparently by a gang who'd been making a habit of this sort of thing. And the weather was going to be more of the same, although it took the weather girl ten minutes to convey that information.

Nothing about anyone named Hudepohl, or Heaney, or Crowe.

* * *

At first he thought Denia had retired for the night. The ground-floor lights were mostly turned down, and he used the key she'd given him and softened his step once he was inside.

The dining room table was cleared, the room dark. He padded across the carpet toward the staircase when she spoke his name. He turned, and saw her in an armchair in the dimly lit parlor. She was wearing a robe, and her feet were bare.

"It won't be any trouble to warm something up for you," she said. "But I've a feeling you've eaten."

"The fellow I had to meet was hungry," he said, "so I kept him company."

"I didn't have any appetite," she said, "so I had a couple of drinks instead and wound up going to bed on an empty stomach. And then I couldn't sleep after all, and I still didn't have any appetite, and I was too restless to lie there and wait for sleep to come. Do you ever have nights like that?"

"Once in a while."

"This is a robe of Jeb's. That's his actual name, incidentally. J-E-B, it's not short for anything, though people assume it's short for Jebediah. I don't think I've ever known anyone named Jebediah. Have you?"

"I don't believe so."

"I'm a little drunk, Nicholas. Why don't you sit in that chair there? I want us to have a little conversation, if you don't mind. That's all I want, just a conversation, but I do want that. Is that all right?"

"Of course."

"It has his smell. The robe, I mean. I ought to give all his clothes to the Goodwill. What am I keeping them for? But I like to smell them. And there's a flannel shirt of his that

I like to sleep in sometimes. And sometimes I put on this robe."

He didn't have anything to say to that.

"Widows are easy. You must have heard that, Nicholas."

"Uh."

"Everybody knows it, too. I'm not sure it's true, but I do know that everyone believes it is, or wants it to be. I'm a reasonably attractive woman, Nicholas, but I'm hardly a movie star or a supermodel. And men who I swear never looked twice at me while Jeb was alive, men who were his friends, men who are married to friends of mine..."

She shook her head, raised her glass, sipped its contents. "Passes were made," she said. "What an odd way to put it. 'Passes were made.' Well, they were, verbal and physical. Made and deflected, with no embarrassment on either side. I was not tempted."

"No."

"But I get lonely, you know. And I miss intimacy. Physical intimacy."

"Well."

"This is whiskey," she said, brandishing her glass. "I usually have a glass or two of wine of an evening. Tonight I've been drinking whiskey because I wanted it to hit me, and it has. Can you tell I'm drunk?"

"No."

"I'm not slurring my words, am I?"

"No."

"Or speaking in too loud a voice, the way drunks do?"

"No."

"What happens in Vegas stays in Vegas. Of course you've heard that slogan."

"Yes."

"My husband and I subscribed to that philosophy. He had to do a certain amount of travel for his business, and if he had an opportunity for a dalliance, he was free to pursue it. When he was at home he was married, and faithful. When he was miles away, he was a free agent."

"I suppose a lot of couples have that sort of understanding."

"I would think so. I'm going upstairs now. I'm sure I'll be able to sleep. I'm glad we've had this little talk, aren't you, Nicholas?"

"Yes, I am."

"And tomorrow's our last day. I can't remember the name of the buyer we'll be seeing tomorrow."

"I believe it's a Mr. Mintz."

"As in pie? Shame on me. It's ridiculous to make jokes about a person's name, and the person will have heard all of them, time and time again. When he's gone we'll open the envelopes. And you'll be able to have dinner, won't you?"

"Yes, of course."

"Boeuf bourguignon, I think. With the little roasted potatoes, and a salad. Good night, Nicholas. No, I can get upstairs under my own power. It's just my tongue that's loosened, that's all. I'll see you at breakfast."

He had a shower. He'd felt the need for one ever since he left the Arapahoe Street loft. He toweled dry, brushed his teeth.

Too late to call Julia. He'd thought of calling her from La Quinta, decided not to, and now it was too late. Was it too late to call Dot? Probably not, but he didn't want to call Dot. It was possible she'd called him, or tried to. He'd turned his phone off earlier and had never turned it back on.

He got in bed, turned off the light. What happens in Cheyenne, he thought, stays in Cheyenne.

He didn't think he was going to be able to sleep, and thought about putting on a robe and going downstairs to drink whiskey. But he didn't have a robe, and didn't much care for whiskey, or for the whole sad business of sitting up late drinking it.

He owned a robe, a very nice maroon one with silver piping. It had belonged to Julia's father, who'd been an invalid during the short time Keller had known him. Mr. Roussard hadn't known quite what to make of Keller, though they got along well enough, and then the man's illness ran its course, more or less, and he was gone.

Keller had admired the robe once, and after her father's ashes had been scattered in the Gulf, Julia got the robe dry-cleaned and told him it was his now. He liked owning it, but he hardly ever wore it. It didn't smell of the old man, or of the sickroom, the dry cleaner had seen to that, but still it stayed unworn in Keller's closet. Robes, pajamas, slippers, they worked fine for some men, not so much for others, and Keller—

Dropped right off to sleep, thinking of robes and slippers.

FORTY-FIVE

The representative of Talleyrand Stamp & Coin arrived twenty minutes late. Keller, on the patio with a second cup of coffee, watched as the fellow parked his black Lincoln Navigator in the driveway and headed for the front door, briefcase in hand. Like his predecessors, he wore a conservative suit and a tie; in manner and body type he fell somewhere between the two.

"Pierce Naylor," he said, first to Keller, then a moment or two later to Denia Soderling. "Lew Mintz couldn't make it. As I understand it, I'm the third stamp buyer to cross this threshold in as many days. Ma'am, you must be sick to death of the whole tribe of us."

"It's been no hardship for me," she said. "Mr. Edwards has enabled me to stay very much in the background."

"You're fortunate," he said. "The less time you spend around stamp buyers, the better off you are. Well, it's my intention to make this as simple and easy for you as I possibly can, and profitable in the bargain. Unless I've been misinformed, you were visited in turn by E. J. Griffey and Martin Rombaugh, and I'd be surprised if either one of them got out of here in less than five or six hours."

Keller was preparing a reply, but Naylor didn't wait for one. "That's far more of your time than I intend to take," he said, "nor will I eat you out of house and home, as I'm sure Marty Rombaugh made every effort to do. One hour's all I'll need."

Oh?

In the stamp room, Keller indicated the chair that had served Griffey and Rombaugh in turn. Naylor stayed on his feet and walked over to the shelved stamp albums. "Spain," he announced, and carried an album to the table. Still standing, he opened it apparently at random, studied the stamps, flipped a few pages, closed the album, and returned it to the shelf. He spent a little more time with Sweden, and not much time at all with Turkey.

"All right," he said, after replacing the Turkish album where he'd found it. "Griffey and Rombaugh, with Griffey leading off. He'd have tried to make his offer preemptive, but that little ploy quite obviously didn't work. And Marty would have tried to add a little sweetener. He'd top Griffey's bid and slip you a little something for your troubles. But that couldn't have worked, either, because the stamps are still here, aren't they?"

Keller agreed that they were.

"How high did Griffey go? And was Marty able to top it?"

"We haven't opened the envelopes."

"You're kidding," Naylor said, and looked intently at him. "You're serious," he announced. "Well, that makes it interesting, doesn't it? Why don't we bring in Mrs. Soderling? I have a suggestion to make."

"You want us to open both envelopes," she said. "In front of you."

"That's right."

"And you'll guarantee to top the high bid by twenty percent. I believe that's what you said."

"It is."

"But you barely looked at the stamps. How can you know they're worth that much?"

"I know the Griff," Naylor said. "I know Marty Rombaugh. If they say the collection's worth X dollars, I know it's worth that and more."

"Twenty percent more," Keller said.

"That's right. I looked briefly at three albums, and that was enough to give me a sense of the quality and the degree of completeness. I'll take the word of my predecessors as to the actual value, and at the same time I'll trust them to have shaded their bid enough to leave ample room for profit. Enough room so that I can bid twenty percent higher and still come out ahead."

"Or back out," Keller said.

"I beg your pardon?"

"Suppose we open the envelopes," he said, "and one bid's three times as high as the other, so high that you wouldn't even want to match it, let alone top it by twenty percent. 'My employers would never go for that,' you'd say, and what could we do about it?"

"Not a damn thing," Naylor allowed. "But so what? You'd go ahead and sell the stamps to Griffey or Rombaugh, whoever's the higher, but that's what you'd do anyway, isn't it?"

There had to be a flaw in the argument, but Keller couldn't spot it. Denia questioned the fairness of it. Wouldn't they be giving Naylor an edge over the competition?

"I had that edge from the start," he said, "because I'm the last of the three players in the game. If I'd already come and gone, and one of the others got to go last, he'd be giving you a version of the same pitch. Ma'am, you want to be fair to yourself, and to do right by the man who gathered all these philatelic treasures together in the first place. Which is to say you want the highest price. And that's exactly what you'll get if you open those envelopes."

It was getting on for noon when they opened the envelopes. By ten minutes to four, the entire cargo compartment of the oversize SUV was filled to capacity, with one additional carton, its seat belt securely fastened, riding shotgun. There was another box on the floor containing a two-quart Thermos bottle and half a dozen sandwiches in individual self-sealing plastic bags.

"I'll drive straight through," Pierce Naylor said. "It's around nine hundred miles to St. Louis, all of it on interstates, and with the sandwiches and coffee I'll never have to leave the vehicle. Very thoughtful of you, Mrs. Soderling. I'll have FedEx get your Thermos back in good shape."

"It's a spare, Mr. Naylor, and the cap's chipped. Don't bother returning it."

"You're sure? Because it wouldn't be any trouble. Well, then. Mr. Edwards, Mrs. Soderling. A pleasure doing business with you."

They stood in silence and watched him drive off. He'd flown from St. Louis to Denver, where he'd reserved the Navigator, making sure he got the largest SUV any of the rental outlets had on offer. If he'd missed out on the collection, he'd have driven back to Denver and flown home. But he'd been successful, so he'd drive home, pay the car rental people a drop charge, waste his return air ticket, and his employers would count it all money well spent.

"It was remarkable how smoothly it went. He called the firm he works for, and someone there called a bank and arranged a wire transfer, and in no time at all Mrs. Soderling's bank confirmed that the money was in her account."

"I guess I knew you could do that," Julia said, "but it never would have occurred to me. And she's happy with the price?"

"Very much so."

"And your other business?"

"All taken care of. I'll be home tomorrow."

She put Jenny on, and he listened happily as she babbled away about a puppy. Was it too early to get her a dog? This was not the first time he'd asked himself this question, and the answer still seemed to be yes, that she wasn't old enough yet. Soon, though.

He rang off, switched phones, called Dot. "You won't believe this," she said, "but the damnedest thing happened on Arapahoe Street in downtown Denver. An ex-con not too long out of Cañon City looked up his old girlfriend and slapped her around enough to leave marks. So she got her gun and put three rounds in his chest, and then I guess she felt remorseful, because she turned the gun on herself."

"These things happen."

"One in the heart. I understand men go for head shots, the mouth or the temple, but a girl wants to look her best."

"So they say."

"And they found something, don't ask me what, that has

them looking at the dead guy for that house that burned down a few nights ago."

"Maybe there was something in his wallet with the address on it."

"Of the house that went up in smoke? That might do it. Whatever it is, my guess is it's enough for them to clear the case. Time for Pablo to head for home."

"Tomorrow," he said. "Uh, as far as us getting paid—"

"Won't be a problem."

"When the husband recovers—"

"That won't be a problem, either."

It took him a moment. "You're saying he—"

"Died, Pablo. *El esposo es muerto.* Or should it be *está?* I think *es,* because it's a permanent condition."

"I thought she hired security."

"She did, amigo, but all the king's horses can't keep a man's kidneys from quitting on him. Acute renal failure, and I gather the only surprise at the hospital was that he lasted as long as he did. And this way she got to forgive him and fall back in love with him and get revenge on the people responsible for his death, and she doesn't have to worry that he'll find some other tootsie and put her through it all over again. Which we both know he would have done sooner or later. I have to say she comes out of this in good shape, Pablo. The little lady got her money's worth."

FORTY-SIX

The boeuf bourguignon was tender and savory, the little potatoes crisp on the outside and soft in the center. The wine was a Burgundy, appropriately enough, full-bodied and hearty, but neither of them managed more than a glass of it.

They talked through the meal, but mostly about the philatelic transaction. Of the two bids they'd opened, E. J. Griffey's was the higher by a substantial margin, and that had surprised them both.

Over coffee, she said she wanted to pay him a bonus. The stamps he'd selected, he told her, were ample compensation for his time. He'd enjoyed the visit, and he'd learned a great deal from the three men, from listening to what they said and from paying attention to the way they operated.

"You made me an offer," she said. "A quarter of a million dollars. And in the next breath you advised me not to take it."

"Aren't you glad you didn't?"

"I wound up with almost five times as much."

"I thought you might."

"You're an honest man," she said, "and an ethical one, but I don't see why that should stop you from accepting a bonus. You have a daughter. You told me her name but I don't remember it."

"Jenny."

"I bet she's smart."

"Like her mother," he said.

"Oh, I think you probably deserve some of the credit. But she's college material, wouldn't you say?"

"Not for a few years now."

"That's just as well," she said, "because what I'm going to do is put a hundred thousand dollars into a trust fund to mature on her eighteenth birthday. It should appreciate considerably by then, and might even increase as much as the cost of a college education. You really can't object to this, Nicholas. It doesn't even concern you. It's between me and Jennifer."

"Jenny."

"Jenny, but isn't it Jennifer on her birth certificate?"

"No, just Jenny."

"And my husband's given name was Jeb, not short for Jebediah, as some people tended to assume. His full name was Jeb Stuart Soderling, though I've no idea why his father, a North Dakota Swede, would name his son after a Civil War general. And Jeb was an acronym to begin with, you know."

"It was J. E. B. Stuart, wasn't it? I don't remember what the initials stood for."

"James Ewell Brown Stuart. I would know, wouldn't I, having been married to his namesake. Well, that's a handful, isn't it? You can see why they went with Jeb. But won't it be awkward for your daughter? She'll spend half her life correcting people who assume her full name is Jennifer."

He'd had this conversation with Julia. "She can always change it," he said. "But for now it's Jenny. See, she was a breech birth."

"I beg your pardon?"

"A breech presentation. She was upside down in the birth canal, and—"

"I understand the term, Nicholas. What I don't begin to understand is why that would make her a Jenny instead of a Jennifer."

He reached for his cup, took a sip of coffee. "I'm not sure this will make any sense," he said, "but that's when we realized she wasn't going to be, you know, ordinary. And there were so many little girls named Jennifer, and we knew we weren't going to call her Jennifer anyway, so—well, that's why it says Jenny on her birth certificate."

"And it doesn't have to be short for Jennifer," Denia said. "Think of Pirate Jenny, in *The Threepenny Opera*. But your little pirate's name is Jenny Edwards. And does she have a middle name, Nicholas? Because I'm serious about putting that money in trust for her."

"It's Roussard," he said, and spelled it. "My wife's maiden name."

FORTY-SEVEN

"Pirate Jenny," he said. "Maybe that's what you'll be next Halloween. We'll get you an eye patch, and your mother can make you a cutlass out of cardboard."

"Daddy home," said the future pirate, bouncing happily on his lap. "Daddy home!"

"Daddy's home," he agreed. "And in fifteen years or so, he'll be the one stuck at home while you toddle off to college."

"And it's all paid for," Julia said. "You really think she'll go through with it? Set up our little bundle of joy with a six-figure trust fund?"

"Well, you never know," he said. "It was her idea, and I couldn't talk her out of it. She could change her mind, but I don't think she will."

"And where will the pirate go to college, do you suppose? She could follow in her mommy's footsteps and go to Sophie

Newcomb, but they went and merged my old school into Tulane. I'm not sure it would be the same. With all that money she could go someplace fancy. All New England preppy. Where would you want her to go?"

"Nowhere, for the time being. Fifteen years from now? I don't know. Some school where there aren't any boys, how's that?"

"Aren't you the dreamer. How about Sweet Briar, in Virginia? I knew a girl who went there, and don't you know she got to keep her own horse there."

"Right in the dormitory?"

"In the stable, you idiot. Jenny, you'll be a pirate on horseback. How does that sound?"

"Daddy home," Jenny said.

"Well, you know what's important, don't you? Yes, Daddy's home. Aren't we lucky?"

After they'd put Jenny to bed and then gone to bed themselves, after the lovemaking and the easy shared silence that followed the lovemaking, she said she didn't think she'd ever known anyone named Gardenia.

"I gather no one ever calls her that," he said. "I believe she said she'd had it changed legally."

"Better than changing it illegally. Jeb, Jenny, Denia—all of y'all have got names that are short for something, except they're not."

"That's true, isn't it?"

"I guess. Is she pretty?"

"Denia Soderling? She's an attractive woman."

"Why didn't you sleep with her? Or did you? No, you didn't. What stopped you?"

"Huh?" He doubled up his pillow, propped himself up

with it. "Where did this come from? Why would that even be a possibility?"

"Oh, come on," she said. "A beautiful lonely widow? A handsome mysterious stranger? 'Stay in my guest room, it'll be so much more comfortable than that nasty old motel.' She didn't offer you the guest room in the hope that you'd stay in it."

"I guess she may have been interested."

"And you weren't?"

He considered the question. "The last night," he said, "when she wanted to set up a fund for Jenny's education, we talked about her name, and how it was just plain Jenny, and not short for anything."

"So they'd get it right on the paperwork."

"I suppose. I told her how Jenny was a breech presentation."

"And she got it right away? Or did you have to explain?"

What he could have told Denia Soderling:

"See, there's a very famous U.S. airmail stamp of 1918, Scott C3a. There were actually three stamps with the same design—a six-cent orange, a sixteen-cent green, and a twenty-four-cent carmine rose and blue. They all pictured a Curtiss biplane, called the Jenny because it was part of the company's JN series of aircraft.

"The high value, the twenty-four-cent stamp, was a bicolor, and that meant each pane of stamps had to make two passes through the printing process, once for each color. Only one sheet went through upside down, and as a result the stamps had what's called an inverted center.

"Now, this was an occasional consequence of bicolor printing. In some countries, where quality control wasn't a priority, or where enterprising employees had learned to make profitable mis-

takes, inverted centers turned up with some frequency. In 1901 the U.S. issued a stamp series to mark the Pan-American Exposition in Buffalo, the one where President McKinley was assassinated, and three of the six stamps could be found with their centers inverted. They all illustrated modes of transportation, so depending on the denomination, you'd have a steamship or a locomotive or an electric automobile, and it'd be upside down.

"Those three stamps were legitimate rarities, and nowadays bring substantial five-figure prices. But they didn't catch the imagination of the public the way that upside-down plane did. These were the first airmail stamps, and aviation was very new and very exciting, and here's this plane putting on an exhibition of philatelic stunt flying. You can buy a decent copy of the regular stamp, Scott C3, for around a hundred dollars. If you want the error, with the plane upside down, you'll probably have to spend over a million.

"Our Jenny was turned around in the birth canal, and they were going to do a caesarean because she was leading with her behind, and that makes for a difficult delivery. But the obstetrician managed to get her turned around some, so that she emerged feet first.

"We'd already decided that we both liked the name Jenny. It was high on our list. And then, when she flew into our lives upside down, well, that cinched it."

"She might have liked it," Julia said. "Don't you think? Her husband was a collector, and she had a million new reasons to like the whole idea of stamps."

"I figured it would take a long time to explain. It was nothing she needed to know, and I didn't feel like going through it."

"So you didn't sleep with her, and you didn't tell her how your daughter got her name. You're some houseguest. Glad to be home?"

"Very."

"And you're exhausted, aren't you? You can tell me the rest tomorrow. And I guess you've got stamps to put in."

"Magic beans," he said.

"I won't even ask what that means," she said. "Good night, my sweet."

But she asked him the following afternoon. He'd caught up with the mail by then, and driven to Slidell to pick up the envelope that was waiting for him at a Mail Boxes Etc. office. Cash, his share of the money Joanne Hudepohl had wired to Dot in Flagstaff.

Back home, he stashed the money, then went to work on his stamps. His office was not nearly so grand as Jeb Soderling's beautifully appointed stamp room, but it suited him just fine. His chair was comfortable, his desk the right size and height, and the light fell on his books and stamps without getting in his eyes.

Jenny took her usual perch on the chair beside his, and he kept up a running commentary while she watched every move he made. He was still hard at it when nap time came around, and Julia led Jenny away and came back to take her place at the stamp table.

"Stamps are educational," she said, "even when it's your father who collects them. I'll bet there's not a kid in her whole day care center who knows a damn thing about the Turco-Italian War and the Treaty of Roseanne."

"Lausanne."

"I was close. Lausanne's in Switzerland, isn't it? Or am I thinking of Lucerne?"

"They're both in Switzerland."

"Both of them? That's confusing, isn't it? Which one is full of magic beans? You don't have any idea what I'm talking about, do you? Well, that makes us even. Those were the last two words you said last night, right before you dropped off to sleep. Or maybe you were already asleep. Are you going to tell me about the magic beans?"

It took him a minute. Then he remembered and recounted his dreamy conversation with his dead mother.

"Magic beans," Julia said. "Well, your mother might not agree, but I think taking your commission in stamps makes perfect sense. What do you figure they're worth?"

"The Scott value's a little over a hundred thousand. On this sort of material, figure retail at somewhere between sixty and seventy-five percent of catalog. I couldn't get that for them, but that's what I'd have had to pay."

"But you didn't have to pay anything. That's nice."

"Very. You know, I don't think it cost her anything, either. I can't believe anybody's bid would have been higher if the stamps I took were still in their albums."

"So everybody wins?"

"Denia wins," he said, "and so do I. Would Talleyrand Stamp and Coin net a few dollars more if these stamps were included in what they bought? I suppose so, but they'll make out fine as it is."

"And they'll never miss what they never knew was there. And you're better off getting paid in stamps, because you'd have spent the money on stamps anyway. So you did fine with the magic beans, and that was only part of your compensation. The next time you talk with your mother you can let her know you picked up some cash while you were at it."

"That'll be a load off her mind."

"Do you want to tell me about that part of it? Jenny's good for another half hour minimum, if you feel like talking about what you did in Denver."

FORTY-EIGHT

I got in a twist over the GPS," he told her. "I'd programmed it with two addresses where things happened."

"The house that burned and where else? Oh, of course. The loft where you wrapped things up."

"And anything digital lasts forever."

"And of course you'd rented the car under your own name."

"I did everything under my own name, including the car rental. So I hatched one brilliant idea after another. I could pull the GPS, smash it with a hammer, drop it off a bridge, and report it as stolen."

"That would work, wouldn't it?"

"You'd think so," he said, "but suppose it's got some kind of cyberconnection to a computer somewhere? Then making it disappear just might lead somebody to check with the mother ship and find out where it had been before it got lost. So I thought of opening it up and messing with its insides."

"To reprogram it? You could do that?"

"Not in a million years. But I could probably find some way to make it stop working. I wouldn't mention it, and nobody would notice until the next person to rent it couldn't get it to work. If he even bothered to try."

"Is that what you did?"

He shook his head. "I just left it alone and gave the car back to them. I decided it was nothing to worry about. If they have reason to suspect me, they won't need GPS records. If they don't, they won't check them. And why should they? As far as they're concerned, the case is closed. Richard Hudepohl is dead as a result of a fire set by the former lover of his jilted girlfriend."

"All of which is true."

"Well, almost true, and there's nobody around to argue otherwise. Trish Heaney and Tyler Crowe are both dead. If the lab crew from *CSI* got on the case, they'd probably spot a few inconsistencies in the murder-suicide scenario, but real-life cops are in more of a hurry than the ones on TV. The case is closed, and the closest thing to a loose end is Joanne, and even if she's crazy enough to tell someone, what can she say? She's got the number of an unregistered phone that no longer exists, and she wired some money to a person who never existed in the first place."

"So it's all over. And yet you seem…"

"What?"

"I don't know. Moody? Dissatisfied?"

"Maybe."

"Did you do that memory exercise? Making the mental picture smaller and bleaching the color out of it?"

He shook his head. "I probably should," he said. "I've spent so little time thinking about them that I didn't even remember to fade them out of my memory. I can barely remember what they look like, Trish and Tyler. Very distinctive in appearance, both of them, and yet it's hard for me to picture them."

"I wonder why."

Later he said, "It was peripheral, all of it. What I was most interested in was getting the best possible price for the Soderling collection. The job in Denver was something to shunt aside and take care of in my spare time."

"When it was supposed to be the other way around."

"I was all involved with the stamps," he said, "and it took me a couple of days to go have a look at the house on Otis Drive. If I'd made it my first priority, there never would have been a fire. Hudepohl would have been a soft target, he wouldn't have had his guard up, so how hard could it have been?"

"For a man of your talents."

"Well," he said. "The point is, by the time I managed to go see where he lived, there was no house there. And then there was nothing to do, so I headed north and went back to work on selling the stamps."

"Which was what you were really interested in anyway."

"Right. And when Dot went proactive and got in touch with Mrs. Hudepohl, I wondered why she couldn't leave well enough alone."

"Because you already had half the money without doing anything."

"And now I'd have to do something. And I did, and it went smoothly enough, but it was a little like watching a movie."

"You weren't really involved."

"I managed to stay in the moment," he said, "because you have to. And I didn't get thrown off at the prospect of making bad things happen to good people."

"Because they weren't good people."

"They weren't just the kind of people you see on *Cops.* They were the kind who call up their friends to make sure they tune in and watch. She was a tramp and he was a glassy-eyed pyromaniac. And they smelled."

"Oh?"

"I don't think he bathed much. Maybe he resented water because people put out fires with it, but you could tell he gave it a wide berth. And she was wearing this overpowering perfume, with a trace of body odor under it."

"Charming."

"I smelled it again a few hours ago, when I made their images get fainter and smaller. I got rid of their faces, but I couldn't get rid of the perfume. Jesus, I'll bet that's what it was."

"What?"

"Jungle Gardenia. It's not as though I recognized it, because I don't believe I'd ever smelled it before, but I mentioned it, didn't I?"

"It's how your girlfriend got her name."

"Her mother wore it," he remembered, "and it evidently drove her father mad with desire."

"But it just made you want to get back to your stamps."

"It made me want to get out of there," he said. "I wish there was a way to get the smell out of my memory. If I can do it with a visual image, why can't I do it with an aroma?"

"Maybe you'll figure out something."

"Or maybe it'll go away on its own. It doesn't matter. The point is my work didn't have my full attention, and I think there's a lesson there."

"Don't try to do two things at once?"

"That's part of it," he allowed, "but there's more. The other thing, the Denver assignment. I don't think I can do that anymore."

"Maybe it's time to let go of it."

"That's what I've been thinking. I thought I was done with it before, when Donny and I were doing okay rehabbing houses. And then I had a reason to go back to it, or thought I did, and it's very seductive."

"Easy money," she said.

"Plus it's easy to get involved. It's problem solving, and you get caught up in it, and there's a good feeling when it works out. Well, there can be a bad feeling, too, but you push that part aside. Except this time I didn't get caught up in it, not really, and the good feeling didn't amount to much. And there wasn't exactly a bad feeling, but there was a bad smell."

"And it's still around."

"I'll tell Dot I'm done. We'll still be friends, but she can call me on the regular line. We won't need Pablo."

"Pablo?"

"It's not important. We've got plenty of money, and I think I can make money in the stamp business, even if that's not the original reason I got into it. And I just realized something else."

"Oh?"

"The real reason I didn't explain Jenny's name to Denia Soderling. It's the same reason I didn't sleep with her."

"It would be long and drawn out and she might not get it?"

"It would be bringing somebody else into something that's just for you and me. I didn't think of it in those terms, I just knew I didn't want to do it. Sleep with her or explain to her.

But that's why." He drew a breath. "I suppose that sounds pretty silly."

"No," she said. "Not to me."

"I'll call Dot."

She put her hand on his arm. "There's no rush," she said. "Call her in a little while."

KELLER'S OBLIGATION

FORTY-NINE

"Well, I guess you could walk there," the bellman said. His tone and expression suggested that the whole idea of walking anywhere struck him as outlandish. "It's not very far," he went on, warming to the notion. "You go out the door, you take a left, you go one, two, three blocks to Allen Street, turn right, and once you cross Pearl Street you're pretty much there. You can't miss it, really."

Keller repeated the directions and the bellman hung on every word, as if he were the one who wanted to get to the Y. "That's it," he said, when Keller had finished. "There's one-way streets involved, but you don't have to pay any attention to that, not if you're going on foot."

That, Keller agreed, was the beauty of walking, along with not needing a quarter for the parking meter. How would he know the building?

"You can't miss it," the bellman said again. "It's three or four stories tall, and it's got a big red *A* on the top of it."

Keller had read *The Scarlet Letter* in high school. Or at least he thought he had, but he might have scraped by with the *Classic Comic Book* version. A couple of years ago he'd read *Adventures of Huckleberry Finn,* which he'd always thought he'd read in school, but the book turned out to be much richer and fuller than what he remembered, and he had a strong visual memory of Huck and Jim on the raft, and decided it owed less to Mark Twain's description than to the broader strokes of a comic book artist. So maybe he'd read Hawthorne and maybe he hadn't, but either way he recalled the woman's name—Hester Prynne, nobody'd ever forget a name like that. And he knew the significance of the title. The scarlet letter was an *A,* and she'd been branded with it to indicate that she was an adulteress.

And the building, the YMCA, was one he couldn't miss. Because it had an *A* on its top.

The bellman's directions turned out to be right on the money, and Keller had no trouble spotting the building, four stories tall, with a classic limestone facade and, no question, the letter *A* mounted on its top, glowing like an ember to tell the whole world what poor Hester Prynne had done. Keller posted himself diagonally across the street and kept an eye on the entrance, then gave it up when he realized he didn't know who or what he was looking for. He crossed the street and mounted a few steps and went inside, and a pleasantly plump woman with a kind face told him he'd find the stamp club on the third floor. "It's to the left when you get off the elevator," she said, "or to the right if you take the stairs."

"One if by land," Keller said.

"And two if by sea, and I on the opposite shore will be, and I forget what comes next. Ready to ride and spread the alarm through every Middlesex village and farm."

"I thought you forgot."

"It came back to me. Why Middlesex? What does a county in England have to do with Paul Revere? Well, let's find out, shall we?"

She tapped away at her keyboard, squinted at her computer terminal. "Ah," she said. "Middlesex is the most populous county in Massachusetts, and was first designated a county in 1643. There's a list of towns, and Concord is one of them."

"Where the embattled farmers stood," Keller heard himself say.

She beamed. "And fired the shot heard round the world, and we've gone from Longfellow to Ralph Waldo Emerson, haven't we? Now *this* is interesting. Since 1997, Middlesex has been a county in name only. The state took over all the government functions. They seem to have done that with all the counties. That's not really terribly interesting after all, is it? I wonder why I thought it was." She sighed. "Between Google and Wikipedia," she said, "you can learn almost anything, and some of it may even be accurate. I'm keeping you from your meeting."

"That's all right."

"This thing," she said, waving a hand at the computer terminal, "is either the greatest time-saver ever invented, or the greatest waste of time. Do you know how long it would have taken me to learn about Middlesex County without it?"

"Ages."

"And then some. I'd have had to go to the library, I'd have had to pull heavy books off high shelves, and in the end I might still not have found what I wanted to know. On the other hand, I wouldn't have bothered. 'Why Middlesex?' I'd have mused, and then I'd have thought of something else, and that would have been the end of it. A time-saver *and* a waste of time. But if you've got a question, the silly thing can give you the answer."

He took the stairs, climbed two flights of them, and turned right, and a sign on an easel pointed him to the stamp club meeting place halfway down the hall. Inside, five men and a woman sat behind tables, while another dozen men and women perched on modular white plastic chairs, the kind you could stack when the meeting was over. The ones at the tables would be dealers, he knew. Vest-pocket dealers, part-timers who helped finance their hobby by selling what they could at local shows and club meetings. The ones in the chairs would be collectors, but some of them might do a little dealing now and then, just as most of the dealers were more interested in their own collections than the few dollars they might make tonight.

Everyone was watching the screen at the front of the room, where a man with a wispy mustache was guiding the audience through a PowerPoint presentation on the various post–World War I plebiscite issues. This surprised Keller; the topic was one that actually interested him.

In the aftermath of the First World War, the victors had redrawn the map of Europe, in accordance with the principle of self-determination of nations as voiced by Woodrow Wilson. Plebiscites were scheduled for disputed regions, and the residents could cast ballots to determine which country they would be a part of.

Until then, each plebiscite region had its own administration, and its own stamps, and they were interesting in themselves, and so was their history. One such district in East

Prussia, Allenstein to the Germans and Olsztyn to the Poles, issued two series of fourteen stamps each in 1920, both consisting of overprinted German issues. Keller owned both complete sets—they weren't expensive, or difficult to find—but an Allenstein collection wasn't limited to those twenty-eight stamps as listed in the Scott catalog. There were color varieties, shades, several of them Scott-listed, some noted in the German-language Michel catalog. And there were other German stamps, five in the first series and one in the second, which had been overprinted, as the rest had been, but had never seen postal service. These unissued varieties were noted in the Scott catalog, with a value given to them, and Keller owned a couple of them and would have been glad for the chance to acquire the others.

And if he did, he might find himself with another specialty—Allenstein, specifically, or plebiscite issues in general. Then he'd find himself seeking out shades, which he didn't ordinarily bother with, and adding items of postal history, such as envelopes mailed to and from Allenstein and Memel and Schleswig and Marienwerder and both Upper and Eastern Silesia.

That seemed to be how it worked. Keller's main specialty was Martinique, the French island in the Caribbean. Keller had never been there, and had no particular desire to visit the place. He'd collected its stamps as he collected those of every other country, and without making any particular effort he'd reached a point where he owned examples of all of Martinique's stamps, except for two high-priced rarities. Then, when both stamps came up in an auction just after he'd had a nice windfall, he'd been high bidder on both lots and his collection of Martinique was complete.

Except it wasn't, because the next thing he knew he was

seeking out additional items, like doubled and inverted overprints. Scott 33, a common one-centime stamp from 1892, bore the island's name in red, but there was a variety—number 33a—with the word *Martinique* in blue. It cataloged at $650, and Keller would have paid twice that for a decent example, but so far he'd had no luck in finding one. And there were other minor varieties, some of which he owned and others he was still looking for, and then there were the covers, envelopes bearing Martinique's stamps. You could go on amassing covers forever, because in a sense every last one was unique, mailed on a certain date, bearing certain stamps, sent from this person to that person, from this place to that place, and carrying the postmarks and stickers and imprints attesting to its peregrinations.

He wasn't sure he wanted to get into all that with Allenstein, let alone Memel and the rest. But he wasn't ready to rule it out, either, and he sat there and paid close attention to what the earnest gentleman with the tentative mustache had to say.

The presentation ran a little under half an hour, and ended with the speaker inviting questions. The first hand raised was that of an older man who wanted to know why the plebiscites almost invariably ended with a decisive vote in favor of the territory's being returned to Germany. The speaker didn't know, and another man suggested that the inhabitants wanted to avoid the harsh Polish winters.

Then a boy raised his hand. There were two boys in the room, both about fourteen, and they were seated side by side, and Keller had been glancing their way from time to time. It was the smaller of the two who raised his hand, and the speaker knew him. "Yes, Mark," the man said. "Do you have a question?"

"There's something I was wondering about the unissued Allenstein overprints," he said. "Two of them are on German stamps with shade varieties. The German five-pfennig stamp can be brown or dark brown, and the twenty-pfennig green also comes in yellow-green and blue-green. Are there shade varieties in the unissued overprints?"

Keller was impressed. Mark had asked a remarkably sophisticated question. Keller didn't know the answer, and neither, apparently, did the speaker, who said he didn't know of any such varieties, and would guess there weren't because so few of the unissued overprints had been produced. But, he added, he couldn't absolutely rule out the possibility, and why had Mark raised the point? Did he have an example of what he thought might be a shade variety?

"I wish," Mark said. "No, I was just wondering."

FIFTY

He'd been at his desk, working on his own stamp collection, when the phone rang. If Julia had been home he'd have left it for her to answer, but she was at the playground with Jenny, letting her polish her social skills even as she refined her sandbox technique. He debated letting the machine answer it, then picked it up in the middle of the third ring.

"Lo siento mucho," said a familiar voice in an unconvincing accent. *"Quiero hablar a Pablo, pero yo tengo el número wrongo."*

Oh?

His caller hung up before he could respond.

"I was beginning to wonder," Dot said. "All you said was 'Hello,' and it sounded like you, but what if I really did dial a wrong number? An hour went by and nothing happened. I figured I'd give you another ten minutes, and here you are. What happened? You couldn't find the phone?"

"I had to recharge it."

"Now why the hell didn't that occur to me? It should have, because I had to charge my own Pablo phone, which I haven't used since you got back from Denver and said *no más.* That's Spanish, it means—"

"I know what it means. It's about as hard to translate as *el número wrongo.*"

"I looked it up," she said, "and what I should have said is *el número equivocado.* But I figured you'd know what I meant. Look, I know you're not doing this anymore."

"Right."

"And I think that's fine. Nobody should stay too long at the fair, and maybe the stamp business will work out for you, and if it doesn't, well, sooner or later construction will be good again, won't it?"

"Probably."

"While I, on the other hand, can't claim a huge interest in either stamps or houses. So I get my hair done and I have lunch with my girlfriends, and when a job comes in I find somebody to do it. And then this one came in, and I decided to call you, and all you have to do is tell me to forget it."

"And you'll find somebody else."

"Nope. I'll forget it."

Well, she had his interest. "Why's that?"

"A child."

"Fourteen years old, and either I saw an old photograph or he looks young for his years."

"Before all this," he said, "that was a line I always drew. I didn't care who the targets were, and the less I knew about them, the better. But no kids."

"It rarely came up," she said. "And when it did, I turned the job down. I didn't always tell you. I just turned it down and that was that."

"So why is this different? Is this kid some kind of bad seed out of a horror movie?"

"I think he's a perfectly nice little boy."

"Then I don't get it."

"Pablo," she said, "the phone rang, and the assignment came, and I drove to Flagstaff to pick up the first payment and the instructions. And there's this photo straight out of *Leave It to Beaver,* and a name and address, and so on. And I thought, well, it's good I didn't have the money in my hand for very long, because that makes it a little easier to send it back."

"But you didn't."

"I was about to," she said, "but then I asked myself a question. You know what the question was?"

"What?"

"'Now what happens?'"

"Oh."

"Right. I don't know why that never occurred to me in the past, when somebody wanted us to hit a kid and I told them thanks but no thanks. But it dawned on me this time that what I was really saying was you'll have to find somebody else, and of course that's exactly what would happen. They'd find somebody else, and the kid would still be dead, even if we didn't wind up with blood on our hands."

"What I always used to tell myself," he said, "was that any job I drew, the guy was dead whether I did it or not. Because somebody wanted him dead badly enough to pay the money, and if I didn't do it somebody else would."

"All of which is true."

"But just because we wouldn't do a kid, that doesn't mean somebody else wouldn't take the job."

"Your average sociopath," she said, "would probably prefer a kid, the same way a mugger would prefer a frail old lady."

"Safer and simpler."

"So let me ask you this, Pablo. What do you figure became of the handful of kids I thought I was saving?"

"Jesus. Not much fun to think about that."

"Not much fun at all. Here's the thing, though. If the voice on the phone had let me know he was talking about a kid, my thinking never would have gotten that far. I'd have turned the job down, and I'd have felt good about it, as if I'd just sent in a big donation to Father Flanagan's Boys Town. Let's hear it for Wilma-Known-as-Dot, who just saved a child's life. And then I'd have gone off to get my hair done."

"How often do you do that?"

"Once a week, whether it needs it or not. But there I was, looking at a picture of the kid, and I know I don't want any part of this one, but if I turn down the job it's the same as killing him myself."

"Not exactly."

"He's just as dead."

"Well, I guess that's true."

"And if I did it myself at least I'd make it as painless as I could. But I wouldn't do it at all, and neither would you, Pablo, and the kind of person who would, well, maybe he's the type who enjoys it. There are people like that in the world, you know."

"Lots of them."

"Even in our line of work, you get the occasional nut job."

He nodded. "By and large," he said, "they don't last long."

"But they get a lot done in their brief careers, don't they? That type of person enjoys his work, takes his time, gets all he can out of it. That's disgusting enough with any target, but when it's a kid—"

He got the point. He said, "What was it that general said? Or maybe it was somebody in the Defense Department. 'We had to destroy the village in order to save it.'"

"Rings a muted bell. But we don't have to kill the kid in order to save him. All we have to do is take the job."

"And not carry it out."

"Have to be a little more proactive than that, don't you think?"

"Carry it out," he said, "but not on the kid."

"Right. On the person who ordered the hit."

"Do we know who that is?"

"No."

"Do we know how to find out?"

"Same answer. We don't."

"Can't you get somebody else?"

"The others," she said, "are just voices on the phone, as far as I'm concerned, and that's all I am to them. If I even broached the subject they'd figure I was going soft in the head. 'Somebody wants a kid hit? So I'll hit him, ma'am. What's the problem?'"

"They call you ma'am?"

She sighed. "What you probably ought to do," she said, "is turn me down. Then you can go play with your stamps and I can send the money back and wash my hands of the whole thing. Isn't that what whatsisname did?"

"Who?"

"In the Bible. The guy who washed his hands. He was famous for it. Never mind. Did I mention where the boy lives? Well, it's Buffalo. I don't even know if you've been there."

"Not in years. I can't remember a thing about it, except for Niagara Falls."

"You went to Niagara Falls?"

"No," he said. "But I could have."

FIFTY-ONE

"You know," Keller said, "I own a couple of the unissued overprints, though I couldn't tell you offhand if I've got the five-pfennig brown or the twenty-pfennig green. Those were the ones you mentioned, weren't they?"

The boy nodded. "Some of the issued stamps come in shades, and sometimes there's a big price difference. A dollar for the common shade and twenty or thirty dollars for the variety. And in both sets, for the two-and-a-half-mark lilac rose, the Scott listing just says 'shades.' I guess that means that the stamp comes in brown lilac and magenta as well, like the German stamp, and that they're all equally common and low-priced."

Keller said that struck him as a reasonable guess. "You know a lot about Allenstein," he said.

"Not that much. I know it was founded by the Teutonic

Knights, which is kind of interesting, but I'm not too clear on who they were."

"I never even heard of them. Was that in Scott?"

"Wikipedia. I actually own one of the minor varieties, Scott 11a, the one-and-a-quarter-mark in blue-green. It's nine dollars, which is no fortune, but it's scarcer than the common green."

"It sounds as though you specialize in Allenstein."

"More like the whole German area," the boy said, and talked about the albums that housed his collection, and how they'd been a present—"Several presents, really"—from his grandmother. "I'm Mark, by the way, but I guess you know that, because Mr. Hasselbend said my name when he called on me. Not that you'd necessarily remember that."

Keller remembered, and hadn't needed to hear Hasselbend, either. "I'm Nick Edwards," he said.

"And what do you collect, Mr. Edwards?"

"You can call me Nick," Keller said, and told him what he collected, and about his Martinique specialty.

"That's one you'll never complete," Mark said. "There are a couple of super-expensive rarities, aren't there? Or am I thinking of Guadeloupe?"

"Either one," Keller said. "There's a Guadeloupe postage-due that's unknown in mint condition, and extremely rare used. And with Martinique you've got Scott 11 and 17, both with five-figure price tags, and that's if you can find them."

Keller could find them. All he had to do was look in his album. He'd bought both at the same auction, after a nice windfall. But that didn't strike him as something he needed to share with Mark.

They chatted, and then Mark excused himself to trade duplicates with a motherly woman who could have been the sister of the Google fan on the desk downstairs. Each had brought a small stock book and a pair of stamp tongs, and they sat side by side at a table and haggled amiably, like Levantine merchants.

"You can still go," Dot said. "Last I heard, the Falls was still up and running. If you fly up to Buffalo on Sunday, you could fit in a day at the Falls."

"I think I'll stay home."

"I figured you'd say that. And I can't say I blame you."

"Why would anyone want to kill a kid? To go and pay money to have him killed?"

"His grandmother died," she said, "and left all her money in trust for him. He gets it when he turns twenty-one."

"*If* he turns twenty-one."

"There you go. So in a sense you've got seven years to do the job, but the client doesn't want to wait that long."

He thought about it. "Shouldn't be too hard to work out who the client is. Who gets the money if the kid's out of the picture?"

"It gets divided up. Three main beneficiaries, so the odds are that one of them's our client."

"Or they're all in it together, like something on *Masterpiece Theatre*. Dot, it's not really my problem."

"I know."

"For all we know, he could be a mean little bastard. Starts fires, tortures animals, wets the bed."

"And whoever kills him will be doing the world a favor."

"For all we know. Why would I fly up there on a Sunday? What happens on Monday?"

"That's when he's easy to find," she said, "because every

Monday after dinner he gets on the bus and goes downtown to his stamp club meeting."

Keller checked out the offerings of some of the vest-pocket dealers, but didn't see anything he could use. He fell into a couple of conversations, none of them as absorbing as the one he'd had with the boy. At an adjacent table, he overheard the other lad, taller and heavier than Mark, contemplating the purchase of a set of World Cup stamps from Transnistria, the breakaway province of Moldova, which itself had broken away from the Soviet Union. Transnistria, its autonomy recognized only by Russia, didn't field a World Cup team, and Keller wasn't sure the inhabitants cared much about soccer, but that didn't keep them from issuing stamps, and selling them to collectors.

The meeting ended with an auction—a handful of members' lots, with listless bidding and the highest sale price under $10. And then there was a raffle, and Mark's trading partner won a souvenir sheet from Saint Vincent and the Grenadines, donated by one of the dealers.

And that was that. Keller took his chair to the back of the room, where some men were stacking them, and Mark made a point of coming over and extending his hand. "I enjoyed talking with you, Nick," he said. "Will you be coming again next week?"

"I'm afraid not. I'm just in town on business."

"Next time bring your duplicates. Maybe we can trade."

"I'll do that," Keller said. "You spend a lot of time on stamps?"

"As much as I can. I do okay in school, so homework doesn't take much time, and I'm hopeless in sports, so that doesn't take any time at all."

"I see your friend collects World Cup issues."

"He likes soccer. He even likes to play it."

"But you don't."

"I like to sit at my desk and work on my stamps. Pretty boring, most people would say."

"Not in this room."

"Well, that's true," the boy agreed. "When I come here I don't feel like a misfit. I don't even feel like a kid." He grinned. "In here," he said, "I'm just another philatelist."

Downstairs, Keller found himself pausing at the desk on his way to the door. The same woman, who did in fact strongly resemble young Mark's trading partner, smiled brightly. Keller said, "Why an *A?*"

She didn't hesitate. Because she could read his mind? No, more likely he was not the first person to ask. Possibly not even the first person that day.

"It used to say YMCA," she said.

"Before the tornado struck?"

"Only metaphorically. YMCA stands for Young Men's Christian Association."

"And?"

"And gradually one word after another became problematic. 'Christian'? That might put off potential Jewish or Muslim members, and irritate atheists. Not to mention the Druids."

"I never mention the Druids."

"Then came 'Men's.' There was a YWCA as well, but the two merged a while back, to eliminate sexism, and cut costs in the bargain. So what's left? 'Young Association'? In addition to sounding stupid, and vaguely ageist, it was just plain inaccurate. This place is more of a senior center than a young association. So all the letters came down."

"Except for the *A*. Is that what they call it now? The A?"

"No, of course not," she said. "Everybody calls it the Y, the same as they always did. Don't you love it? And aren't you glad you asked? But not so glad as I. Because now I feel useful, having just supplied some information you probably couldn't have found on Google."

Keller walked back to his hotel, went up to his room, turned on the TV. He found a Spanish-language channel showing a soccer game, and turned it off when he realized he wasn't paying it the slightest bit of attention. The only part he was enjoying, in a sort of subliminal way, was the audio, and that was because he couldn't understand it.

He called home, spoke to Julia. "I was hoping I wouldn't like him," he said, "but he's a very nice boy. And serious about his stamps."

"So I guess you'll be a few days."

"I could turn around and come home," he said, "except I can't."

He switched phones, called Dot. "Well, I'm in," he told her. "I got here, and I met him, and I'm in."

"I figured the stamps would cinch it."

"I was probably in anyway. What choice do I have? It's an obligation."

"That's just waiting to be turned into a joke," she said, "but I'm not going to touch it. Where do the two of us get off talking about moral obligations? But there's no getting around it. That's what it is."

He thought for a moment. "There are three people who collect if the kid doesn't, right?"

"Two aunts and an uncle. They each get a fourth, and that's a lot, because Grandma was a wealthy lady."

"That's three people each getting a fourth."

"The boy's mother would get the last share, but—"

"But it's probably not her."

"Unless we're back to *Masterpiece Theatre,* and she's the classic Least Likely Suspect."

"If I brace them in turn, I should be able to pick a winner. I guess I'll start with the uncle."

He took a shower, turned the TV on, turned it off again. Instead of arriving on Sunday, he'd flown in that very morning. So he hadn't been to the Falls, and probably wouldn't get there, either. If he hadn't been working, he'd have brought Julia and Jenny along, and all three of them could have made the trip. Put on those yellow slickers, rode the *Maid of the Mist* right under the Falls, did all the tourist things.

But if he hadn't been working, how likely was it that he'd have come to Buffalo at all?

Two aunts and an uncle. He could hang around for a week, then go home. Maybe the client would change his mind, maybe the broker would tell him to look elsewhere. Maybe it would take seven years before the uncle (or the aunt, or the other aunt) found somebody to do the job, and by then there'd be no job to do.

Maybe what he himself ought to do was take out all three of them, the uncle and both aunts. The odds were they all three had it coming. If one of them happened to be the client, that was just because he (or she or she) thought of it first, or knew a number to call.

He'd thought he was done with all of this crap. And all it took to draw him back in was a kid with a pair of tongs and a magnifier, a kid who knew a lot of useless information about Allenstein. (And wasn't that redundant? Was it possible to know any *useful* information about Allenstein?)

Was he going to be doing this sort of thing for the rest of his life? Couldn't he just pack up his things and go home?

Evidently not. And Mark was a nice young man, with a keen interest in his hobby, and philately needed a next generation. The torch had to be passed, and every issue of *Linn's* held a lament for the paucity of future torchbearers.

Not to worry, Keller told himself. He'd think of something.

ABOUT THE AUTHOR

LAWRENCE BLOCK published his first novel in 1958 and has been chronicling the adventures of Keller since 1998. He has been designated a Grand Master by the Mystery Writers of America, and has received Lifetime Achievement awards from the Crime Writers' Association (UK), the Private Eye Writers of America, and the Short Mystery Fiction Society. He has won the Nero, Philip Marlowe, Societe 813, and Anthony awards, and is a multiple recipient of the Edgar, the Shamus, and the Japanese Maltese Falcon awards. He and his wife, Lynne, are devout New Yorkers and relentless world travelers.